RELUCTANTLY
Royal

NICHOLE CHASE

AVON

An Imprint of HarperCollinsPublishers

This is a work of fiction. Names, characters, places, and incidents are products of the author's imagination or are used fictitiously and are not to be construed as real. Any resemblance to actual events, locales, organizations, or persons, living or dead, is entirely coincidental.

AVON BOOKS
An Imprint of HarperCollins*Publishers*
195 Broadway
New York, New York 10007

Copyright © 2014 by Nichole Chase
ISBN 978-0-06-231749-0
www.avonromance.com

First Avon Books mass market printing: September 2014

Avon Trademark Reg. U.S. Pat. Off. and in Other Countries, Marca Registrada, Hecho en U.S.A.
HarperCollins® is a registered trademark of HarperCollins Publishers.

Printed in the U.S.A.

10 9 8 7 6 5 4 3 2 1

One Kiss from a Prince

"You should be running from me as fast as you can." She whispered the words. "I'm everything you don't want."

"I'm not so sure."

"I live for the spotlight, it's my food." Her eyes were half lidded as she edged closer to my mouth. "And you've seen my family. I'm trouble, Max."

Did I care? I wasn't sure I was capable of making a real decision as her smell wrapped around my senses. The only thing I knew was that I wanted to taste her, to touch her, to press her against my body. To hear her say my name again.

Dipping my head, I grazed her lips with mine and I was lost. On a sigh, she leaned into me and wrapped her hands around my neck. Tilting her head back, I brought my mouth to hers carefully, softly, tasting. I wanted to deepen the kiss, to hear her moan, to feel the way her body could wrap around mine, but I kept it soft, sweet, and simple. She was in such a hard place, she needed to be protected, treasured by someone.

And right now, I was that person.

By Nichole Chase

SUDDENLY ROYAL
(Royal Series, Book One)
RECKLESSLY ROYAL
(Royal Series, Book Two)
RELUCTANTLY ROYAL
(Royal Series, Book Three)
MORTAL OBLIGATION
(Dark Betrayal Trilogy, Book One)
MORTAL DEFIANCE
(DARK BETRAYAL TRILOGY, BOOK TWO)
IMMORTAL GRAVE
(DARK BETRAYAL TRILOGY, BOOK THREE)
FLUKES
(THE FLUKES SERIES, BOOK ONE)
ON CHRISTMAS HILL
(A CHRISTMAS HILL SHORT STORY)

For my Deemaw, the first person to believe
in my writing.

RELUCTANTLY
Royal

ONE

$\mathcal{I}$ WAS CLEOPATRA ABOUT to change the fate of the world. I was Queen Elizabeth the First proving that a woman could rule an empire. I was Meredith Thysmer and I was about to sing.

Bathed in the spotlight's warm halo of attention, I reveled in the moment. Standing on stage waiting to sing was one of the highlights of my life. That pause as the audience waits, the anticipation—it fueled me. Of course, opening my mouth and letting the music flow out of me was even better. I loved the way the audience sat up a little straighter as the first notes hit the air, and the look of surprise and delight on their faces as I launched into the meat of the song. It was intoxicating, a drug just for me.

I opened my mouth and let the words pour out. I sang with my heart, feeling the awe and hope of the song. We were practicing for our holiday show, and the songs, the bells, the sweet feelings all touched something inside of me. I used it—that sense of magic—to propel my song, my voice, to something more than just a singer singing words. I wanted everyone in the auditorium to feel what I was feeling, to sense the emotion behind the lyrics.

The next verse was soft, with the barest amount of background music to play with my voice. Because of the quiet I heard the squeak of a door opening and the slow steps of a person entering the auditorium. I saw a figure pause as he walked down the side aisle. The lights made it impossible to make out the face, but from the height and stature I was sure it was a man. He took a seat next to the director and I tried to ignore their whispered exchange. It was a closed practice, but I wasn't going to complain if someone wanted to listen. Music had a way of easing the soul, and you never knew when someone needed the break it could offer.

As the song ended and my voice trailed off, I stood there and took a deep breath. Several of the other cast members clapped, but my eyes were trained on the director. He was the best there was, here in England. There was nothing that he missed and his teaching was invaluable. I'd been thrilled when I found out I made the cut for the show, much less been given a spot in one of his advanced classes.

He leaned back in his chair and smiled, but there was something in his eyes that left me disappointed.

"What is it now?" I put a hand on my hip and frowned.

"Nothing." He sat up in his chair and shook his head. "It was perfect."

"But?" I raised an eyebrow.

"But nothing." He frowned at me. "You did everything right."

"You have that look." I gestured in his direction. "That look that says something is wrong but you don't want to tell me."

"Your performance was perfect." He stood up. "Everyone take ten. Meredith, come down here with me."

Nerves churned in my stomach as I wondered what I had done wrong. Had the director changed his mind about me?

I felt my eyebrows pull together as I walked down the steps and looked from the director to the man sitting next to him. Max? Why had Prince Maxwell of Lilaria come to my practice? We'd met at his older brother's wedding and shared a dance, but nothing more. Just visiting the area, perhaps?

Checking up on some of the newer royals? That seemed unlikely though. From all accounts, Max tended to stay away from royal duties.

The last couple of years had been a whirlwind and I still couldn't imagine why a prince would be at my rehearsal, much less in England where I was busy building a career and new life for me and my son. When my grandfather had been contacted by the Lilarian royal family to tell him he was from a long-lost line of royalty, I had been certain it was a ploy to get his bank account number. Not that it would have done anyone much good. The old man had been broke and barely able to keep his heat turned on. I smiled at the thought of my grandfather's face when he found out it was real.

"Lady Meredith." Max unfolded his long frame and stood up before holding his hand out to me. "That was a beautiful performance."

His warm fingers wrapped around mine before lifting my hand to his mouth. His bright green eyes looked up at me from under his light brown hair. For half a second I almost swooned before yanking myself back to reality. A handsome face was the perfect shield for a player's heart. I knew that from experience. Knew all too well how quickly that smile could turn into a sneer.

"Thank you." I smiled at him, feeling the eyes of the people still in the auditorium on us. "What brings you to town?"

"I was here for a gallery opening—"

"Oh! Do you have a piece on display?" I smiled. I'd heard that the prince was a magnificent artist, but hadn't had the chance to see any of his work.

"I do—"

"I'll have to stop by and see it." I bit my lip and berated myself for cutting him off. I had a bad habit of doing that when I was excited.

"I didn't know you liked art." His eyes lit up for a moment and his serious expression brightened. I hoped that meant he wouldn't hold my rudeness against me.

"I appreciate art in all its forms." I smiled. I also appreciated the way his jacket and shirt stretched across his broad shoulders.

The director cleared his throat. "I believe His Highness had something to tell you."

"Uh, yes." Max frowned. "Is there somewhere we can talk privately?"

I blanched. Why would he need to talk to me alone? "Is something wrong with Marty?" Adrenaline filled my veins and I fought the impulse to run from the room looking for my son.

"No, no. I'm sure he is fine." Max touched my

shoulder and I was shocked by the warmth in his expression.

"God, for a minute I thought you came to tell me he was dead . . ." My heart froze and I looked up into his green eyes. "Grandfather?"

Max's fingers on my shoulder tightened. "I'm sorry, Meredith."

"No. Oh no, no, no." Tears filled my eyes and my legs grew weak. "Was he alone?"

My grandfather had been the one person I could always count on. Always, I knew that he would be there for me no matter what. When I had found out I was pregnant at seventeen he hadn't freaked out or been angry—unlike my dad. Instead he had held me while I cried and told me how beautiful and smart any child of mine would be. To think he had died without someone by his side broke my heart. Or worse, with only my drunkard father to ease his passing.

"He passed away in his sleep." Max moved me with a gentle tug so that I was sitting in one of the audience chairs. "The doctors believe it was his heart."

I squeezed my eyes shut and took a ragged breath. Where I had felt whole and centered merely a moment ago, my entire world had been taken and turned upside down. The very floor on which my life was planted had been torn away. My grandfather was gone.

"I need to see Marty." I scrubbed at my eyes, not caring that the mascara I had worn that day was smeared across my cheeks. "I have to be the one to tell him."

"I have a car out front." Max stood and held his hand out to me.

I took it, barely registering the way his fingers curled protectively around mine and didn't let go.

"Can I do anything to help?" My director placed a comforting hand on my shoulder.

"No, no. Thank you." I shook my head. "I'll be in touch."

"Take your time," the director offered, but I knew better. My understudy would be on that stage in a matter of moments, warming up.

"Right, thanks." I let Max urge me out of the room.

"How is your son going to take the news?" Max asked quietly.

"He's going to be devastated." I whispered the words, my heart aching for the pain I was about to bring to my son. That almost hurt worse than the actual loss—knowing how many times my son had lost people in his life; knowing how much my grandfather had meant to Marty. "Devastated."

"I'll help in any way that I can," Max said. "Let's get you out of here."

I let him guide me out of the auditorium and down the hallway. I pulled my sweater closed and couldn't help my shiver. An arm wrapped around my shoulders and I leaned into the warmth. His long, strong fingers squeezed my arm gently. It made me feel safe and not so alone.

"Thank you." I sniffed and tried to hide it when I wiped my nose on my sleeve.

"You're welcome."

I looked up into his eyes and gave him a watery smile. "I know this must be torturous. Dealing with a stranger who just lost a loved one can be a nightmare. You must have drawn the short straw."

"I was in the neighborhood." He wiped a tear from my cheek with his thumb and lingered for half a heartbeat. "Plus we didn't want you to hear it from strangers. Take it from me, I know what it's like to have the media tell you that someone you love has died."

I bit my lip as he opened the door for me. I knew that his father had died in an accident, but I wasn't sure if that was who he was referring to. A shudder racked my body. The thought of the media telling me that my grandfather had passed away was something out of a nightmare. And the media wasn't exactly known for being gentle.

The limousine idled just outside and Max chivalrously helped me into my seat. I chewed the lipstick off my bottom lip while I swiped at my eyes with my sleeve. I couldn't believe that my grandfather was gone. What would I say to Marty? He was only six years old. Would he understand?

The tears formed in my eyes, and despite my desire to stay calm and collected in front of a prince, I was lost. They ran down my face unchecked while I stared out the window and sniffled.

"Here." He handed me a hanky and I took it with a watery smile.

"Thanks." I dabbed at my cheeks while debating how rude it would be to blow my nose. "I'm such a mess."

"You just lost your grandfather. I think you're holding yourself together remarkably well." He offered me a soft smile.

Trying to smile back, I felt like snot was going to run down my face, and I quickly looked away. Giving up, I used the hanky to quickly rub my nose. I'd have to buy him a new one. And from the looks of it, it would be an expensive one, and for a moment my old mindset kicked in and I worried about the cost. Snorting, I barely caught a little snot that escaped.

Max looked so uncomfortable sitting next to me, pretending that he wasn't listening to me quietly cry. It would have been comical if it wasn't for the hole in my heart.

As the car drove up to the school Marty attended I wiped at my cheeks again. Turning to look at Max, I tried to pull myself together.

"How do I look?"

"You couldn't look anything but lovely if you tried." Max's smile was honest.

"Will I scare him?"

"Scare him?" He looked at me confused.

"Marty." Had he forgotten I had a son? "I don't want him to panic when he sees me."

"No." He shook his head. "You look serious, but lovely."

"Thank you." I took a deep breath and tucked his hanky into my pocket. "I owe you a new one."

"Of course not." He helped me out of the car. "Would you like me to accompany you inside?"

I hesitated. I didn't want to be rude, but this was something that I needed to do alone. "I think it would be easier if there was no one else there when he finds out. He was very close with my grandfather."

"I'll stay with the car then."

"No, I'm sure you have more important things to do. I can get a taxi back to our flat." I shook my head.

"I'm not leaving you at a time like this, and I'd rather have you in the air on the way to Lilaria before the press catches wind of things." He closed the door and leaned against the car.

"I guess you're right." I chewed on my lip again. "I'll book tickets from my phone."

"The royal plane is waiting for us. I'll be seeing you home." He tucked his hands in his pockets and his eyes bored into mine. "I'm not leaving you alone to deal with this."

I watched him for a minute, surprised by his vehemence. "I owe you thanks again."

"You owe me nothing." His eyes were sincere. "It's my pleasure to help."

"Such a princely thing to say." I felt my mouth pull up in a small smile.

"Well, if the shoe fits . . ."

"Is it crystal?" I looked down at his feet.

"Leather." He lifted one foot and smiled. "Much more comfortable than Cinderella's slipper."

"And manly." I laughed and straightened my shoulders. I would have believed my own performance if I didn't ruin it by sniffing. "Well, time to face the music."

Taking a deep breath, I rooted through my soul for a role that would fit this moment. A strong woman, a capable mother who could be the rock her son would need.

Without a look back I strode up the steps and through the double doors. The further my feet took me, the stronger I felt. I could do this, tell my son that his best friend had died, and be there to hold him when he fell apart. By all that was holy, I hoped my strength would hold and I wouldn't turn into a sobbing mess.

The woman at the front desk was more than understanding and took me to a small conference room while someone fetched my son. When the door swung open, Marty ran straight into my arms.

I pressed a kiss to the top of his brown hair and squeezed him tightly. "Hey there, big boy."

"Why are you here? Do I get to go home early?" He looked up at me with eager eyes.

"Yes." I smiled and knelt down so that we were eye to eye. "Something has happened and we need to go back to Lilaria."

His face froze. "Something bad?"

"Yes, baby." I placed my hands on his shoulders. "We can talk about it in the car."

"Is it Great-Grandfather?" His big eyes looked up into mine and shimmered with understanding. "I had a dream about him last night. That he was telling me good-bye."

My mouth fell open for a minute, but I managed to pull myself together. "Yes, it's Grandfather."

"He died?" Fat tears pooled in his eyes. "He's dead, isn't he?"

"Yes, baby. He died in his sleep." I pulled him against my chest and buried my face in his hair while he cried.

"But I'm going to mi-i-iss him so-o-o much." His little arms wrapped around my neck and part of me broke right there on the floor of his school. "He can't be dead."

"Shh." I smoothed his hair and placed a kiss on his forehead. "Remember how much he loved you? He's always going to be with us."

"It's not the same." His little body shook against mine and tears filled my eyes. "It's not the same!"

"I know, baby. I know." I sat down and pulled him into my lap, letting him cry. "But he'll be here in our hearts, in the little things that remind us of him."

"Like fishing?" He sniffled and rubbed his

nose on the back of his arm. Apparently that was a family trait.

"Oh, you know it. Every time you catch a big one, he'll be right there watching." I rocked us gently and fought to keep a smile on my face.

"What about the little ones? I always manage to catch tiny ones."

"Even the little ones." My chuckle sounded wet so I cleared my throat. "Remember what he always said?"

"Can't catch the big ones without the little ones." He lowered his voice.

"That's it. Bait fish make the fishing go round!" I mimicked his tone.

"What does that even mean?" Marty looked up at me with red-rimmed eyes and a curious expression. "What goes round?"

"I don't know." I shook my head. "It's just what he always said."

"Now we'll never know." His little voice sounded so sad.

"I bet we'll figure it out." I squeezed him tightly once more, before getting up off the floor. "Are you ready? There is a plane waiting for us."

"Can I have your pretzels?" He rubbed his nose on his sleeve again. I really needed to cure that habit.

"We have a lot more than pretzels." Max's deep voice rumbled from the doorway.

I looked up at him, annoyed that he had come to check on us—thinking that he had been tired of waiting—but the anger melted away at the sympathy in his eyes as he looked at Marty.

Max leaned against the door frame with his hands stuck in his pockets, looking like a *GQ* model.

"What are you doing here?" Marty looked up at the prince in surprise.

"Prince Max is the one that came to tell us." I shook my head at Marty's lack of decorum, but right now wasn't the time to correct him.

"Did you draw the short straw?"

I laughed. He was obviously my son.

"Rock, paper, scissors." Max knelt down and smiled. "I chose rock."

"Paper is the sneaky answer." Marty nodded his head as if that made the most sense in the world.

"I do believe you're right," Max agreed.

While Marty was distracted I quickly wiped at my cheeks and dragged the tips of my fingers under my eyes to make sure I didn't have any runaway mascara.

"Are you ready?" I held my hand out to Marty

while Max picked up the tiny backpack by the door.

"Does this mean we're going to fly on a private jet?" Marty looked at me with a little more of his usual excitement.

"I think so." I squeezed his fingers and tried to not think of why we were being escorted "home" by Max.

"Awesome!" He bounced a little as we walked down the hallway. "Do you think I can drive it?"

"Um, that would be a no." I laughed, but it was a show.

People had lined the hallways to watch us leave. Some of them had sad expressions as they watched Marty and me, but the rest were out in full force to get a glimpse of the royal guest. Not that I blamed them. Max filled out his suit perfectly.

"Have a safe flight." The woman from the front desk nodded in my direction before turning around and making shooing motions at the people in the hallway.

"Thanks." I blew out a breath. At least the private jet would be a good distraction for Marty. I was already mentally preparing myself to deal with my father. If I was lucky he'd be passed out in his office and leave everything to me. Coaching Marty through the funeral on top of making all the plans would be difficult enough. Dealing with my father at the same time would be almost impossible.

TWO

$\mathcal{B}$AD.

My feet were planted just like they had been in the auditorium while listening to Meredith sing. It felt like my shoes had been glued to the floor. My legs refused to move.

Wrong. My brain refused to tell my legs to move.

This was a terrible idea.

I should leave. Why were my feet not moving?

"Marty, go up to your room please." Meredith's foot tapped against the stone entryway.

The little boy shot a look at the people in the sitting room, another at his mother, and beelined for the stairs. I didn't blame him. The heat coming off the top of his mother's head was enough to make me want to turn tail and run. But there was also something tempting in that white-hot anger. Which was an even better reason to flee. Even in her grief, Meredith Thysmer was enticing.

"What is *wrong* with you?" Meredith was glaring at the blurry-eyed man sitting on the couch. The reporter perched across from him looked torn between excitement and fear. The room smelled strongly of liquor and stale cigarette smoke.

"I'm telling my father's life story." The man who must be Meredith's father sat up a little straighter and pulled at his rumpled suit jacket. I thought his name was Arthur, but I could be wrong.

"He's not even in the ground!" Meredith shook her head. "And you're selling interviews?"

"What does that have to do with anything?" Arthur leaned forward. "And who is that?"

He pointed at me with disdain and I felt my eyebrows rise. It wasn't often that I wasn't recognized in my own country. The journalist looked at me with wide eyes and began to collect his stuff.

"That. Is. The. Prince." Meredith bit out the words. "His Royal Highness, Prince Maxwell of Lilaria. He was kind enough to come tell me that my grandfather died before the media did. Then he brought us home." The frustration and hurt in her voice was unmistakable. While her father was trying to make a quick buck, she had just found out a loved one had passed away.

"I'm sorry for your loss, sir." I bowed my head.

He snorted, and his red eyes traveled over me

in disdain, but he didn't respond otherwise. His blurry attention went straight back to his fireball of a daughter. That was self-preservation at its best.

"I was here dealing with everything that happened." He picked up a snifter from the table and twirled the contents before dumping the amber liquid down his throat.

"You left us to find out—" She stopped abruptly and looked at the journalist. "I'm sorry, but now is not a good time. Could we reschedule? I'm sure you can understand that this is a difficult time for all of us." She paused and I could see her temper flare again. "Being that my grandfather *just* passed away, none of us are in the right state of mind to be giving interviews. And I'm sure that anything you print would say the same thing."

Damn. She had just put that journalist in his place better than my sister-in-law's sidekick Chadwick. That man had a way of making people feel small. It was a gift that apparently Meredith shared.

Another reason I should be making a hasty retreat and leaving her to deal with her family drama.

"Of course, Lady Meredith." The man bowed his head as he stood and almost tripped on his own feet. "I'll be in touch, Duke Thysmer."

I could hear Meredith grind her teeth from where I stood. Apparently being reminded that her father was now the duke of the estate was the last thing she needed.

"You can't excuse my guests, Meredith." Her father stood up, much steadier than he should have been considering the smell of alcohol coming from his breath. "You heard the man. I'm the duke now."

"The only thing you're fit to be duke of is the wet bar," Meredith scoffed at him.

"I think that's my cue to leave." I took a step backward. It wasn't that I hadn't seen my share of family drama, but it was another thing to deal with someone else's.

"Oh God. I'm sorry, Max." Meredith shook her head and composed her face, but I could see the embarrassment underneath her calm mask. "Thank you for everything."

"I was happy to help." I bowed my head. That might be an exaggeration. I was glad that I could keep her from learning about her grandfather's passing in a horrible way, but I hadn't been happy to do it. "If you need anything else, please let me know."

She chewed on her lip for a minute, and I had to fight my fascination with the way it plumped around her teeth. "I had an e-mail from the palace about funeral arrangements. We should be fine." Straightening her shoulders, she shot me a more assured smile. "Thank you, again. Martin loved riding in the jet."

"I'm glad I could brighten his day a little." And that was the truth. Seeing his eyes clouded with pain had brought back a lot of memories. It was nice to be able to give him something else to focus on for a little while. Hopefully Meredith's father wouldn't cause too much trouble for what was left of their little family.

"He got to sit in the pilot seat. I'm not sure I'll ever be able to top that." She smiled up at me, and her smile was so radiant that for just a moment I felt my breath catch in my throat.

"It was the least I could do." I bowed my head to her and then to her father before turning and leaving. My steps echoed in the hallway, but thankfully there was no more shouting from the sitting room.

"Psst."

I paused at the door, my fingers gripping the handle, and looked up at the small balcony near the stairs.

"What are you doing?" I cocked my head to the side as I regarded the little boy.

"Are they still fighting?" He looked at me from between the railing of the staircase with narrowed eyes.

"I don't hear them." I shook my head.

"That just means they're being quieter." He sighed and slumped down on his butt. "They're probably still arguing."

"Aren't you supposed to be in your room?" I let my hand fall from the door and I turned to give Marty my full attention. If his mother was still arguing with his grandfather, I was sure she wouldn't want him to know.

"It's not fair."

"What's not fair?" I moved so that I could see his little face better, and the tear stains on his cheeks made me wince.

"I don't want to be alone up here." He wrapped his arms around his stomach and bowed his head.

I teetered on the bottom step. This was one of those moments when a normal adult would have something reassuring to say, some soft words that would make this little boy feel better. But I was drawing a blank, and, worse, Marty had started to sniffle.

"Hey." Giving up on my escape plan I took the stairs two at a time and sat down next to the little boy. Okay. I was here, now what? "Hey. Um, I'm sure your mum will be up here to see you soon."

He just shrugged.

That was no good. I needed him to calm down, and to do that I needed him to tell me what was really bothering him—though I was fairly certain I knew. How to get a little boy to open up to a stranger? I seemed to remember my sister, Cathy, going on and on about using open-ended questions for her school program. Something about asking questions that couldn't be answered with a yes or no.

"Where is your room?"

"There." He pointed at a door that was cracked open.

"Um, do you have any video games?" Damn it. That was not an open-ended question.

"Yeah." He shrugged like that was the stupidest question in the world.

"What kind of games do you like?"

"All kinds." He peeked up at me through damp eyelashes.

"Racing ones?" I was forming a plan. At least I think that was what was happening.

"Yeah, those are cool. I'm really good at Race Indy Two Thousand." He wiped his nose on the back of his arm. "You wanna play?"

"You wanna lose?" I bumped him with my shoulder.

"You wish." He stood up, lightning-quick, and ran toward his room. "C'mon."

I shook my head as I followed him into his room. The little guy chucked me a controller and took a seat on his bed. I pulled the desk chair out and turned it backward to sit in before looking at the controller in my hands.

"This is going to be a bloodbath." The little boy chuckled.

I loosened my tie. "We'll see about that."

Marty didn't hesitate to start. We picked our cars and it was go time. The little pooper was good, but so was I. If there was one thing I had never outgrown, it was video games.

"Hey!" Marty cried in outrage. "How'd you know about that?"

I used the hidden power strip to zip around his avatar. "You thought just because I'm old I didn't know about the speed strips?"

"Uh, yeah." He shrugged while I laughed.

"Get used to it, little man. I'm going to leave you eating my dust."

I had no idea how much time passed while I played with Marty. After I lost to him twice, he talked me into playing another game. It wasn't until someone cleared their throat at the bedroom door that I realized we were being rowdy.

"Max?" Meredith leaned against the door frame, her red hair half obscuring her face as she watched us with an amused expression. She might have been smiling, but I could see the red that rimmed her gorgeous eyes. "I thought you left."

She crossed her arms, and I had to pull my attention away from the way it highlighted her breasts. Sure, I liked breasts as much as the next guy, but the woman was grieving, for Christ's sake.

"I was challenged." I flicked my eyes back to the screen, more in an attempt to get them away from her chest than to be involved in the game. "A man can't turn down a challenge." .

"He's losing!" Marty fell over on his bed with his tongue sticking out of his mouth as he furiously worked his controller.

"I'm losing?" I used my character to shoot a gust of frozen wind in his avatar's direction. "Is that what you call losing?"

Marty groaned loudly. "Quit doing that!"

I laughed, but let him get the upper hand. No reason to beat him into the ground the day he lost his great-grandfather. Marty had needed a little distraction, and surprisingly, I had enjoyed providing it. Children weren't really my forte, but Marty made it simple. He wasn't needy or hard to understand. He also spoke a language I understood—that of the gamer.

"Well, we're about to have dinner if you'd like to stay."

I looked away from the game and heard the explosion as my car ran off the road. Her eyes were cautious, but not warning me to say no. For a moment I considered it, considered spending a little more time with Meredith and Marty, and I was man enough to admit it made me nervous.

"No, thank you. I have some things I have to finish tonight." I reached over and ruffled Marty's hair when he groaned. I was itching to get back to a drawing I had started on the plane ride.

"C'mon. They won't fight if you stay."

"Marty!" Red colored Meredith's cheeks.

"What's a family dinner without some bickering?" I stood up and set the controller down. "I really do need to leave though." I glanced at my watch and winced. I'd missed an important phone call that I'd have to make up.

"Maybe another time." Meredith walked over and hugged Marty's head to her stomach. He put his little arms around her waist and smiled at me.

"Sure." The word popped out of my mouth

before I could think twice. Dinner with them was not on the agenda. Not unless it was a formal occasion with a hundred other people. I wouldn't have hesitated to take Meredith on a candlelight dinner where I could devour her instead of our food, but not when she had a little boy to think about. Not when she was a mother and brought all of the baggage a mother would bring. Nope. Not going there.

"That would be awesome!" Marty held his hand out to high-five me and you didn't leave a little boy hanging, so I returned the gesture.

"I'll see you out." She gently pushed Marty back toward his bathroom. "Wash up and meet me downstairs."

"Ugh." Rolling his eyes, he turned and walked like a zombie.

"Roll your eyes at me again and you'll get no dinner," Meredith snapped.

"Sorry, Mum." Marty picked up his pace and disappeared.

I followed her out of the room and tried to keep my attention away from the way her perfect ass swayed as she descended the stairs.

"Making sure I actually leave this time?" I forced my eyes to the back of her head and watched as her red hair bounced with each step.

"Well, it seems like you might need a little supervision." She smiled at me over her shoulder and my groin twitched. Down, boy.

"I need a lot of supervision." There was no mistaking my innuendo.

"I can imagine." Even her chuckle was sexy. She turned at the door and her eyes ran over me in appreciation. "I bet you keep the girls on their toes."

"Sometimes." Sometimes on their backs, or their bellies. Even better when they were bent over and holding on to my headboard. Shit, I needed to leave. The thought of Meredith in my bed was making me hard.

"Hm." She raised an eyebrow, and if I didn't know better I would swear she was reading my thoughts.

"Well, thank you for letting me hang out with your son."

"Thank you for distracting him while I dealt with my father." She held her hand out to shake. Her face turned serious and I could see the tiredness behind her eyes. "I'm sorry you had to see that."

"Don't think about it again. Trust me when I say I've had my fair share of family drama." I took her hand and pressed a kiss to her knuckles. It was an archaic gesture, but I couldn't resist touching my lips to her in some way. "Please let me know if you need anything."

"Anything?" Her eyes sparkled, but I could see the sadness shining through.

"Anything at all." I squeezed her fingers gently before letting go. "I'm at your service."

"I'll keep that in mind." A genuine smile lit her face. "Good night, Your Highness."

"Good night, my lady." I bowed my head before leaving.

My car was waiting outside and as I climbed into the back, I berated myself. A little flirting was one thing, but this felt dangerous. Good thing I wouldn't see them again until the funeral.

THREE

HOLY HOTNESS, THAT man was trouble. Tall, lean, but with broad shoulders, and a face that made me want to do naughty things. He was the walking personification of a fallen angel; handsome beyond measure, with the promise of hot, sweaty nights in his eyes. I leaned against the door and blew my hair out of my face. Every fiber of my being was exhausted from grief and anger, but one look from Max had yanked me back to the land of the living. There was something in his eyes that made me nervous but excited.

I was no stranger to flirting. Hell, I'd had a baby at the age of seventeen. I knew my way around men, which was basically easy; use them for what you want, expect nothing else, and discard them as fast as possible. I had learned that from watching men do the same thing to women. Though they were usually just after sex, and that wasn't something I was willing to give to anyone again.

So I strung them along with the promise of some-day and then dropped them like a bad habit as soon as I got what I needed; whether it was a ride to work or a new job. Hell, I'd even flirted down the rent payment on my apartment a couple of years ago.

Once Grandfather had been granted his title and lands back, I had dropped men altogether. The only good one I knew was now gone.

Tears gathered in my eyes and I rubbed at them with the heels of my hands. Crying wasn't going to get this family through everything. I might have to quit school so I could make sure that Dad didn't ruin our new chance on life. If things hadn't changed I'd still be working at the same restaurant waiting tables in Southampton. I leaned my head back against the door and closed my eyes. I could still finish a degree, just not in performing arts. Any degree would be better than no degree, and I'd never thought I'd have the chance to even think about going to university.

"My lady, dinner is ready." The butler stepped into the hallway and motioned toward the dining room.

"Thank you." I stood up from the door and wished that we were having dinner in the kitchen around the island with Granddad instead. He hated eating in the formal dining room. We used to eat around the television in the living room. The formal furniture, place settings, and silverware were all foreign to us.

"Mom! What are we having for dinner? Nothing gross, right?" Marty bounded down the stairs and I straightened my shoulders and smiled. "I'd really like pizza."

"No pizza." I shook my head and smiled. "I think we're having roast chicken."

"Ah, man."

"Wah." I pulled him against my side as we walked to the dining room. "How are you holding up?"

"I dunno." He shrugged. "I'm sad, but Max made it a little better. I liked playing video games with him."

"I saw that. It looked like you were both having fun." Guy time was hard to come by for Marty. His father had ditched me as soon as I saw the plus sign on the pregnancy test, and my father had little to do with Marty from the day I announced I was pregnant. It had been my grandfather who had stepped up and taken us under his wing. I had been scared and lost, but Granddad had always steered me in the right direction. He'd been our rock.

"He's pretty cool for an old guy."

I laughed. "He's not old, and you're just saying that because he let you fly his plane."

"Oh man. That was so awesome!" He skipped a step. "I should have made a loop."

"I don't think those kind of planes are meant to make loops." Though there had been a couple of moments when Max had made my stomach make loops.

I put my hands on his shoulders and ushered him into the dining room. To my utter relief my father wasn't to be seen. Considering how much he had been drinking today, he was probably passed out in his wing of the manor. Dinner was quiet but peaceful, and considering the day we had, I couldn't ask for more than that.

Marty was yawning by the time we finished the chicken and his little eyes were rimmed in red. After I tucked him into bed, I walked down the long hallway of our wing and hesitated by my grandfather's bedroom door. Taking a deep breath, I pushed it open and leaned against the door frame. Everything looked normal, like he would be back any minute. Someone must have changed the sheets and made the bed after he was taken away.

Tears ran down my cheeks as I imagined no

one here to mourn his passing, no one to care as he was loaded into a hearse. I had to remind myself that it was impossible to not love the old man. The staff went out of their way to make sure he was happy. In fact, I had noticed more than one pair of red and watery eyes since I had gotten back. He hadn't been alone. He hadn't been in pain. It had been quick.

I covered my mouth as I cried. It hurt that he was gone, like something had been ripped away from my body. I'd known he was sick—his heart hadn't been the same since his first heart attack—but it still hadn't seemed possible that he would really leave us. Leave us to deal with my father.

My asshole of a father.

Rage flooded my body, the grief only heightening my anger. Drunkard. Selfish idiot. I couldn't believe what I had seen when I had walked into the home this afternoon. Selling a story to some sleazy reporter for a few bucks? It made me sick. Without my grandfather, my father would be in jail—or dead. The man couldn't care less about a person, except for when it could possibly benefit himself.

I balled my hands into fists at my sides and squeezed my eyes shut. What the hell was I going to do with that man? Grandfather had refused to believe he wasn't worth saving—that he wouldn't turn around at some point—but I knew better. I knew that my old man would sell us for a pint. Hell, he had sold his father's life story before the man was cold and in his grave.

Soft footsteps broke my train of thought and I looked up into the face of one of the housekeepers. Quickly I wiped my cheeks and fought a sniffle.

"Can I help you?"

"My lady, I just wanted to let you know that Gerard, the head butler, accompanied your grandfather today. He wasn't alone." She smiled apologetically. "I know you worried about him, with you being so far away, but we all treated him like he was our own family."

"Yes, you did." I smiled and stood up a little straighter. It did help to know that he wasn't alone. "Thank you."

"You're welcome." She dipped her head briefly. "If you need anything, let us know. Gerard will help get everything ready for the funeral."

When she left I slumped back against the door frame. I was tired; mentally, emotionally, and physically. I had no idea how to plan a funeral, but needed to get started. How long did Lilarians wait before having the service? Would it be scandalous to cremate my grandfather? Or did the family have some kind of special tomb? A royal burial ground? I smacked my head against the door frame once before standing back up.

There was too much to do to stand here having a pity party. Granddad would tell me to stop worrying and to get going. He'd be right, of course. Worrying wouldn't get anything accomplished.

Inside my room, the blankets were already turned down and there was a packet of information lying on the foot of my bed. I picked the envelope up from the white duvet and pulled the papers out. There were different packages of services that could be held. Notes had been made in the margins to let me know what would be expected for a duke's burial.

Even after the last few years it was hard to keep my eyes from bugging out of my head at the totals that were highlighted. My grandfather was going to have a burial fit for a king. Well, a duke anyway. Good grief, there were requirements for the type of ceremony he should receive. And one of the royal family members would be present? Were they serious?

Granddad would have wanted something small and simple. Probably with a round of pints for all. The ceremony these papers outlined was far from an intimate family gathering. There were

lists of flowers, how many pallbearers were required. Pallbearers? Six were required. Penciled
in next to the words were three names; men who
had worked for my grandfather, including Gerard,
who had made the notes.

I closed the package and dropped it on the
nightstand. I needed to find three more pallbearers. Sadly, I couldn't assume that my father would
agree to the job, and while I hated to even think of
it, I wondered if I should let Marty be one of the
pallbearers. Would that be appropriate? Hadn't
Prince William and Prince Harry walked with
their mother's carriage? Was I a bad mother for
considering this, or a bad person for comparing
my grandfather's death to that of the People's
Princess? Shit, I was just a bad person all around.

I threw myself back on my bed and used
my toes to kick my shoes off. I loved this bed. It
wrapped around me like a warm cocoon, without making me feel like I would suffocate. It was
heaven.

I blinked slowly, my eyes tired and gritty from
tears. Rolling over on my side I tucked my hands
under my head and looked at the photograph on
the nightstand. It was all of us in front of our old
house. Even Dad had stood there with a smile on
his face; one of the rare moments when we'd all

been getting along. Reaching out, I grabbed the frame, tucking it against my chest, and choked down a sob.

I never got to hug my grandfather good-bye. Tears were my only company as I cried myself to sleep.

The soft glow of sunlight peeking through my curtains woke me up just before the sound of feet running down the hall.

"Mom!" My door flung open and Marty ran into my room. Tears streamed down his face.

"C'mere." I held my arms open for him. He climbed on my bed and buried his face against my shirt.

"I'm sad." His voice was muffled and thick with tears.

"I know, baby." I squeezed him tight and dug deep to find the strength to not cry too. "I'm sad too, but he wouldn't want us to be upset."

"Why?" He rubbed his tear-streaked face on my shirt and I didn't stop him. Even though I was sure that there was snot mixed in with those tears. It didn't matter. The only thing that was important was my baby's broken heart.

"Did Great-Granddad ever want you to be sad?" I tsked. "He would have done something silly to make you laugh, then give you a big hug."

"But he's not here to do that now." Fat tears welled in his eyes.

"Well, I'm not really good at silly stuff, but I can give you big hugs." I lay back on the bed and tucked him against me. "You know what helps me?"

"What?" Sniffle, sniffle.

"Well, I know that he's watching over us." I snuggled closer to him and placed a kiss on his head.

"Like from heaven?"

"In some form or fashion he will be here watching us, trust me."

He rolled over to look at me. "Do you think it upsets him that I'm so sad?"

"I think that he would hate for you to be sad, but would understand." I kissed his nose. "It's never easy when someone we love leaves us."

That was something I knew all too well. How many times had I been left over the years? My mother for one, and then there was Marty's father, who had run as soon as he found out I was pregnant. And now. Now my granddad. It didn't matter that it wasn't his choice, the hurt was still just as real.

"Will you fish with me?" He looked up at me with big eyes.

Uh-oh. I hated to fish. That meant handling worms or little bugs. I suppressed a shudder and looked at my son's hopeful eyes. "I'll try."

"I'll bait your hook!" He smiled, and my relief was immediate. Marty would be okay with time. As long as I was okay and calm, we would get through all of this.

"Deal?" I held out my pinky finger, which he latched on to with his own.

"Deal!" He kissed his thumb and I kissed mine. My fate was sealed. I'd be fishing sometime in the near future.

"Then get out of my bed and go get dressed." I pushed his shoulders gently. "I have a lot to do today."

"Like what?" He straightened his Darth Vader pajama shirt.

"I've got to get everything set up for the funeral." I looked at him for a minute, deciding that I wouldn't ask him to be a pallbearer. I also made a mental note to buy him new pajamas. The ones he was wearing were getting short.

"Are you going to cement him like Great Grandma?"

I couldn't help the sputter of laughter that escaped me. "Cement him?"

"You know, put him in a vase like Grandma."

"Cremate." I shook my head. "Not cement."

"Weird." He shook his head. "Can I wear regular clothes?"

In other words, could he wear jeans, not khaki pants and a button-up shirt.

"Yes." I waved my hand at him. "Now scat. I need a shower."

"And to brush your teeth." He giggled when I blew in his direction.

"You too, monster."

As soon as he was out of my room and running down the hallway, I swung my legs over the edge of the bed and stretched. I was still in my clothes from the day before, and I frowned. I must have been exhausted to be able to sleep in the form-fitting skirt and blouse I was wearing. Normally I preferred giant T-shirts and sweatpants for sleeping. Nothing tight or revealing for me. All of that stuff was reserved for the stage or special occasions.

I didn't take long in the shower, just long enough to get clean. No lazy morning bath for me. I had too much to do. There were a lot of decisions to be made. Including one that left me feeling frustrated. Who could I ask to help carry Granddad's casket?

There was his old friend Patrick. I could call

him and see if would be willing to help. Patrick and Granddad had been very close before we moved to Lilaria. If he would help, that would leave me with only two spots to fill.

I had to ask my father. There was no way around that. He should be one of the men to carry the casket, and I'd hide all of the liquor in the house if he said no. I could always super glue his hands to the casket—or maybe bribe him with scotch.

One more person. I needed one more person.

I looked around my room like someone would spontaneously appear. An idea began to form in my mind and I looked down at the jeans I was wearing and shook my head.

There was one person that I could ask. He had told me to tell him if I needed anything. Well, I needed something all right, but it wasn't the kind of thing you could ask over the phone. I needed to go to him and present my case.

I undid the button on my jeans and kicked them off before walking to my closet. If I was going to ask for such a big favor, I needed to reevaluate my wardrobe decision. The right clothes could go a long way to getting me the answer I needed.

FOUR

"**I** SWEAR TO GOD, I'm moving all of my stuff to the palace. I can't take one more night of your loud, tub-thumping sex." I pointed my finger at my brother and sister-in-law.

Sam laughed loudly as she heaped more bacon on to her plate. "Good. Our plan is working."

"That's not funny." I slathered butter on my croissant.

"Sure it is." She shoved a piece of bacon in her mouth and smiled at me. "We've been trying to get you out of D'Lynsal Manor for months."

"It's not my fault that my bathroom is right next to your room. And besides, the bathtub is the only place Samantha is comfortable—"

"Enough!" I cut Alex off with a horrified look. "I don't want to know where you two have sex, much less pregnant sex."

"Well, how do you think I got this way?" Sam gestured to her baby bump.

"Knowing and hearing are two different things." I rolled my eyes. I'd never admit it to her, because it would go to her head, but she made an adorable pregnant woman. It looked like she had a basketball hidden under her shirt.

"Then go back to the palace." Alex pointed at me with his fork.

"I came here for the same reason you did." I shoveled some eggs in my mouth before continuing. "The place is covered in visiting dignitaries. I ran into the Duke of Edinburgh in our family kitchen. He was drinking out of the milk carton."

Sam laughed. "Was he naked?"

"Thank you very much for that horrible visual." Alex set his fork down.

"No. He was wearing sleep pants." I grabbed the coffeepot and refilled my cup. Sam's love of coffee had infected the entire family.

"I hate you." Her eyes were full of lust as she eyed the coffeepot.

"You're hating on the wrong brother." I made a big show of sipping from my cup. "I didn't knock you up."

"Let me smell it." She held her hand out. "I just want to remember what it tastes like."

"Don't torture yourself." I laughed while Alex playfully slapped her hand.

"I don't miss the wine, or being able to stay awake past eight o'clock in the evening, but I do miss my coffee." Her sigh was so sad it almost made me feel bad for her. Almost.

"You could always drink decaf," I said.

"Blech. That's like Oreos without cream in the center. Just a mean tease." She made a face.

"What is it you keep saying?" Every time she came across something she couldn't or shouldn't do while pregnant she would mumble under her breath with gritted teeth.

"It'll be worth it." She closed her eyes and took a deep breath. I wasn't sure if she was trying to calm herself or catch a sniff of the coffee. "It'll be worth it."

"What's your mantra going to be when the baby is up at two in the morning?"

She didn't answer, just flung a piece of apple in my direction.

"Leave her alone," Alex said. "She didn't get any sleep last night."

"Yeah, I heard, remember?"

"I mean it, smart ass. The baby kept her up all night." Alex looked at Sam with a disgustingly sappy look. It normally made me sick, but we were all protective of Sam, especially now. Her morning sickness was more like all-the-time sickness.

Not to mention it had lasted way past the first three months.

"Sick again?" I tried to keep the concern out of my voice.

"A little." She shrugged and rubbed her belly. "The little bean was grumpy."

"Might have been all that bouncing around." I bit into my croissant and hoped they didn't notice that I was worried. Sam was usually active and lively, but lately she seemed to be dragging.

"Oh, shut it." Sam glared at me. "You're just jealous that you're not getting any."

"I don't have time for the drama." Setting the croissant down, I took a big slurp of coffee. That would teach her for picking on me.

"Aren't you supposed to be doing a lunch event with Mother?" Alex asked.

"I canceled." I shrugged. It wasn't like it was the first time I'd backed out of an event she'd tried to force me into. She probably had expected it.

"I told her you would." Alex shook his head.

"And yet she keeps trying to get me to do things." I frowned. "You'd think she'd figure it out."

"Mother just wants you to be more comfortable with it."

"That's never going to happen."

Sam opened her mouth to say something but was interrupted by the dining room door being opened. The butler stepped in and cleared his throat.

"Lady Meredith of Thysmer." He bowed his head before motioning for someone to walk in the door.

I stood up and set my napkin down as the feisty redhead walked into the room. Was it my imagination, or did the room seem to brighten just a little? I couldn't help the way my eyes traveled over her perfect legs and along her delicious body. The skirt she was wearing hugged every curve, and the slight sweater over her shirt draped open in an inviting way. Her hair hung over one shoulder in gentle waves, and I found myself wondering if it was as soft to touch as it looked.

Alex cleared his throat as he too stood, and I quickly tried to cover up the fact that I had been staring.

"Meredith." I bowed my head before motioning to the table. "Would you care to join us for a late breakfast?"

"I've eaten, but some tea would be nice."

"We have some peppermint tea, if you'd like." Sam motioned to the teapot near her.

"That would be great." There was a sway in

Meredith's walk as she crossed the room that was almost hypnotizing. I looked over at Alex to see if he had noticed, but his eyes were trained back on Sam as she poured tea into an empty cup and passed it across the table.

Hurrying around the table, I pulled the chair out for Meredith and slid it back in as she sat.

"Thank you." Her voice was husky as she looked up at me with half-lidded eyes.

"You're welcome." I cleared my throat and moved back to my seat.

"You look wonderful." She smiled at Sam and I felt that tug again. As if she had captured me in a web, something pulling at me—pulling me toward her. "I'm guessing from the peppermint tea that you're still having morning sickness."

"Ugh, yes." Sam frowned. "And thanks, but I don't feel wonderful. I feel fat and tired."

"How far along are you?" Meredith poured cream into her tea.

"Five months." Sam smiled. "I thought I'd feel better by now."

"Hang in there. I had morning sickness for what felt like forever, but by the middle of the fifth month I woke up one morning and felt wonderful." She reached out and squeezed Sam's hand.

"God, I hope that happens to me." Sam smiled wistfully.

"It'll be worth it," Meredith said, and I chuckled.

"That's her mantra," I explained when she turned to look at me.

"It's a good one." Meredith picked up her tea and took a sip. "I'm sorry to crash your breakfast."

"Not at all," Alex offered. "I was very sorry to hear of your grandfather's passing. He was a bright, humorous man."

"Thank you." Her eyes dimmed. "He will be missed."

"Do you need anything?" Sam asked. Her voice was thick and I realized she was fighting tears. Though it had been over two years since her father's death, it was obvious that it was just as raw.

"Actually, I do." Meredith looked at me with large eyes and leaned forward just enough that I got a peek of cleavage. "I was hoping that you, Max, would be one of the pallbearers at my grand-dad's funeral."

I pulled my eyes away from the glimpse of breast and frowned. I had barely known the man and she wanted me to carry his casket?

"Trust me, I know it's a lot to ask, but we don't

have much family, and to be honest, we haven't really been in Lilaria long enough to make many friends." She looked down at the cup in front of her. "I don't have anyone else to ask."

I cut my eyes at Alex but kept my face blank. How the hell was I going to get out of this? Funerals gave me the heebie-jeebies and being in the spotlight made me irritable. Center stage at a funeral? Fuck me.

Alex gave a small shrug as if to say there was nothing he could do, but it was Sam who sealed the coffin, so to say.

"Of course he will!" Sam reached out to touch Meredith's graceful hand. "We wouldn't leave you alone in a time like this."

"You don't mind?" Meredith's face lit up with relief, her eyes turning to me with hope. "It's so much to ask and I know you don't do a lot of public appearances."

"Um, no, I don't." I shot a look at Sam and hoped she could read the promise of torture before smiling at Meredith. "But I can make an exception for you."

Damn, I meant to say for him, not for her. What the hell was wrong with my mouth? It kept saying things I didn't mean. I didn't mean that I would do it because it was for her. Did I? Shit.

"That means the world to me." She smiled, and the room brightened again. "I owe you big-time."

That I could work with. There were lots of big things she could do for me . . .

Stop it, I told myself. The last thing I wanted was an erection at the breakfast table. At least not while my brother and sister-in-law were in the room. Now if it was just me, Meredith, and a little raspberry jam . . . Fuck me. I was hard.

"Don't mention it. A little media won't hurt me." I waved my hand. Caskets. Dead people. Media galore. Yep. That killed my excitement.

"Do you need any help with the arrangements?" Sam asked around a mouthful of bacon. You could give her a crown, but she's still good ol' Sam.

"I think I have most of everything covered. There is someone from the palace coming to Thysmer Manor to help with the major things." She looked at her watch. "Speaking of which, I should probably be heading back. Marty has probably made the nanny cry and there is no telling what my fa— my favorite kiddo has gotten into."

I knew instantly why she had hesitated. She was more worried about leaving her father alone than about what her son was doing to the poor nanny. I couldn't imagine that little boy being that difficult. All you had to do was sit him in front of his video games and he'd probably never move. How hard could that be for the nanny?

"Let me see you to the door." I stood and helped pull her chair out.

"I'm sorry for interrupting your breakfast," she said to Sam and Alex. "I hope I didn't ruin your day."

"Not at all." Alex stood and held his hand out to her. "If we can be any more help, please let us know."

"Thank you, but you've already done enough." Meredith looked at Sam. "If you need someone to bitch to about being pregnant, I'm your girl."

Sam laughed. "Oh, you might regret that. I'm not exactly the glowing pregnant woman."

"Pfft. You look fantastic, but a spa day never hurt anyone." Meredith raised her eyebrows. "And if you need company, I'm your girl!"

"That we will definitely have to do." Sam laughed. "But no waxing."

"Have you ever tried threading?" Meredith stepped next to me, and it felt strange but good to have her petite frame next to mine while we chatted with my brother and his wife.

"Oh hell no. I'm never doing that again." Sam shuddered.

"I see you have tried it." Meredith's laugh was contagious and I felt my mouth pull up into a smile.

"Never again." Sam shook her head.

"Well, we can stick to the calmer things. A prenatal massage for you."

"That sounds wonderful." Sam smiled. "I'll have Chadwick, my assistant, contact yours."

"Oh, I don't have an assistant." Meredith laughed. "Just tell him to call me and we'll hash it out."

"You're going to need some assistance in the coming days." Sam frowned. "I could send someone over to help out."

"No, we're fine. Besides, the palace has already called me about helping arrange the funeral." Meredith edged a little closer to the door.

I wondered what had made her uncomfortable. Not that her face showed it in the least. I was beginning to suspect that a lot of today had been a performance. It was the little, real-life moments that let me get a peek at her real emotions.

"If you're sure." Sam frowned.

"I am, but thank you." Meredith stood a little straighter and smiled. "Thank you again for letting me join you this morning."

"Of course." Sam raised an eyebrow I could

see the wheels turning in her head and knew that Meredith was most likely going to end up with a bevy of assistants.

"This way, my lady." I held open the dining room door and let her walk through ahead of me. The faint smell of lavender floated past me and I took a deep breath.

"I really appreciate you saying yes." Meredith seemed to drop some of her strong appearance when she looked up at me. "I'm not sure what I would have done had you said no."

"No need to worry." I cleared my throat. She looked so vulnerable in that moment I would have agreed to anything.

We stopped at the front door and I saw her car idling out front.

"It's a lot to ask of someone. You barely know me and hardly had any time to see my grand-dad." She frowned up at me. "He was a good man, though."

"I'm sure he was." I reached out and touched her cheek. Her eyes closed briefly, before reopening with a soft smile.

"So, I think, are you."

"I have my moments." Warning bells filled my head and I took a step back. "Are you sure you don't need anything else?"

"Not right now." Confusion passed across her face before she straightened her shoulders and her winning smile curved her lips. "Thanks again."

"My pleasure." I watched as she walked down the stairs, her perfect ass swaying gently. Definitely my pleasure.

She got behind the wheel of her car and gave a small wave before pulling down the long driveway. Closing the door, I turned around and came face-to-face—well, face to the top of the head—with my sister-in-law.

"I'm sending Chadwick over there to help." She looked up at me with stubborn eyes.

"What did Alex say?"

"That I should respect her wishes. But no one should have to deal with all of this on their own and I've heard that her father isn't much help." She put her hands on her hips, making her baby belly stick out a little further. "Plus Chadwick will just make a place over there. No one tells Chadwick no."

"Chadwick will likely tell you no, though." I shook my head.

"Why?"

"He's not going anywhere while you're pregnant. Are you kidding me? He barely leaves the house without an emergency baby kit." Her assistant was almost as excited about the baby as Sam and Alex were, and his planning skills had turned to all things infant.

"Then he can pick someone to send over there." She narrowed her eyes. "Or you could go."

"What?" I felt my eyes widen.

"You could go. Make sure she doesn't need anything. Hang out and keep her father from going off the deep end. Your mother had to pull some strings to keep an interview he did from going live." Sam shook her head. "I can't imagine what all Meredith is dealing with right now. And her son must be devastated. Good boy, that one. Smart too."

"He is." I thought about Marty being stuck in that house while everyone talked about the funeral and his grandfather drunkenly said stupid things. "Okay."

"Okay?" Her brown eyes widened. "You'll do it?"

"I'm no Chadwick, but I think I can help with some of it. Get the boy out of the house anyway."

"Oh, that was way easier than I thought it would be." She turned around and hollered, "You owe me twenty!"

"What?" I frowned.

"I bet Alex that I could get you to go help her

out." She smiled smugly. "Mr. Drama-Free-Zone has the hots for a single mother."

"I do not have the hots for anyone."

She poked me in the chest. "Don't lie to me. I'm not stupid and I'm hormonal. Lying to me is a bad idea."

Turning away from me, she headed back to the dining room. She had a slight waddle to her step which I found adorable, but again, I wouldn't tell her that. Especially now that she had tricked me into doing what she wanted.

FIVE

I took a deep breath and let the charade fall away. I was so relieved that he hadn't told me no, I had thought I would faint. Walking into that home—the home of a ruling family—had been strange enough. Hell, Alex was next in line for the throne and he'd seemed normal enough. But to walk in and ask for something as odd as for one of them to carry a casket? Yeah, that had given me a sour stomach. Who else did I have to ask, though?

And now. Now I needed to go home and let my father know that he would also be a pallbearer. I had no idea how that would go over. It probably depended on how much he'd had to drink already. A shudder racked my body and I fought the tears that quickly followed. I needed to be able to see to drive. Taking a mighty sniff, I reined in my tears. My father was the one person who never did anything I needed. And if I asked for something? All hell usually broke out.

Damn you for leaving me with him, Granddad. Anger made me grip the steering wheel a little tighter and I had to take several breaths to calm myself. It wouldn't do to run off the road because I wasn't thinking straight. I was the only person Marty had left.

Lead filled my stomach at the thought and my hands steadied on the wheel. The only other person who was a fixture in Marty's life was my father and he wasn't exactly what you would call steady or secure. The urge to update my will and up my life insurance policy hit me hard. Sometime during all of this planning of the funeral, I needed to make sure Marty would be okay if something happened to me.

As I made the two-hour drive home, I had the horrible thought that I really didn't have anyone to help with Marty were something to happen to me. Before I had moved to Lilaria with Granddad, I would have thought my best friend, Karey, would take care of him, but now I wasn't sure. We had grown apart as I'd tried to carve out a place of my own in this new world where I was living. Was she even in a place where she could raise a boy?

By the time I got home my stomach was in knots. I thought I'd feel better after asking Max to be a pallbearer but instead I had obsessed over scary things.

"Mom! I beat level six!" Marty ran down the stairs and held his arms up in victory. I clamped down on worries and focused on the happy little boy staring at me.

"Way to go! That's the one with the evil robot doctor, right?" I followed him up the stairs so he could show me.

"Doctor Gear. He's been kicking my butt for weeks!"

"Don't say *butt*." I frowned. Living in a home like Thysmer Manor and rubbing elbows with royals and rich people, I'd begun to realize how different we talked and behaved. I'd started correcting Marty so that he would fit in a little better, but at the same time, I didn't want to change his personality. I wanted him to fit in, but not conform. No reason to lose his sense of self. After all, he was a pretty awesome little boy, if I do say so myself.

"Should I say a—"

"Don't finish that if you want to ever see your game system again." I raised an eyebrow.

"Sorry, Ma." He jumped on his bed, not even a little bit worried. "Look! I left it on the screen with the medal. I can't believe it. Isn't that awesome?"

"Completely." I reached out and tickled his side.

"Mom!" He wiggled out of my grasp. "I'm being serious. This was hard!"

"Huh. We should celebrate." I tapped my chin. "How about ice cream for lunch?"

"Really?" He looked at me with big eyes.

"Really." I'd do anything to keep that happy look on his face.

"You. Are. The. Best!" He jumped off the bed and did a little dance. "Oh yeah!"

"I'll tell Sarai." I stood up off the bed. "Go beat level seven while I handle some stuff."

"Okay, but don't forget the ice cream." He held out his pinky and I twined mine with it.

"Pinky promise." I kissed his forehead and pulled his door half shut as I left.

"My lady," the head butler called.

"Yes?" I turned to smile at Gerard. He was the one who had accompanied my granddad to the funeral home. I owed him so much for not leaving him alone.

"I wanted to let you know that the palace called and their aide is on her way to help with the arrangements. They've also asked that you be willing to say something to the town of Thysmer. It's tradition that the next in line for the title address the people after a death."

"I see." He didn't go to my father. He came to me. There was a lot left unsaid in his explanation. "And when do I need to do this?"

"Soon, preferably. Before the funeral, I'd say. The palace aide will be able to help you come up with an appropriate response." He stood up a little taller. "I'd also like to offer my condolences. Your grandfather was a fine man."

"He was a rambunctious old devil with bad habits." I smiled. "But you're right. He was a good man."

"Yes, ma'am." The doorbell chimed and he turned. "I'll see to that."

"Thank you."

I walked down the hall to my room and kicked off my high heels. The things were making my toes go numb. I pulled on some slippers while peeling off the skirt and tugging on a pair of comfortable jeans. I might be a lady now, but I'd just lost a loved one, and all I wanted to do was curl up in my bed and cry. Unfortunately, I had to take care of details. That meant I'd have to forgo my pajama pants, but I wasn't giving up my jeans. I ditched the cardigan and unbuttoned the gray shirt I had been wearing to reveal the tank top underneath. That was more like it.

Pulling my earrings off, I put them in a small

dish next to my bed, but left the pearl ring on my right middle finger. It was a small, cheap ring. Just wire wrapped around a small freshwater pearl, but I always wore it. Granddad had given it to me when I had Marty. It meant more to me than any of the new jewelry I had acquired since we'd hit the royal jackpot.

As I headed back down the hall, I heard a voice I hadn't expected.

"Is Lady Meredith available?" Max's deep voice rumbled up the stairwell.

"I'm not sure, Your Highness. Would you mind waiting a moment?"

I peeked around the corner before ducking back. There he was, standing there in khakis and an untucked button-up shirt. The sleeves rolled up to his elbows. Hearing the butler coming up the stairs, I ran back to my room quickly and kicked off the fuzzy slippers I'd been wearing. Why was Max here? Was he going to back out of being a pallbearer? I couldn't imagine any other reason for him to show up right now. Or ever, really. Not that I was complaining. He was nice to look at and his smile caused parts of me that had been dead for years to heat up. But why?

"Lady Meredith?" The butler knocked on my

open door frame. "Prince Maxwell is here to see you."

"Thank you. I'll be right down." I looked around my room for suitable shoes. "Would you take him to the sitting room and order some tea?"

"Of course, my lady." He started to turn.

"Um, where is my father?" I didn't want to throw Max to the wolves.

"I believe he left this morning to visit the village pub." His voice and face never changed, but I could see the pity in his eyes.

"That's for the best, I suppose." I shrugged. "Thank you."

"Yes, ma'am." He bowed quickly and left.

Rummaging rapidly through my closet, I found a pair of dark red flats that wouldn't squish my toes but looked cute with my jeans. I liked it when my shoes stood out. It was something like wearing armor. Good shoes made me feel good, which in turn made me feel like I was in charge.

But why was Max here? I walked slowly down the hall. What was I going to do if he backed out? I still hadn't talked to my father about the funeral, though I was sure he assumed I'd just take care of everything.

I hesitated just outside of the sitting room and

took a deep breath, letting nervous Meredith melt away and replacing her with strong Meredith. I could play this role for a little while until he left, but eventually I needed some time to fret and panic. Just to get it out of my system.

"Max?" I opened the door and let surprise show on my face. "I didn't expect to see you so soon."

He stood up and his eyes ran over my open shirt briefly before fixing on my face. "I wanted to talk to you about something."

"Oh, I see." I sat down and motioned for him to do the same. "I ordered tea."

"Thank you." He sat down and leaned forward so that his elbows rested on his knees. "I know that at the house you said you didn't need any help."

"If you're uncomfortable being a pallbearer, I completely understand. My feelings will not be hurt if you'd rather back out." I smiled at him and hoped that my performance was compelling. I wasn't exactly at the top of my game right now.

"No, no. You misunderstood what I meant." He shook his head. "I'm offering to help out with all of the planning."

"What?" My eyebrows drew together.

"I'd like to help while you get things settled. Even if it's just taking Marty fishing to keep him away from the more depressing things." He shrugged.

"You want to help plan a funeral?" I shook my head, confused.

"Or help keep Marty distracted." He looked at me with serious eyes. "I know what it's like to watch everyone around you deal with the death of a loved one."

"I see." I leaned back in my chair. "Have you ever watched a six-year-old boy?"

"I don't think I did too bad yesterday afternoon." He looked mildly offended, and it took a lot of control to keep from smiling.

"Yes, it's easy when video games are involved."

"Well? What do you say?" He rubbed his palms on his pants and I noticed that there was paint under his nails.

"That's really sweet, but I already feel like a burden." I frowned as one of the staff members brought in our tray of tea.

"You're not a burden." He picked up the pot and poured us both a cup. "Besides, it's me or Sam is going to send a bunch of staff over here to take care of you. Her mommy instincts are in full swing right now."

"I see." So the princess was behind his offer

of help. "Really, I can't accept. I'm sure you have much more important things to do—"

The front door swung open with a bang and a crash as a picture fell from a wall in the foyer.

"Where t' hell are you, Mere? You think you can jus' plan everythin' withou' me?" Dad's voice carried through the house like a tidal wave. "An' who da hell's car is blockin' my driveway?"

I jumped to my feet and motioned for the staff to disappear. The maid melted out of the room, but the butler refused to move when I shot him a look.

"I'm sorry, Max, but I think it's time for you to go." God, I didn't want him to see this. It was like having my dad show up at school drunk. Only worse.

"I don't think that's a good idea." Max stood up and moved to stand behind me as the sitting room door was thrown open.

"There's my lil' girl. All cozy in here, playin' woman of the house." My father swayed into the door frame. "Who da hell is he? Another boy toy, eh? 'Cause that worked out so well for you las' time."

"Father, you've met Prince Maxwell, remember?" I kept my voice even and calm, despite the shaking of my hands. There was no hiding the way the blood drained out of my face. Bringing up Marty's father was a low blow. It had been a while since my father had been this drunk, and that time I'd almost broken my arm when he threw me out of the house.

"Don't remember no such thin'," he said.

"He brought me from England." I didn't mention Marty and prayed that he was safe in his room.

"I don' care." He pointed at me. "I care that you're actin' all high-and-mighty. I'm the duke of this manor. Ain't no duchess here."

"I'm just helping you plan the funeral." I kept my voice low but never broke eye contact.

"You're tryin' to cut me out! You think you're gonna take over? I'll show ya." He might be drunker than a skunk, but he moved faster than a football player. With two giant steps forward he swung his right arm at my face and would have made contact if Max hadn't stepped forward.

Pulling me back against his chest, Max let Father stagger past us before letting me go and pinning my father's arms.

"Let me go, ya bas'ard." Father struggled uselessly.

I sucked in a deep breath, my composure cracking. It had been years since he had hit me, but I still remembered that moment with fear. It felt like someone had broken my face and I had thought my eyeball would explode. My cheek had been swollen for weeks. The bruises had taken forever to fade and I'd had to lie to all of my friends.

"That's enough." Max's words rang with authority. "Stop struggling or I will have you escorted to the jail."

"This is my home, you stupid git."

"And I'm a prince of this country. Who do you think the police will listen to?"

"Someone will listen to me!" Father's movements turned sluggish. "Someone should but no one does." Tears filled his eyes and I had to look away from him. I should feel pity for someone so out of control, but all I could muster was hate. And shame that Max had seen just how horrible my father really was.

"Easy now." Max half dragged, half carried my father over to a chair. "I'm going to put you down now, but if you make any more trouble, I'll have my bodyguard take care of you."

I hadn't even realized that a large man filled the empty doorway my father had just vacated.

"I jus' wanna be left alone, ya hear me?" My father's voice grew quiet before turning into a snore.

I stood there for a moment, completely at a loss for how to handle what just happened.

"Are you okay?" One of Max's hands gripped my shoulder with gentle fingers while the other lifted my chin so that he could look in my eyes.

I nodded my head but couldn't hide the tears. I wasn't a good enough actress after all. There was too much happening to and around me. I wasn't strong enough.

"I—I'm fine." I shook my head and his hand slid from my chin but he kept his grip on my shoulder. I couldn't meet his eyes. I was so embarrassed for myself and my family. "Thank you for stepping in."

His eyes searched my face, worry creasing his brow. I felt exposed, naked under his scrutiny. He had just seen my darkest secret.

With his free hand he reached up and brushed away a tear. "You're not fine and I'm staying. You need the help and there's no way I'm leaving you here with him."

SIX

Rage flowed through my veins, accompanied by the strong desire to protect Meredith. I stared down into her brimming eyes and fought my need to wrap her in my arms. It was hard, though, because she looked so delicate and frail. Nothing like the firecracker I had seen in the past.

"Thank you, but you really don't have to stay. This isn't the first—" She stopped and looked away from me. Her cheeks colored a delicate pink and my fury boiled just under the surface.

"Not the first time he's done this?" I growled the words. "He's hit you before?"

She looked at me with large eyes and I could see her trying to close doors, lock away the emotions, but it was all too raw, too real. And she was failing. The perfect image she had crafted for herself had been blown to bits by her father.

"Of course he's hit me before. Didn't your parents spank you?" She stepped away from me and I let my hand fall to my side.

"You know what I mean."

She shrugged and walked over to the couch, where she fixed a pillow that had been knocked over. "He's a drunk."

"Meredith." I ran a hand over my face. "You can't live in these conditions."

"I don't. I live in England." She frowned and a shudder racked her body. Her voice sounded tiny and distant. "Well, I did."

"Did your grandfather approve of this?"

"He saw the best in my father," she said. Never once looking me in the eye, she fiddled with things that had been knocked astray. "He saw the best in everyone. It never got this bad when my grandfather was around. It was like my dad knew better."

Looking over my shoulder, I nodded at Charles, my bodyguard, to let him know that he could leave. I turned back to look at Meredith as she continued to work around the room, righting what had been upturned in the scuffle.

"Has he ever hit Marty?" The moment she turned around I knew I had crossed the line.

"Who the hell do you think you are? Just because you're a prince doesn't give you the right to come barging into our lives, asking personal questions." She moved across the room to poke me in the chest. Anger filled her eyes with strength and passion. "But for your information, no. He's never hit Marty. I would never allow that to happen. Do you understand? I would die before I let someone hurt Marty."

I looked down into her red eyes. "Of course you wouldn't. But if you let him hurt you—"

"If he takes it out on me, he doesn't take it out on anyone else. Got it?" She stood up on her tip-toes, her nostrils flaring. Her finger dug a little deeper into my chest.

"Got it." I reached up and wrapped her finger in mine before moving it down to our sides. "I'm sorry."

"Are you?" She squinted at me. "Because I'm not sure if you just talk without thinking or if you really think I'd let him hurt my son. Why do you think I moved to England? It wasn't just to go to school."

"I have an unfortunate habit of speaking before thinking." I squeezed her finger gently before letting go. "I'm sorry for implying that you would let someone hurt Marty."

She snorted but didn't move away from me. Her delicate features belied the strength in her eyes. This was a woman to be reckoned with, someone who could move mountains by sheer will. She belonged on a stage, bathed in the spotlight.

She was everything I should avoid, but it seemed like she kept ending up in my path.

"What are we going to do with him?" I broke eye contact and nodded my head toward her father. His snore was growing louder.

"Leave him." She wrapped her arms around her waist and moved a step backward.

"What are you going to do?"

"Go about planning the funeral and ignore him." She shrugged. "There isn't much else to do."

"What about rehab?" I looked at the man and couldn't help the frown that pulled at my mouth. Someone who put himself above his family was disgusting. It went against everything that Lilaria stood for. I'd grown up learning that family always came first. Always.

"You have to want it to work for it to actually make a difference." She shook her head. "And he doesn't want it to work. He doesn't care."

"You're saying that he wants to be a drunk who beats his daughter?" I couldn't wrap my mind around something like that.

"I'm saying he doesn't care." She glared at me. "Are you going to keep on about this? I'm sorry you had to see it, but thankful that you kept him from doing any real damage. But it's not your problem to worry about."

"I promised that I would come help you." My chin lifted. "And I keep my promises."

"That's really sweet but I didn't ask for your help—"

"Yes, you did." I shook my head. "You asked me to participate in the funeral, and that's something I take very seriously. I don't just agree to things. Besides, it looks like you might need a little help."

"I can manage—"

The chime of the doorbell had her freezing in place, and a wild panic filled her eyes as she heard the thundering sound of footsteps down the steps.

"I'll get it!" Marty's little voice carried down the short hallway.

"That's probably the assistant from the palace." Meredith chewed on her fingernail and looked at her father before turning to me. "Out. Out!"

She shooed me out of the room and quietly closed the door behind us. "Not a word. Do you understand? I don't want Marty to know. I don't want anyone to know."

"You can't just sweep this under the rug, Meredith." I looked down into her bright eyes and frowned. Again. "That man needs to be dealt with."

"I am dealing with him. I've been dealing with him for my entire life," she hissed between clenched teeth.

My ire churned as I thought of her dealing with that poor excuse of a father. Leaning down so that the people at the door would not hear me, I lowered my voice and breathed against her ear.

"I will not leave you to deal with him alone anymore. I will not stand by while you and Marty are in danger. I may be reluctant to claim my title but I am a prince of this country and the protection of its people is my duty." I pulled back to look in her eyes. "I will do everything in my power to keep you and Marty safe. Do you understand?"

Her eyes widened in shock as she stared up at me. As footsteps neared the bend in the hallway she took a step backward and bumped into the wall. With a quick nod in my direction, she looked down and smoothed out her shirt and sweater. As I watched, she lifted her chin and her face melted into something softer, happier, and relaxed. It was like watching a person slide on a mask.

When the palace aide rounded the corner I watched as Meredith smiled and held out her hand, but I didn't get to hear the introductions.

"Max!" Marty bounded down the hall, sliding

to a stop in front of me. "Did you come back to play video games?"

"Well—"

"Actually, that would be great." Meredith turned and smiled at me. "It would be a big . . . help."

"Your Highness, I didn't realize you would be here." The older woman bobbed her head and smiled. I thought her name started with an R. Rebecca? Rachel? "It's so nice of you to help a friend during such a difficult time."

"Maybe I could play games after I help your mom." I smiled at the boy, but I could see a tiny storm cloud forming over his head. His stubborn expression matched the one on his mother's face. "Or maybe not."

"Yeah! C'mon." He grabbed my hand and tugged me toward the stairway. "I finally beat the last guy. This new level is totally awesome."

"Are you sure?" I shot a look at Meredith. She might look calm and collected but I knew what was roiling below the surface.

"I promise to take good care of her." The aide smiled at me. "I already have everything lined out. She just has to approve which options she would prefer."

"Thank you. If you need anything, let me

know." I said it to the aide, because I knew that Meredith wouldn't ask another thing of me if she could help it.

"Of course, sir." She dipped in a short curtsy and I fought a grimace.

"Thank you." With that I let Marty lead me up the stairs and to his room.

He closed his door and leaned against it with a look of relief. "Did he hurt Mama?"

"What?" My senses came alive, like a cornered dog. This was dangerous territory.

"Grandfather. Did he hurt my mom?" His little face was a thundercloud of rage. "I just wanna kick him so hard . . ."

Turning away from me, he kicked a toy across the room and clenched his little hands at his sides.

"No, your mom is okay." I sat down on the bed and folded my hands in my lap. I thought the scariest thing in the world was my job as a prince, but it turned out that this, this right here, talking to Marty about his mother and grandfather made me break out into a cold sweat.

"Did you beat him up?" Marty looked at me with eyes that were too old for his little face. "I'm too little, but when I get bigger I'm going to make him sorry for being so mean to my mom."

"I didn't beat him up, Marty." I looked around

the room, trying to find the right words. "It wouldn't have helped. The only way your grandfather is going to stop is if he realizes what he is doing is wrong."

"You could show him what he is doing is wrong." Marty looked at me with the angry eyes of his mother. "He makes my mama cry. I'm not supposed to know, but I do."

I stared at the little boy, surprised by the mix of emotions running through my gut. Anger was definitely at the top of the mixture. Anger that this little boy was growing up too fast, rage that Meredith had spent so long dealing with this by herself. Had the old man, her grandfather, truly let her deal with all of this alone? I was half tempted to ask Marty, but that would be wrong. He needed to be protected, sheltered from this storm.

"I'm not going to let him hurt your mom again." I looked him in the eyes so that he would know I was serious. And there it was. The moment I realized I was in deep trouble. Because I meant every word. I wouldn't let that man downstairs hurt Meredith again. And I wouldn't let Marty have to worry about his mother again.

"I knew you'd help." The little boy launched himself across the room and into my unsuspecting arms.

"Oof." I froze for a moment, surprised, and then wrapped my arms around him. I was blown away by his complete trust. When was the last time I had trusted someone so much? Someone other than family? "I'll do my best."

"Mom says that's all anyone can do." He shrugged and crawled out of my lap. "You want to play the race game?"

"Do you want to lose?" I raised an eyebrow as I took the controller he handed me. Relief flooded my system. Racing I could handle.

"No way." He popped the game into the machine and waited for it to load. "I've been practicing."

"Show me what you've got." I narrowed my eyes.

"You asked for it." He laughed maniacally, which prompted me to chuckle. The boy was a handful. Then again, considering his mother, you couldn't expect anything else.

Time with Marty sped by faster than the cars on the screen. I shifted in my seat and shook my left leg because it had fallen asleep. It was dark outside before I knew it. The light barely filtered through the shades covering the windows.

A maid brought up a tray of food, which the boy dove into with a vengeance.

"Has Lady Meredith finished?"

"Not that I know, sir. The last I checked, the dining room table was still covered in papers and they were discussing flowers." The woman bobbed her head and started to leave.

"And Duke Thysmer?" I said the words quietly. Hoping that little man, my new nickname for Marty, wasn't listening.

"Still in the front parlor, sir." She frowned, her eyes shifting to Marty. "We'll see him to his room when he is ready."

I started to ask if that was safe but stopped. She tilted her head in the boy's direction. "It's no problem, sir."

"Thank you."

She smiled at me. "My pleasure, sir."

"Are you going?" Marty asked around a mouthful of sandwich.

"Not yet." I pulled his desk chair out and turned it around to straddle. "That food looks too good to pass up."

"The cook here is awesome." He laughed. "It's so weird to have a cook!"

"I suppose it is." I helped myself to a sandwich and a handful of crisps.

"Yeah, before this place we ate lots of leftovers and easy stuff. Mom didn't have a lot of time to cook." He took another bite. "She was always working. It's way better now. She just has school and that means we get a lot of time together."

"What kind of things do you do?" I sipped the soda that had been brought up for us.

"Movies, games, she even plays with me at the park across from our flat." He smiled. "She's rubbish at football, but she tries."

"Well, everyone has different talents," I offered.

"Yeah. Mom's is singing." He pointed at me. "You should ask her to sing for you. People really notice how great she is when she sings."

"I heard her in England," I said. I'd more than heard her. I'd felt her words like she was singing just for me. I couldn't imagine anyone not noticing how great she was when she sang. "You're right. She's fantastic."

"Yeah." He finished his sandwich. "Another round of battle racing?"

I glanced at my watch. I didn't want to leave until I'd spoken to Meredith again. "Sure."

"Hey, do you like to fish?" Marty asked as we raced our avatars around the track.

"Yeah." I was focused on beating the little punk. He had gotten better since the day before. Or he had been taking it easy on me. I really hadn't been fishing in years, but I remembered it being fun.

"Me too. Wanna go with me?"

I looked over at him, but he was paying attention to the game. "Sounds like a plan."

"Cool."

Marty sat back in his pillows and got comfortable while we raced. It wasn't until his car ran off the track that I realized he was asleep. Chuckling, I turned down the sound and got up from my seat. My back complained from having sat in one position too long, so I stretched the kinks out.

Carefully I pulled Marty's shoes off and tugged his legs up onto the bed. Slowly I covered him with the blanket on the bed and looked down at his sleeping face. The moonlight that streamed through the window highlighted his cheekbones and cast long shadows of his eyelashes along his skin. It was that moment that I realized just how young the boy was. He didn't deserve to worry about his mother. He deserved the life he had in England, where he played football with his mother and went to school with regular kids.

As I turned to leave the room, my eyes fell on a sketch pad and I couldn't help myself. Sitting back down in the chair I flipped it open and smiled at the drawings inside. Marty had promise for such a young kid. Turning to a blank page, I glanced around and searched for a pencil. Charcoal would be best, but pencil would do.

I started with the lines of his forehead, the curve of his impish nose, the roundness of his cheeks. I was lost in the sketch, enjoying the shadows, the tenderness in his expression, working to capture that moment of utter innocence.

"That's beautiful." Her voice was soft.

I looked up from what I was doing, not surprised that she had snuck up on me. When I'm lost in a project, the world disappears; the only thing I'm aware of are the layers of the project I'm working on.

"He's a good subject." I turned back to the paper and finished up the shading of the blanket.

"Only because he's asleep and not moving." Her quiet laugh sent shivers over my body.

"That does help." I smiled up at her. "But it's the contrast. The contrast of him awake versus him asleep. He looks so young right now, so innocent."

"What do you mean?" She leaned closer to look at the picture.

"He's so mature, quick-witted." I whispered the words. "But here he is, looking like the child he is."

"His teachers say that," she said. "That he's quick to pick things up."

"I'd say so." I turned and handed her the sketch pad. "I hope you don't mind that I drew him. The light and shadows were too perfect to resist." Sort of like her right now. The way the moonlight glinted in her eyes and shone along her hair. Her perfect features would make any artist ache to draw them. Her pixie nose, the heavy eyelashes, the curve of her body hinted at by the oversized sweater she had wrapped around herself. It made my palms itch. Partly because I just wanted to touch her, to see if she would taste as sweet as she looked in that moment.

"Thank you for keeping him entertained." She stood up. "Can I keep this?"

"Of course." I stood up and stretched. Her eyes swept over my chest and then back up to my face. Maybe I wasn't the only one tempted to touch. I hated to admit it, but I had a flare of pride. "I enjoyed hanging out with him."

I was surprised to realize I meant it. I never would have thought spending time with a six-year-old would have been enjoyable.

"Looks like he did too." She moved away from the door and I followed her into the hallway.

"Did you get everything settled?"

"I think so." She frowned.

"What's wrong?" Her expression worried me.

"Granddad would have hated a large ceremony." She sighed and headed for the stairs. "But I guess that as a duke there are some things that have to happen."

"I don't blame your grandfather." I followed behind her. "I would want a small ceremony, not to be made into a production."

"I'm starting to think you don't like any type of production." She looked at me over her shoulder.

"Not really, no." I wasn't going to lie. "I don't like being the focus, being the center of attention. It makes me uncomfortable." I wasn't going to lie, but I hadn't intended to tell her so much about me.

"And yet you agreed to help me with my grandfather's funeral." She turned to me at the bottom of the stairs and set the sketch pad on a table. "Why?"

I stared at her for a minute, enjoying the way her eyes looked up at me, the tilt of her chin, the way her hair cascaded around her shoulders. "I don't know."

Unable to help myself, I reached out and touched her cheek with my fingers. Her pupils dilated and she inhaled softly. With one thumb I traced the dip under her plump bottom lip. Her hand reached up to trace my jaw and she took a step closer to me.

"You should be running from me as fast as you can." She whispered the words. "I'm everything you don't want."

"I'm not so sure."

"I live for the spotlight, it's my food." Her eyes were half lidded as she edged closer to my mouth. "And you've seen my family. I'm trouble, Max."

Did I care? I wasn't sure I was capable of making a real decision as her smell wrapped around my senses. The only thing I knew was that I wanted to taste her, to touch her, to press her against my body. To hear her say my name again.

Dipping my head, I grazed her lips with mine and I was lost. On a sigh, she leaned into me and wrapped her hands around my neck. Tilting her head back, I brought my mouth to hers carefully, softly, tasting. I wanted to deepen the kiss, to hear her moan, to feel the way her body could wrap around mine, but I kept it soft, sweet, and simple. She was in such a hard place, she needed to be protected, treasured by someone.

And right now, I was that person.

SEVEN

DECADENT. TENDER. PERFECT.

I hadn't been kissed in so long I'd almost forgotten how wonderful it could be. Or maybe it was just Max. His teasing lips, the soft touch of his hand on my hip, the way he tasted. It was enough to make me forget the stress, the worry, the pain of the day.

I knew it was wrong. Knew that I was bad for him, but there was something in the way he looked at me, the way he touched me, that killed my reasoning. When I slid my tongue out to touch his bottom lip, his fingers tightened on my hip, his thumb rubbing soft circles just above the top of my jeans. The kiss deepened, our breaths mingling together. I couldn't help the soft moan when he pulled me to his body; feeling his lean muscles pressed against me was more than I had experienced in years. I let one of my hands run down his chest and around to his back.

He pulled away from me just a little, his lips kissing me softly once more before looking at me with serious eyes.

"I'd say I'm sorry, but I'm not." His deep voice made me want to wrap it around me.

"Good." I let my hand run along his jaw softly before falling to my side. "I'm not sorry."

That thought was surprising. I didn't kiss men. But boy was I glad that I had let him kiss me.

"I should go." He didn't move.

"You should." I looked up at him but didn't step away. "This is a bad idea."

"Maybe." Leaning forward, he pressed a kiss to my cheek. "Will you be okay tonight?"

His eyes darted to the shut door of the sitting room.

"Yes." I sighed, the moment broken. Nothing like the thought of my asshole father to kill the mood. "He's been taken up to his room. I doubt he'll remember anything from today."

"I'm coming back tomorrow." He stated it like I should just expect it.

"No you aren't. You have other things to do." I narrowed my eyes. "I don't need you in the way while I handle everything."

"You need help." His jaw tensed.

"No I don't. Everything has been set up for the funeral." I took a step away from him. "I don't need you until then."

"I'm offering to help you." His face took on a stubborn cast.

"And I'm telling you I don't need any." He wasn't the only person who could be stubborn.

"You don't need to take all of this on by yourself."

"I've been doing just fine without you." My chin jerked upward.

"Like today? When your father tried to beat your face in?" He took a step toward me. "Stop being stubborn and let me help you. You can't live like this."

"What are you going to do? Throw Duke Thysmer in jail?" She laughed. "Trust me, he's been there before, and all it did was make him hit harder."

His jaw clenched and his head jerked toward the stairs.

"What are you thinking, Max?" I stepped forward and touched his tensed shoulder.

"That maybe it's time someone hits him back." He turned to look at me, and I was surprised by the amount of anger in his green eyes.

"It won't do any good." I pulled on his arm to get him away from the staircase. "Besides, I don't want Marty to think that's how to solve problems."

His vision cleared a bit, but he looked back at the stairs. "That man is a ticking time bomb. When are you going back to England?"

"I don't know." I looked away from him. "I might stay here."

"What?" Max turned back to me. "You can't stay here with him."

"I can't let him destroy the family." I willed him to understand. "This is our chance to be more than a poor family with no hopes. I can't let him ruin that. Not for Marty."

"There have to be other options."

"What? Going back to waiting tables? Double shifts?" I put my hands on my hips. "I never saw Marty. He was growing up without me. I was working extra shifts just to pay the babysitters to watch him while I worked those shifts. It took me an extra year just to finish high school. There was no way I'd be able to go to university. This is our chance for more."

"He's going to hurt you or Marty. You won't be able to stop him." He frowned. "If I hadn't been here today he would have hurt you."

"It's only when he's drunk." I shrugged.

"Don't shrug. We're not talking about him smoking a cigar when he drinks." He put a hand on my shoulder. "What's to say he doesn't wake up tomorrow and do the exact same thing?"

"He won't." I stared up at him. "He'll sleep it off tomorrow and then go back to normal."

"Did your grandfather leave you any money?" He let his hand slide to his side. "Did he put any aside for you?"

"I have what's in my bank account, but I don't think he had a will. It all goes to my dad." My breath hitched in my throat. "The title, the house, the money. Even the township falls on my dad. Don't you get it? It's not just about me and Marty. I can't let him ruin all of that. I can't let him make your family look bad for bringing us back."

His eyes darted down to my lips and I swear I could still feel his kiss. A breath shuddered out of me.

"Don't worry about my family. My mother knew what she was doing when she brought you back." He stepped close. "You're not the first family that has had a problem with alcohol. There are ways of handling this if you'll let me help."

"I . . . I don't know, Max." I licked my lips. "Having you around will just make him feel threatened."

His chest rose in an angry breath. "This is insane, Meredith."

"Just . . . just trust me." I put a hand on his chest. "Look, I appreciate you wanting to be my knight in shining armor, but I know what I'm doing." No, I didn't. I had no idea how I was going to handle my father, but the last thing I needed was someone swooping in and making it harder.

"I'm leaving, but I'll be back." He took my hand. "I have to." His eyes willed me to understand.

"Give me a day." Compromise. I could do that. "I've got to speak to the township tomorrow." God, I still had no idea what to say. I could fake it, though. I was good at that.

"When is the funeral?"

"Three days."

Reaching around me, he pulled my phone out of my back pocket. Quickly he typed into the phone and hit send. His phone beeped and he pulled it out of his pocket and checked something before handing my phone back to me.

"Call me if you need me." He looked at me earnestly. "Even if it's just to sit with Marty."

"Okay." I took my phone back and slipped it into my pocket. I hoped he couldn't tell that I was lying. I wasn't on my best game right now. The last thing I wanted to do was involve a member of royalty in my family drama.

"Meredith . . ." He sighed and shook his head. "I'll be back."

His eyes searched my face for a minute and then he was gone, the door closing softly behind him. I leaned against the stair railing and took a minute to catch my breath. That man kept me on my toes. God, I was the wrong kind of woman for him. And what had I been doing when I let him kiss me? Kiss me! I didn't kiss men. It was too raw, too real.

Sweet Lord, it had been delicious. The kind of kiss that made you feel like a woman.

Dangerous. He was dangerous. I'd broken my main rule for men after two days of being around him. How the hell had he wormed his way where other men couldn't get with a bulldozer?

I looked over where I had set the sketchbook and felt my breath catch. He had captured Marty in just a few strokes of the pencil. Down to the baby fat still in his cheeks and the way his mouth hung partially open. It was beautiful and he had done it with a child's sketch pad and number two pencil. I picked up the book and carefully pulled the picture out.

Taking the steps two at a time, I opened the

door to Marty's room and slid the sketchbook back on his desk.

"Mom?" His voice sounded so small in the dark room.

"Yes?" I opened the door wider and looked at my son. "What do you need?"

"Is Max gone?" He rubbed at his eyes.

"Yes, baby." I walked over and sat down on his bed. "He had to go home."

"I like him." He rolled over and reached out for my hand. I wrapped his fingers with mine and squeezed gently.

"Me too." It was true. I liked Max. More than I had liked anyone in a long time. Which was scary.

"Good." He yawned. "Will you stay until I fall asleep?"

"Sure." I kicked my shoes off and curled up next to him.

"Thanks."

I kissed his head and pulled him against me. His legs were hitting another gangly, awkward phase, his ankles peeping out of his pants. It wouldn't be long until he was taller than me.

His little fingers gripped my wrist and I smiled. He might be growing faster than a weed, but he was still my baby right now.

It wasn't until the sunlight streaming through

Marty's window hit my face that I woke up. Marty was sprawled across the bed, his leg draped over mine and one arm thrown above his head. Carefully I extracted my body from his bed and rubbed the sleep out of my eyes.

I tiptoed down the hall and into my room, where I hurried into the shower. I still needed to figure out what I was going to do for the speech later that afternoon. I needed to wake up my father and see if he would be willing to do it, or if he would at least come stand with me in family solidarity.

I closed my eyes and let the water run over my face. There were only three outcomes that I could foresee. One, he would tell me to do it myself and go back to sleep. Two, he would insist on doing it himself and drunkenly slur through the whole ordeal. Or three, he would come and stand beside me while I handled the responsibility and then blame me for something not going right.

Getting dressed, I put on what I considered "lady" clothes. A skirt and blouse, dark, to show mourning, but I couldn't resist wearing some kick-ass heels. I needed something to make me feel strong and pulled together, and those shoes were just the thing. Looking in the mirror, I nodded in approval. I pulled my hair up into a simple twist and chose very bland jewelry. Simple studs and the ring Granddad had given me.

Taking a deep breath, I walked down the hall and to my father's side of the house. I could hear his snores before I even got to his room. I knocked on the door and waited. There was no answer so I knocked again. It would be best if he woke up before I went into the room. I'd learned the hard way as a child that you didn't wake my father up from a bender by touching him. It always ended poorly.

"Father?" I opened the door a crack and knocked louder.

"Wha . . . ?" His groggy voice turned into a snore.

"Dad, I need to talk to you." I peeked in the room and grimaced. He was sleeping on top of his blankets, still in his suit from the night before.

"Jesus." He rolled over. "Can't a man sleep in peace?"

"We have to address the township today about Granddad." I stepped into the room, but stayed well out of reach.

"What? Why?" He didn't roll over to look at me.

"It's tradition for the family to address the township when the duke passes away. A sign of respect and solidarity." I clasped my hands in front of me.

He grunted but didn't say anything else.

"I was told that it typically falls to the new duke or duchess."

"I'm not going out there to tell them something they already fucking know." He growled and sat up. "You do it. You're so set on being Duchess of Thysmer anyway."

"I'm not trying to be duchess. I'm just trying to help." I eased a little closer to the door. "There's a lot to do."

"No one asked you." He kicked his shoes off angrily.

"It's my duty as part of the family." I opened the door a little and he threw his arm up to block the light.

"Listen to you." He snorted. " 'Duty as part of the family.' What bullshit. You're from the poor side of town, Meredith. Putting on fancy clothes won't change what we are, who we are."

"This could be our chance to do more with our lives." I took a deep breath.

"You sound like my father. Talking about making the best out of this 'gift.' " He pulled his suit jacket off. "Get the hell out of here. Go do your *duty*."

"Yes, sir." I couldn't keep the disgust out of my tone, but I doubted he heard it. He was already snoring when I closed the door. He would likely not remember any of our exchange. Just another thing for him to be angry about later. But for now I could just focus on the important tasks at hand.

"My lady, Rachel, the palace aide, has arrived." Gerard met me at the top of the stairs. "I believe that she has put together a press conference to address the township."

"Yes, thank you." I looked toward Marty's door and frowned. I didn't want him to have to attend the event with me. It was going to be hard enough at the actual funeral.

"Shall I see to your father?" The butler's face remained blank.

"No, he won't be attending." I glanced at a mirror on the wall before descending the stairs.

"Yes, ma'am." The butler followed behind me, careful to keep his distance.

"Would you make sure that the nanny is available for Marty? I'm not sure how long today will take."

"Of course, ma'am."

"And would you see to it that breakfast is served in the dining room?" I smiled at him.

"I believe the cook has everything ready. Including, a proper pastry for the young Marty." His eyes twinkled.

"You mean a Pop-Tart?" I laughed. Marty had begged for his favorite food when we'd first moved into the large, strange house. He'd just wanted something familiar. The chef had been horrified that he'd rather eat something out of a box than one of her creations. It had taken a lot of explanation and placation on my part to keep feelings from being hurt. "Did the cook cry while putting it in the toaster?"

"She was distinctly not amused, my lady." His lips curved upward.

"Well, Marty will be grateful." I brushed at my skirt. "Is Rachel in the sitting room or the dining room?"

"I believe she is waiting for you in the sitting room." He stepped forward to open the door for me. "Do you require anything else?"

"No thank you."

Gerard let me walk through the door before pulling it closed.

"Good morning, my lady." Rachel stood up and bobbed her head.

"Please, call me Meredith." I tried to not let the curtsy give me the heebie-jeebies. There was something very weird about having a dignified, older woman bow to me. Especially when not that long ago I might have been her maid. Or a cocktail waitress at an event she was hosting.

"Thank you, Meredith." She smiled.

"Have you eaten breakfast? The cook has prepared something for us." I motioned toward the dining room.

"Oh, that would be lovely." She started gathering her papers. "I had a quick cup of tea and hurried over here. I didn't want to leave you to handle all of this on your own."

"Leave the papers. We'll come back here to go over stuff." I smiled, despite my annoyance. Why did every one seem to think I couldn't handle the situation on my own? "No reason to ruin good food with paperwork!"

"Well, thank you so much." She looked around the house as we walked to the dining room. "Thysmer Manor is a beautiful home! A friend of mine was one of the caretakers over the years. He took great pride in keeping the house in the same shape it was left."

"I've never lived in a place as grand as this one." I opened the dining room door for us. The smell of food wafted across my face and made my stomach growl. "It's been interesting to learn some of its secrets."

"Did you know that there used to be a servants' quarters behind the stables?" She took a seat next to the head of the table. Avoiding the ornate chair, I sat across from her instead. The last thing I wanted was for my father to walk in and see me sitting in the duke's spot.

"I did! You can still see where the original foundation sat." I poured some tea into my cup. "Supposedly, the place was burned down by a rival."

"Yes, just before the Thysmer family left." She shifted food on to her plate. "It was during all of that terrible mess with the would-be usurpers hundreds of years ago. Thankfully all of the servants were unhurt and it is said that the duke left them each a sum of money before he left. The Thysmer family treated their workers well."

"It still must've been hard for them to find themselves homeless and jobless." I frowned thinking about it. "And the township could have fallen into disrepair."

"The crown saw to the townships, appointing stewards and finding jobs for those who were left without anything." She shrugged her delicate shoulders. "It was a terrible time for many, and no one could blame the families for leaving to protect themselves. If your children are in danger, you drop everything and find a way to shield them."

"Yes, I suppose you're right." I frowned. Wouldn't I do anything to protect Marty? Even if it meant giving up everything we'd been given? Damn straight I would. We'd find a way to make it work.

"Anyway, I've always heard stories about Thysmer Manor and its grounds. Supposedly some of the best gardens in the country." She turned to look out a window.

"It's beautiful in the spring." I glanced out the window. "Marty loves the backyard. He can catch all kinds of little critters to play with."

"Is there a pond back there? I bet there are frogs aplenty." She grinned.

"Frogs, bugs, lizards. You name it and it's back there." I shook my head. "I never know what he's going to come back with."

"It's good for them to play outdoors. Fresh air for their lungs. Have adventures."

"Do you have children?"

"Oh yes, three. All grown now with their own young ones." She smiled fondly. "But I remember when they were bringing me their own frogs."

"Mom!" The door pushed open and Marty walked in. He was still wearing the rumpled clothes he had fallen asleep in last night.

"Hungry?" I turned to look at him and tried to

not smile. His hair was sticking up off the top of his head.

"Starving." He sat down next to me and I put his preferred breakfast on his plate.

"Good morning." Rachel smiled at Marty. "Did you sleep well?"

"Yep." He shoved half of his Pop-Tart in his mouth.

"Marty." I leveled a glare in his direction and he hurriedly chewed what was in his mouth.

"Sorry." He wiped his mouth with the back of his hand. "Yes, ma'am."

"Thank you." I bumped him with my arm. "Ms. Rachel is here to help with some things I have to take care of today."

"Is that why you're all dressed up?"

"It is. I have to go speak in town."

"Speak? Like a speech?" He frowned. "Do I have to go?"

"No, you can stay here, but don't bother your grandfather and take it easy on the nanny."

"Yes, ma'am." He bit into his food with a big smile. The boy had not inherited my love of the spotlight. Though to be fair, I wasn't exactly looking forward to doing this particular speech.

"Is your father not joining us?" Rachel watched me with a calm face.

"No, I'm afraid it will just be me." I stomped on the anger that flared up. It was better this way. I'd rather people remember my granddad, not the way my father slurred through a speech.

"I suppose that he is taking the death of his father very hard." She sighed. "Don't worry, though, you're in good hands with me."

"Thank you." I nodded my head. "I hate to be a burden."

"Nonsense! When one of our own is suffering, we all pitch in to help." She set her fork down. "I'm not here to take over, just to help. This is not the first royal funeral I have planned."

"You were a great help yesterday. You had everything planned out." I sighed. "I had no idea what all went into a funeral."

"Lots of details to take care of, but then I'm a detail-oriented person. That's why they sent me." She reached out and patted my hand. "Don't you worry, dear. We'll make sure you're well taken care of."

"Thank you." The rest of our breakfast consisted of small talk and questions for Marty. It was sort of peaceful, like having a long-lost grandmother show up. She obviously knew her way around the royal scene, but her demeanor was so comfortable I was able to relax. Even the day before had been painless, with the exception of what happened with my father.

When Marty had finished his breakfast, he disappeared with the nanny to get dressed and find something to do.

"Have you thought about what you would say to the township?" Rachel sat down on the chair across from me in the sitting room.

"Um, a little." I frowned. "Actually I was going to ask you if there was a certain protocol or how it would normally be handled."

"Just a short acknowledgment of his passing, expressing your family's sorrow, and promising that the township would be taken care of no matter what." She frowned. "It's a little unusual that his granddaughter would be the one to pass on the information, but not so much that people will complain."

"Would they really complain?" I frowned as my stomach churned.

"No, no. It's usually the first duty that the new duke takes on, but no one will question that it's you making the address." She looked down for a minute before looking back at me with shrewd eyes. "Might I speak frankly, my lady?"

"Please call me Meredith and yes, by all means." I sat back in my chair.

"Are you planning on staying and covering for your father forever? Or are you going to go back to England?" Her grandmotherly demeanor seemed to sharpen. "I know that's terribly blunt of me to ask, but it might make the township feel better to know one way or the other."

"I don't want to. I have a life in England . . . but I can't leave the township with no one to help." Sighing, I leaned forward and tried to dispel the fear that thought brought. "Is this why the palace sent you?"

"It is known by certain people that your father has a problem." She poured herself a cup of tea. "And he is certainly not the first person to deal with this particular problem. When needed, people are employed by the palace to help."

"And you're one of those people?" I felt my smile tighten.

"I am." She looked at me over her glasses. "One thing I want you to know is that this is not a reflection on you. Quite the opposite. I'm here to help you and Marty during a difficult time. In any way you need me to."

"What do you mean exactly?"

"I'm here to help with your father, to make sure he doesn't do anything too far out of line. We'd hate to see him stripped of his title and his township passed down." She sat back in her chair. "Passed down to you."

"Oh Jesus, no." I felt my eyes widen. "Do you know what that would cause?" I looked over my shoulder to make sure no one else heard. Panic raced up my spine as I thought of how my father would react.

"I assume that he would be greatly upset." She nodded her head. "But from the fear in your eyes, I'm guessing it goes beyond that."

"My father's temper . . . it's not something to take lightly." I tried to calm my thumping heart.

"Are you aware that your grandfather left a will?" She cocked her head to the side. "It was done in secrecy and entrusted to the crown."

"No." I shook my head and took a deep breath. Shock sharpened my response and I wanted to shake her for not telling me sooner. "What does it say?"

"There will be a formal reading the day after the funeral. As of now, only the attorney, witness, and Her Majesty know what is included."

"Who was the witness?" I narrowed my eyes. Who would my grandfather entrust with a will? And for the love of all things good, why hadn't he told me about it?

"I don't know." She shook her head.

"You're worried about what is in the will." I frowned. "You're worried that my grandfather left everything to my father. Nothing left to me and Marty which would leave us at my father's mercy, or I'd have to start all over. Which I would and could do." My sadness was replaced by determination.

"It is possible." Her face was blank and I fought the urge to shake my head. Granddad had been blind to his son's follies. However, I couldn't really say it surprised me. He would expect my father to take care of me and Marty, not the other way around.

"I cannot stay here with my father forever." I could feel the determination stiffen my back. "I can't."

"I understand." She was so calm, so patient. It was at complete odds with how I was feeling.

"Why are you here?"

"I'm here to help however *you* need it."

She was here for me. Not for my father. Message delivered.

"And if I ask you to leave?" Would the crown object?

"If that's what you'd prefer, then I will go, but I'm asking you to let me help. I can stay out of the way, attend to the basic paperwork, act as an event planner. But if you need something else, I'm here. Simple as that."

"So you're here to spy for the queen?" I ran my fingers over the upholstery of the chair I was sitting in. "And I'm supposed to just let you?"

"I'm here to help." She frowned. "The queen did send me, but it wasn't to spy for her. I'm mainly here to help you through a difficult time. She didn't tell me much more than that. Though— she was worried about your father's problem."

My frustration was at an all-time high. "Is there any one left that doesn't know my father is a drunk?"

She didn't respond, just watched me with sad eyes. I stood up and paced the length of the room.

"He's going to ruin the family." I turned and looked at her. "With Granddad gone, there is no one to stop him."

"There is you." Her words were quiet.

"I am not my father's keeper." I growled the words and rubbed at my temples. "I should not have to take care of that man."

"No, you shouldn't." She set her teacup down. "But I'm here to help."

I looked at her and laughed. "You have no idea what you're signing up for."

"Then tell me."

"My father . . . he's an angry drunk, Rachel. And he takes it out on the closest person he can find." I sat down in the chair, defeated. Telling someone such a deep, dark secret was physically painful. I felt drained to the point of exhaustion. "It's why I moved to England with Marty."

"Sweetheart, you're not the first person to deal with this. Hell, you're not the first royal to deal with this."

I couldn't help but snort when she cursed. "I know that, I do."

"There's a reason that they chose me to come out here. My father was a right bastard." Those words said in her motherly tone made me shake my head. "My mother worked for the palace, so it wasn't a big secret. It wasn't until she went in to work with a black eye that anyone did anything about it."

"What could they do?" I shook my head.

"They offered him treatment. He refused." She shrugged. "So they gave her the means to leave him without worrying about her children."

I didn't say anything. I had left. I had moved away and was starting to make a new life for me and my son. Now here I was dancing around my father and feeling the weight of the world on my shoulders.

"You see, sweetie, family isn't just what you're born into. It's also the friends and loved ones that find you along the way." She smiled. "And the crown feels that way about you."

"Is this something Max set up?"

"Max?" She frowned. "No, not as far as I'm aware."

"Then he's also here under orders from the queen?" The thought made me far sadder than it should.

"I don't know Prince Maxwell very well, but I would assume whatever he is doing is because he wants to. I don't believe he takes on many tasks that might require he be in the spotlight."

"And why is that?"

"No one's told you?" Rachel sighed heavily. "Max loathes the media."

"Why?" I knew he hated the media, just not why.

"Max was at a school tournament when his father died. Before anyone could get to him, the media bombarded him." She paused. "He found out his father died from a reporter who wanted a quote."

EIGHT

I SWUNG MY LEGS over the side of my bed and ran my hands through my hair. I'd had the same dream about Dad again. He was riding his horse and fell just before I could get to him. I hadn't been able to move, frozen in place as it happened in slow motion in front of me. I could hear the snap of his back as he hit the ground . . .

Standing up, I stretched to work out the kinks in my back. It felt like I had been asleep for days instead of a few hours. Those dreams always did a number on me. There was only one way to get rid of the pent-up tension, and that was to draw. I pulled my stool over to my desk and let my mind wander. Faint lines became darker lines, and it wasn't until I was shading that I realized who I was drawing.

Meredith's bright eyes were cut to the side as she looked at me, her hair trailing over one shoulder. My fingers itched to find a red that would do her hair justice, but I stopped myself. Why had it been her? The woman surrounded by trouble, the mother of a little boy.

But that kiss last night—that had been something else. It had hit all the right points. I could still remember the way she smelled, how she fit against my body. No wonder I was still thinking about her.

I stood up and left the paper on my desk, not sure what to do with it. Not ready to answer why it had been her face that had soothed my brain.

I slipped on some pants and headed outside. A run would get rid of the last of my lingering stress. When I got outside, I was surprised to see Cathy stretching while chatting on the phone. She quickly said good-bye and hung up when she saw me.

"What are you doing here?" I asked.

"Good morning to you too."

"Shouldn't you be at Rousseau Manor? Shacked up with what's his name?" I sat down next to her. I knew David's name, hell, I even liked him, but that didn't mean I wasn't going to give her a hard time about it.

"He's doing a guest lecture in Minnesota." She leaned over to touch her head to her knee. "And then going to visit his family."

"You didn't go with him? I thought you two

were joined at the hip." I shook my head as I watched her stretch. "You know, tall people aren't supposed to be that flexible."

"I guess I missed that memo." She rolled her eyes at me. "And we're not joined at the hip."

"Yes you are. It's disgusting." I couldn't help but smile. "You're as bad as the other two."

"Gee, are you jealous?" She stood up and made anime eyes at me. "Feeling wonewy?"

"Shuddup." I laughed. I was not lonely. Nope. And if I was, it was because I liked it that way.

"Why are you out here then?" She pointed at my bare chest. "Trying to impress the ducks?"

"Har, har." I bent down to retie my shoe. "Just needed some fresh air."

"Rough night?" Her eyes took on a sad glint. She was one of the only people who knew about my nightmares.

I shrugged. To be honest, I wasn't sure if it was the nightmare or Meredith's face that I needed to run out of my system.

"Are we going to run or what?" I asked.

"See if you can keep up." She took off and I followed. Actually, it was nice to spend a little time with one of my siblings without their "other half" being around. Not that I was jealous. As much as it pained me to admit it, I missed them.

There was no talking on the run, just the sound of the wind in the trees, the soft tweets of birds, and the lapping of the water along the lake. It was exactly what I needed. Well, it would be if my brain would shut the fuck up.

Apparently I had lost my balls overnight, because all I could do was worry. Worry about Meredith dealing with her father. Worry about Marty not having his great-grandfather to go fishing with. Worry about the way that stubborn woman made me feel. I was going to have a period any minute.

We rounded the corner and the sun glinted off the lake in a bright array of colors. It had been a while since I had worked a landscape painting. Lately I had been working on portraits. The nitty-gritty of real life, the beauty in the normal and real. It was part of a project I had started to counter all the stereotyping done in media. The touched-up pictures of movie stars, the airbrushed images of cover models. I wanted for people to see the beauty of the here and now, not how things could be better.

But maybe a landscape would be a nice change. Something rough, with a palette knife instead of the smooth stroke of a brush. It would capture the choppiness of the water much better.

By the time we made it back to the house, my muscles were burning. That good burn that meant they'd been used after a hiatus. I'd been wearing a suit and doing family duties too much lately. It was starting to mess with my head. No wonder I'd had that dream about Dad again. My mind felt less cluttered as well. I was already plotting out where I would set up my easel and the colors I would need.

"Anything you want to talk about?" Cathy sat down on a stone bench and took a swig of water from the bottle she had left behind.

"What would I want to talk about?" I walked around the clearing, my hands on top of my head.

"How did the opening in London go?" She put her hands on her knees. "I saw the portrait you did of Mom. It was amazing."

"Thanks." I sat down next to her and grabbed her water bottle. "I was surprised she let me do it."

"Why?"

"Most portraits of the crown are pretty, perfect pictures of them in their full regalia." I shrugged. "She didn't even blink an eye when I told her to wear regular clothes."

"You know, I think that's the first time I've ever seen her in a T-shirt and jeans." Cathy laughed. "I didn't even know she owned jeans."

"I saw her wear them once when I was little. It was before she was pregnant with you." I shrugged. "I think we were playing at a park."

"Did it go over well at the opening?" Cathy took the bottle back from me and took a sip. "Were people shocked?"

"That's the fun part. People either walked right by her, not a clue who she was, or knew immediately that they were looking at the Queen of Lilaria." Mother was the only family member I had included in the show. The rest of the people were models, homeless people, rich bankers, students from the local schools.

"So people just assumed she was another model?"

"A banker asked if she was married."

Cathy burst out laughing. "You're joking."

"No, I'm not. He had no idea who she was. One of the London bankers I used as a model." I laughed along with her.

"Did you tell him?" She looked at me with her big blue eyes.

"I told him she was a widow." I grinned.

"I wonder if he ever figured it out." She leaned back.

I shrugged. It had been fun to watch the gallery owner, Eddie, gape through the entire conversation. Whether or not Eddie had told the man later, I didn't know.

"Why aren't you still in England? I figured you'd be there for a while."

"Alex asked me to do him a favor."

"Ah, that's right. You had to tell Meredith about her grandfather." She sat up straight. "Alex shouldn't have asked you to do that."

"Why? I was the closest one to her." I looked away from Cathy. "Better than her finding out another way."

"Yeah, but—"

"Cathy, I'm a big boy." I threw my arm around her. "I don't need you to stick up for me."

"Gah. What you need is a shower." She scrunched up her face.

"Do I?" I squeezed her tighter. "You don't smell so great either."

"God, you're gross." She wiggled out from under my arm and stood up. "Are you going with us today?"

"Going with you where?" I undid my tennis shoes and kicked them off.

"Meredith is addressing the township today."

"Of course not." I rolled my shoulders. Suddenly anxious to get back to my room.

"Why not?" Cathy narrowed her eyes. "Sam

wants to show solidarity. Apparently Meredith's father isn't going."

"He's not?" The wheels turned in my head. That meant that Meredith would have to do the speaking by herself and deal with the talk about her father. "I don't do those types of things, Cathy. You know that. But you guys should definitely go."

"Come with us." Cathy put her hands on her hips.

"I want to paint."

"Paint later."

"No." I stood up and picked up my shoes.

"You have a hole in your sock." Cathy looked down at my feet.

"Yep." I wiggled my big toe.

"You're probably the only prince in the world that doesn't throw away his holey socks." She laughed.

"So?" I felt my eyebrows furrow. "They still work."

"Come with us and I'll buy you new socks while we're out."

"I can't." Shit on toast. I hadn't meant to say that.

"What? Why not? You can paint later."

"I need to catch the light right now." I turned to walk back in the house but she kept pace with me.

"She's not speaking until later." She practically bounced. "That's perfect. It's been forever since we've all been together."

Oh, low blow. She might look all sweet and innocent, but she was working the guilt angle now.

"It hasn't been that long." I ducked my head in the kitchen to make sure the cook wasn't in there. She wasn't, which meant I could drink straight out of the milk carton.

"Come with us." She sat on the counter and frowned at me.

"No."

"Come with us. Please." She gave me her best smile.

"No."

"Why are you being even more stubborn than normal?" She pouted.

"I'm not." I lifted the carton to my mouth to forestall any more talking.

"Yes you are. What's going on?" She crossed her arms. "Do you not like Meredith?"

"No." I shook my head.

"No you don't like her or no you do like her?" She watched my face carefully.

"She's okay." I shrugged again. I was shrugging a lot today.

"Okay? She's gorgeous, funny, and can sing like an angel."

"Didn't notice." I turned away from her and opened a cabinet looking for cereal.

"You didn't notice that she's a hottie?" She followed me around the kitchen. "You?"

"Did you just call a girl a hottie?" I raised an eyebrow.

"I'm straight, not blind." She grabbed a handful of my cereal before I poured the milk in the bowl.

"Okay, she's attractive." I looked at her with a frown. "You're really annoying, you know that?"

"I've been told before." She leaned back against the kitchen island. "I thought you told Sam you would help her out."

"Is that what this is about?" I shoved a spoonful of colored squares into my mouth.

"Well, you said you'd help, and she obviously needs help."

"Look, I know what I'm doing." I turned away from her and poured the rest of my cereal in the trash. "I don't do public appearances. You know that. God, when does David get back so you can annoy him?"

"Come with us." She stepped in my path to the door. "If Sam thinks you aren't helping Meredith right now, she's going to send over a ton of people to take over."

"Mother already sent someone from the palace."

"Then come with us."

"How old are you?" I glared at her.

"I'm twenty-two." She smiled. "Why won't you come with us?"

"I promised I wouldn't." I sighed. She wasn't going to leave me alone.

"Promised who?" She stopped in her tracks.

"Meredith." I growled her name. Knowing that she was doing all of this today on her own made me angry. Even more angry knowing that she had made me promise when she had such an important thing happening.

"Why?" A sly smile curved my sister's lips. "Did you annoy her that fast?"

"Shut it." I glared down at her. "She doesn't want our help."

"But does she need it?"

My chest clenched and something in my face must've shifted because Cathy smiled like the cat that swallowed the canary.

"You can't force people to take your help," I said.

"We don't leave our own to deal with horrible

stuff alone." Cathy crossed her arms. "And look at you! It's bothering you so much you were up at dawn."

"I had a nightmare." There, I'd give a dog a bone and let her gnaw on that. It would be better than her going on about Meredith.

"I wonder why." She smiled up at me. "Be ready at two."

"I'm not going with you." Putting my hands on her shoulders, I moved her out of my way.

"Wear something nice. We want to look civilized."

I shook my head. Little sisters were something else.

I showered and changed back in my room before gathering my stuff and heading to the lake. I hadn't been lying about wanting to paint. The idea had stuck in my head and I needed to get it out.

I used one of the four-wheel terrain vehicles to get my supplies to where I wanted. It was a decent walk and would have been made difficult by carrying an easel, canvas, and paints.

Once I was set up, I tuned into the painting and let everything else melt away. And as I smoothed paint on the canvas, everything did melt away, except my nagging need to protect Meredith while she gave her speech today. It was in the back of my mind the entire time I worked. Like a quiet whisper stuck on repeat.

And I knew damn well there was only one way to deal with it. If I didn't go to that damn event, I'd be pissed off for days. I also knew that if I went it would push Meredith even further away from me. Which could be good. Or at least that's what I was trying to convince myself of. On the other hand, I didn't break promises. It bothered me to think that I was even considering it right this moment.

As I slapped paint on the canvas, slowly carving out the waves along the bank, I went through the possible scenarios. Tell Sam, if Cathy hasn't yet, that I promised to give Meredith some space. Surely Sam would understand that. She knew what it was like to end up royal all of a sudden. Explain that I thought they should go and I would keep myself busy.

Or I could go and try to stay out of sight. Which would be impossible with the media around.

Yet, maybe there was a third option. I could help without helping. Sort of behind-the-scenes help. That would allow me to not feel guilty, do something good, and hopefully make someone happy.

That solution went a long way to making me

feel better and I was able to concentrate on my painting. Yes, a compromise would be a good solution. I would give her a day. A full twenty-four hours. If she wasn't speaking until that afternoon then it would be at least a few more hours before she got home. Which would mean I'd have done what I said. I would have avoided her for an entire day.

Smiling to myself, I continued my work on the painting. Yes, painting had been exactly what I needed. I felt much better.

Once I was finished, I packed up and headed back to the house. Sam was sitting on one of the sofas near the fireplace, a book propped up on her stomach. She really wasn't very big, but the baby bump was unmistakable.

"Oh, let me see what you did today." She closed her book and leveraged herself up off the sofa.

I turned the canvas around so she could get a look at it.

"God, you're so damn talented. It's not really fair." She smiled at me to take the sting out of her words. "I love the colors."

"I'm happy with the way it turned out." I leaned the painting against one of the walls and rubbed my hands on my jeans. "What are you reading?"

"*Pride and Prejudice.*" She smiled.

"I thought you just finished it." I shook my head.

"I did." She shrugged. "I wanted to read it again."

"You're a wee bit weird." I raised my eyebrow and held my finger and thumb up to show a small little space between the two.

"Says the artist covered in mud and paint." She laughed. "You look just like your brother when you do that." She motioned toward my eyebrow.

"That won't do." I wiped my face clean. "I wanted to tell you, I'm not going to the speech today."

"Cathy told me." She sat back down on her spot. "I get it."

"Cathy told you? She acted like I had to go." I threw myself down in one of the armchairs. "She wouldn't leave me alone about it."

"She just wanted to know what had you so upset." She waggled her finger at me. "You only run when something is bothering you."

"You've officially been around too long." I glared at her.

"Bah. You love me. I'm the sister you always wanted." She giggled.

"I already have one annoying sister." I closed my eyes so she wouldn't see my amusement.

Though I had a feeling that she knew me too well at this point to doubt it.

"Exactly." Her tone turned serious. "I didn't mean to put you in a bad spot, Max. I really can send someone else over there to help out."

"No, I'm fine." I'd said it too quickly. Why hadn't I just let her send someone else? "It would just make her frustrated to have a bunch of new people around."

"I get it." She frowned. "I think I've started to get used to having so many people around. Which is scary."

"You're just glad you don't have to bend over to pick up anything you've dropped." I opened one eye to look at her.

"Oh, you're so funny. You try to bend over with a basketball stuck in your stomach. See how easy it is."

"Not really my thing." I closed my eyes and was caught unsuspecting by the giant pillow that landed on my head. "I deserved that."

"No kidding."

"Sorry, pregnant lady." I shot her my best smile.

"You're lucky you're cute." She rolled her eyes. "Seriously though, Cathy said your mom sent someone to help out. If you aren't comfortable going over there, or think that it will upset Meredith, then leave it alone. I didn't mean to make things difficult. I just wanted to help."

"I know." I looked at her. "But she's stuck with me now."

"Heh." Sam narrowed her eyes.

"Don't 'heh' me." Hehs from Sam were dangerous. It meant she was working something out in her head.

"Is it bad over there?" She frowned.

I shrugged. It really wasn't my place to say and I didn't want to upset my highly hormonal sister-in-law. The truth was that Meredith and Marty needed somewhere else to live, preferably back in England where she had been building them a life. But for now, I'd just have to try to be a wall between them and the worst of it.

"That bad, huh?" She frowned. "It must be if your mom sent someone to take charge."

"Oh, that'll go over well." I snorted. Meredith was not going to let someone come in and just run rampant. "Good luck with that."

"She's stubborn, huh?"

"As stubborn as you." I wasn't surprised when she laughed.

"That's rough. You'll have your work cut out for you." She paused, and I could see her rub her belly out of the corner of my eye. "How is Marty?"

"He's coping." The thought of him in that big house with his grandfather made me ill. "Is she bringing him to the speech?"

"I don't think so." She frowned. "Not really a great place for a little one."

"Good." I stood up. "I thought I might go take him fishing."

"Fishing?" She looked at me with surprised eyes. "You're going to go take a little boy fishing. Heh."

"Stop it. I told him I'd take him. His great-grandfather used to take him all the time." Plus it would get him out of the house with his grandfather. Not that I was going to tell Sam that. She might show up with the cavalry if she thought there was a little one in danger. I was sure that Meredith had left him with someone who would watch out for him, but still. It would make me feel better if I was there. I could leave as soon as she got back and still feel like I had done my duty.

It would also alleviate my guilt at not being there for Meredith while she made a difficult public appearance.

I would leave as soon as she got there. I wouldn't hang around hoping for another kiss, like a lovesick schoolboy. Nope. Not going to happen. I'd hang out with Marty and then come home. So what if it was a two-hour drive? It didn't matter in the long run. What else was I going to do today? Plus it would mean that I could avoid the media.

I stood up. "I'm going to go change."

"Okay." Sam held her hand out to me and I helped pull her to her feet. She wobbled for a minute and I steadied her with an arm around her shoulders. Leaning down, I kissed her on her head.

"What was that for?" She looked up at me with a smile.

"Just because." I looked down at her for a minute. Alex had been extremely lucky when he found her. Or had she found him? The only thing that mattered was that they were happy.

"Well, don't think I'm going to name the baby after you just because you helped me stand up." She laughed.

"Oh, I know I'm at the bottom of the list." I winked at her. To be fair, I was pretty sure I wasn't on the list. They hadn't told anyone if they were having a boy or girl and had kept their name choices to themselves. If I was a betting man, I'd put money on her father's name and my father's name for a boy. Or I would if anyone would actually bet me. They all assumed I already knew the answer.

After changing, I called for my car, and headed toward Thysmer Manor. My ever-present body-guard, Charles, was in a car behind me. It seemed silly, but being able to drive in a car by myself was one of the things I refused to give up. There was no uncomfortable need to make small talk. Though Charles wasn't exactly the type for long, drawn-out conversation. It was one of the reasons I'd chosen to keep him around.

I timed it just right and saw Meredith pass me on her way to town. I barely caught a glimpse of her red hair in the back of a black sedan. She didn't see me, which was perfect. It probably would have upset her, or made her worry, which was the opposite of what I wanted to accomplish.

I pulled up in front of the house and parked off to the side so that I wouldn't be blocking anyone else. The front door was thrown open and Marty came running out, followed by a woman with an armful of toys.

"Max!" The little guy stopped just before he got to me and I could tell he was trying to decide whether to hug me or play it cool.

I held out my fist instead. "What's up?"

He bumped my fist with his tiny one and smiled at me. "I was building a fort in the front room, but saw your car coming up the drive."

I looked over at the woman standing in the doorway. She bobbed her head quickly before marching down to where Max was standing.

"You can't just run out like that, Marty." She knelt down and looked him in the eyes. "It's dangerous."

"But it's Max!" The little guy turned around and bumped his shoulder into my hip.

"Yes, but other people drive that type of car." Her voice was patient and it became apparent why Meredith felt confident leaving Marty in her care. There was an undercurrent of love in her words.

"Yes, ma'am." He frowned. "I'm sorry. I won't do it again, Ms. Katie."

"Thank you." She stood up and smiled at me. "You just missed Lady Meredith. She's on her way to the township."

"I passed her on my way here. I'm actually here to see Master Marty." I smiled down at the boy and put my hand on his shoulder.

"Oh, she must have forgotten to tell me that you were coming." The nanny looked confused.

"Well, I hadn't really planned on it." I hoped I didn't look guilty. "I just decided to go fishing and remembered that Marty liked to fish. So I thought I'd come see if he wanted to throw the rod a little. If that's okay?"

"Yeah!" Marty pumped his fist. "Can I?"

"You're going to stay here at Thysmer?" Katie looked from Marty to me.

"Absolutely. I brought all of my stuff with me." I walked over and opened the back of my SUV. "But only if you're comfortable with it."

"I think that'll be fine." She smiled. "He wasn't happy being cooped up all day anyway."

Sometimes being a prince had its perks. "Thank you, Katie."

She blushed a little and bobbed her head again. "Come along, Marty. Let's get you changed."

"I'll meet you inside." I winked at Marty and turned back to the equipment. I'd raided Alex's stash, because it had been forever since I had been fishing. He and Sam used to go from time to time, but never came back with any fish. Either they sucked at it or were doing something else out there by the lake.

I juggled the tackle box and two poles into the house and stopped in the foyer. I could hear Marty talking excitedly upstairs, but wasn't sure where to wait. I didn't want to just make myself at home. That seemed rude. I looked around the opening and noticed that the drawing from the night before was gone. I couldn't help but wonder what she had done with it. It certainly hadn't been my best work. Just a quick pencil sketch.

Marty raced down the stairs in a pair of fishing boots, jeans, and long-sleeved T-shirt. Katie followed behind him making shushing sounds. His grin was infectious.

"Ready?" I asked.

"Gotta get my stuff out of the shed in the back." He took off down the hallway.

"Are you sure you can handle him? He's a handful." Katie looked up at me with a small smile.

"Yeah. It'll be fine." I shrugged. "Besides, we won't be far from the house. You'll hear my screams for help."

"I'll keep an ear open while I clean up the fort in the living room." She laughed. "He's a good kid."

I followed Marty's path to the back of the house and then the sounds of him rummaging through a shed near an old barn.

"Did you find your stuff?" I leaned my poles against the metal wall in case I needed to climb in there and help him.

"Yeah." He grunted as he pulled on something. "But it's stuck."

"Here, let me try." I reached over his head and pulled the rod in question up and out of the offending metal stand.

"Thanks." He rummaged along the floor and came up with a well-worn tackle box. "This was my great granddad's."

His face clouded up and I felt my heart tighten.

"Do you think it's okay if I use it?" He looked up at me with shimmery eyes and I panicked. I hadn't meant to make him upset.

"Hey, I think he would be glad to know it was getting use." I knelt down and picked up a twig and rolled it around between my fingers. "When my dad died, there were lots of things that made me think of him. His favorite TV show, a pair of binoculars we used when we'd go birding. At first it was hard to see those things, but then I realized they were little pieces of him still left behind."

"My heart hurts." A tear ran down his cheek.

"I know, buddy." I reached out and pulled him into a hug. "It'll get better though."

He sniffled against my shoulder and I let him have a moment. It felt so strange to be holding such a small person, but right, too. There was this odd tug on my own heart, the desire to make him feel better, but I knew the only thing that would help would be time. So instead I held him and offered my support the only way I knew how.

"I think he'd want me to use it." He leaned back and rubbed his nose along his sleeve.

"I think you're right." I stood up and grabbed the tackle box and held it out to him. "Ready to go catch some fish?"

"Yeah." He grabbed his pole in one hand and the tackle box in the other. We made our way out to a small pier that jutted out into the pond.

"Nice place." I set my box down and looked around.

Thick trees circled the pond, providing lots of shaded areas for the fish to hide. Wildflowers were scattered around, hogging the areas where the sunlight filtered through the branches.

"Great Granddad loved it. He said it was the best part." Marty opened the tackle box and looked through the different lures.

"Here, let me help with that." The last thing I wanted was him to stab himself with a hook.

I searched through the lures, not sure which ones were appropriate for this type of water. The last time I had gone fishing I had used a worm and hadn't really cared about catching any fish. I'd been busy taking pictures for a project.

"No, not that one." Marty's little hand darted into the box and pulled up a different lure. "This one."

"Okay." I took the one he handed me and went about attaching it to the line of his pole. I fumbled a bit, but eventually got the piece attached. I looked up triumphantly and noticed Marty was giggling. "What?"

"You're not really good at that, are you?" He pointed at the pole I was holding.

"What?" I frowned at the lure. Sure it was a little crooked, but that wasn't a big deal. Was it?

"Here." Marty took the pole from me and I watched in amazement as his little fingers fixed my mess. "Great Granddad showed me how to do this when we moved here."

"Huh." I looked at the lure and then at Marty. "I guess you're right. I'm not very good at it."

"Nope." Marty stood up and grabbed my pole. "But that's okay. Everyone has their own talent."

"True enough." I stood up and took the pole he offered me.

I hadn't really thought about the actual fishing until I was out on the dock with Marty, but I had more fun than I had thought I would. The kid was quickly becoming one of my favorite people. He said the craziest things that made me laugh and would then turn around and say something that was so profound I wondered if he understood it himself. I couldn't help but wonder if all kids were like that or just Marty.

"Dinner is ready!" Katie walked toward the pier

and stopped on the edge. "You two better come on in! The bugs are big enough to carry you away."

"Whoops." I looked down at Marty. "I didn't think about bug spray."

"I'm okay." He smashed a mosquito on his cheek, leaving a bloody trail, and I cringed.

"I hope your mom's not back yet. She'll kill me." I wiped at his cheek with my thumb but he wiggled out of my grasp.

"Nah." He started picking up the mess we had made on the dock. "She likes you."

"Oh yeah?" I looked away from him so he wouldn't see my smile.

"Yeah. She never likes guys, so it's weird." He looked at me with narrowed eyes. "Do you like her?"

"Sure. You're mom's cool." I shrugged.

"But do you like-like her? Like the older kids at school?" He handed me his rod and I juggled it into my other hand, because his little fingers closed around mine.

I looked down at his little hand and back into his big eyes. "Um."

He just looked at me, not offering me an out, and I felt like pulling at my shirt collar.

"Your food is getting cold!" Katie called from closer to the house.

"We better hurry." I pulled him with me as I started up the dock.

"Yeah, Ms. Katie is serious about dinner. She doesn't like it when I'm late." His little legs picked up the pace.

We dropped off his fishing gear in the old shed and headed back into the house. Marty pushed the door open for me, laughing as I fought with the two poles in my hand.

"What are you doing here?" Meredith stood in front of the door with her arms crossed.

We both froze like two kids caught with their hands in the cookie jar. Well, one kid and one adult.

"Just came to do a little fishing." I leaned the poles against the wall next to the door.

Marty threw himself at his mom and hugged her around her hips. "We had so much fun!"

"I'm glad to hear it." She looked down at her son and smiled. "Go get washed up."

"Can Max stay?" He looked up at his mom with big eyes. "Please?"

"Sure." She smiled again. "Now get. I want to smell soap when you come back."

"Yes, ma'am." He smiled at me over his shoulder as he ran toward a bathroom.

When I looked back at Meredith she was not smiling. In fact, she looked irate.

I cleared my throat and looked down at my watch. "It's technically been a full day."

"You know what I meant." She tapped her foot and I had to keep from smiling. I didn't think she realized that she was still in mom mode. The amusing part was that I found it just as attractive as when she was being alluring in a dark hallway.

"It was either this, or I had to go with the family to your township." I let my hands hang at my sides. My fingers itched to pull her against me, to see if last night's kiss had been a fluke.

"Don't think I didn't notice that you sent your family to check up on me." She glared at me.

"Whoa. That had nothing to do with me." I lifted my hands like I was going to ward off an angry bear. "They wanted to show their solidarity with you."

"Your mother has already sent someone to help out. I don't need to be babysat."

"You've got it all wrong, Meredith." I took a step forward. "We really do only want to help."

"Then why are you here?" She threw her hands in the air. "You said you'd give me a day but here you are! I can't think when you're here." Her eyes widened a little at that last sentence. She hadn't meant to tell me that.

"I thought I'd be gone by the time you got back." I took another step closer. "I promised Marty I'd go fishing with him and since I knew you'd be gone, I thought I'd help by keeping him distracted. I was just trying to help."

"I—I have too much going on for this." She waved her hands between us. "Whatever this is. If there is something. I don't know. And coming back to see you with Marty . . . he's so vulnerable right now. It's just . . ."

It wasn't just Marty that was vulnerable. Meredith felt exposed and it scared her. Fuck, it scared me.

"I should have asked if it was okay to hang out with Marty." I took another step closer to her, but she didn't move. "I'm sorry."

"I just—"

"It's okay." I reached out and touched her hair. I just needed to touch some part of her. "I should have known better."

"You should have." She looked up at me with deep blue eyes. There were circles under her eyes, but they didn't detract from her beauty. Instead they just emphasized everything else that was so perfect. Her mascara was smudged a bit in the corners as if she had been fighting tears, and I let my thumb wipe it away.

"I want to help you." I said the words quietly. "And I'm trying the only way I know how."

"Why?" She frowned. "Why now? Why here?"

"Because you need it."

"I'm not good for you." She bit her lip. "Last night—"

"It can wait." I shook my head. "You have enough on your plate right now."

"I don't just kiss people." She frowned. "That sounded wrong. I mean I don't go around kissing people all the time."

"Well, for being out of practice you're pretty damn good at it."

Rose crept up her cheeks and I felt a stab of pride that I had put it there.

"You reminded me of what I was missing out on." Her eyes darted to my lips briefly.

"Maybe we can try it again sometime." It was taking all of my willpower to keep from trying it again right that moment. "When things calm down."

"Maybe." The word came out a little breathless.

It was like my body was on autopilot. I could only sense what I wanted and right that moment I wanted her. Her breath fanned out across my face and I inhaled deeply. Her hand wrapped around my wrist and she stood up on her tiptoes.

"Mom!" Marty clambered down the stairs.

Meredith jumped away from me as if she had been electrocuted. "Back here."

"Saved by the bell." I winked at her and was surprised when she blushed. I had a feeling that I was getting a rare look at the real Meredith.

"C'mon! I'm starving." Marty stuck his head out of the hallway. "What are you doing?"

"Just talking." I shrugged.

"You can leave your poles there while we eat dinner." She looked at me briefly before gently pushing Marty toward the dining room.

"I hate to impose." I followed behind them not really feeling guilty in the least.

"Don't worry about it. D'Lynsal is two hours from here. You'll starve to death by the time you reach your family's home." She shook her head at me. "Besides, we have enough for everyone."

"If you insist." I smiled at her.

"We insist!" Marty said firmly. He opened the door to the dining room and quickly jumped into a chair.

She sat next to her son and I took a seat opposite them. She started dishing out the food, despite Marty's grumbles about beans and broccoli. Between mouthfuls he told her about fishing.

"And he can't tie a lure on!" He laughed. "Can you believe that? I had to do it for him."

"It's not nice to make fun of someone," she admonished, but couldn't help a small smile.

"To be fair, I'm complete rubbish." I held up my hands. "It's been years since I've gone fishing."

"I thought you liked to fish!" Marty looked at me accusingly.

"I do! I just haven't had the free time in a while."

"Well, you should definitely practice some more." He stabbed a bean with his fork and stuck it in his mouth. "You should come back tomorrow."

"We'll have to check with your mom about that." I looked at her as she tried to decide what to say.

"I believe your sister and sister-in-law are coming tomorrow." Meredith shrugged her shoulders uncomfortably. "They want to pay their respects."

"That doesn't surprise me." I had to fight to not laugh. "They like to take care of people. Both of them. If you're not careful, they'll wrap you up, send you to bed, and take over everything."

"What is it with your family?" She looked at me with disbelief.

"We take care of our own." I wondered if she

realized that she had been adopted by my family. Because that is exactly what had happened. And once they set their hooks in you, you were never alone. Something she had no experience with.

NINE

$\mathcal{M}$Y HEART BOUNCED in my chest as Max teased Marty. They had obviously bonded over the last couple of days. They got along effortlessly, like they'd always known each other. I felt a little like the third wheel.

But he had called us their own.

As if that was normal. The way it should be.

Theirs.

That was such a foreign concept. Other than Granddad, Marty and I had forged our way through life with just the two of us. It wasn't until Granddad found out about our lineage that we'd all come back to Lilaria together. Dad had just gotten out of jail after being caught in an underground gambling ring. At first I had thought that maybe things would work out. Granddad insisted that Dad would shape up, but I knew better. I applied to schools, looked for other options. The night I got my acceptance e-mail for university in England, Dad came back to Thysmer incredibly drunk. I'd been so relieved to have a way to escape.

"Mom?" Marty's voice broke into my thoughts.

"What, baby?" I looked at him and realized he must have been asking me something before that.

"Is there anything for dessert?" Marty looked at me hopefully.

"Hm. I don't know." I pursed my lips. "Did you clean your room today?"

"Um, mostly?" He looked at me hopefully. "I ate all my beans though."

"Well, that is something to celebrate." I laughed. "Go see if we have any ice cream."

"Yes!" He was out of his chair faster than lightning.

I fiddled with my fork on my plate, not sure what to say. I was normally full of words, full of things to talk about, but today I just wanted to crawl in my bed and hide under the blanket. I couldn't do that even if Max hadn't been sitting across the table from me. I needed to stay strong, work hard to keep everything level and calm for Marty.

"Are you sleeping?" Max's deep voice rumbled quietly.

"Right now?" I offered him a smile.

"You know what I mean." He leaned forward, concern etched on his face. "You look tired."

"Not exactly what every girl wants to hear, Prince Charming." I rolled my eyes and leaned back in my seat.

"You're one of the most beautiful women I've ever laid eyes on." The sincerity in his words sent my heart into overdrive. "That doesn't mean you can't look tired."

I closed my eyes for a minute. "I don't have time to be tired."

"How'd the speech go today?" He put his arms on the table and leaned forward.

"Fine." I shrugged. It had been one of the most painful things I'd ever had to do. Telling a crowd of strangers, cameras, and reporters that my granddad had passed away had been emotionally draining. Answering their questions had been like having someone dig around in an open wound.

"You don't have to pretend." He clasped his hands in front of him and looked down at the table. "I'd need a stiff drink."

"I don't drink." My eyes shot toward my father's room.

"Then maybe a long, hot shower." His lips curved into a small smile. "Or a bath. I imagine that would go a long way to soothing your tense muscles."

"That does sound nice." I sighed at the thought. "But I have to go scrub down a little boy who smells like fish."

"I'll do it." He shrugged.

"You'll give my six-year-old boy a bath?" I laughed.

"How hard can it be? A broom, little dish soap, and the hose are all I need." He raised one eyebrow when I laughed. "It'll only take a couple of minutes."

"Nice. Would you just let him run naked through the house like a crazed person to dry off?"

"How else would you do it?" His smile grew a little.

"I can only imagine the housekeeper's face at the puddles all over the place." I chuckled.

"You could get a dog and blame them on it." He laughed.

"No, those leave their own sort of puddles." I shook my head and fought my grin. "And don't you dare mention that in front of Marty. I've been fending off the dog request for a while now."

"Duly noted." He bobbed his head and looked up at me through his brown hair, with a grin. "I remember wanting a dog at his age. I drove my parents crazy."

"Did they let you have one?"

"It took a lot of convincing, but I finally got a Lab." His eyes turned thoughtful. "We had some great adventures. He was my best friend."

"Are you trying to convince me to get my son a dog?" I leaned forward and leveled my eyes at the prince sitting across from me.

"Is it working?" His teeth flashed white in the light.

"Not even a little bit." I laughed.

"Well, I tried." He shrugged as his eyes glinted with mischief.

"Marty would appreciate the effort." I smiled but looked away from him. He was doing it again. Breaking through my barriers. I couldn't remember the last time I had discussed Marty with a man who wasn't family.

"I found ice cream!" Marty bounded through the door with a stack of bowls in his hands.

The cook followed behind him with an amused expression. She was carrying a tub of ice cream.

"We only have vanilla, but I can make a chocolate syrup if you'd like." She set the tub on the table and folded her hands in front of her.

"Do we have any sprinkles?" Marty set the bowls on the table and climbed into his chair.

"We have some from the last time you were here." She pulled a bottle out of the pocket of her apron and set it on the table. "Enjoy."

"Yes!" Marty reached for the tub of ice cream but I was faster.

"I'll put some in your bowl." I lumped some ice cream into his bowl and handed him the bottle of sprinkles, which he liberally applied. Without thinking, I grabbed Max's bowl and filled it with ice cream. "Do you want sprinkles too?"

"No, thanks." He smiled at me when I handed him his bowl.

By the time I'd gotten my own dessert, Marty was ready to lick his bowl clean. Max reached across the table and flicked a sprinkle off my son's nose, making him giggle.

"Okay. It's time for a bath." I shook my head when Marty groaned. "You're filthy, buddy."

"But it's a good, healthy filthy." Marty grinned.

"Go upstairs and pick out some pajamas." I shook my head.

"I'm going." He hopped out of his chair and ran around the table. To my complete surprise, he hugged Max and whispered something I couldn't hear. Max laughed softly and hugged my son back. A stab of pain filled my chest and I squashed it. Other than Granddad, Marty hadn't had a man in his life that he could count on. I didn't let anyone get close enough to hurt him.

To hurt us. Marty's father and my own had shown me how quickly men could leave you or hurt you.

"I'll be up there soon," I told Marty as he flew out the door.

"He's a smart kid."

"I know." I looked over at Max and tried to sort through all the emotions that were bombarding me. To not hold the past against this man. "Thank you for taking him fishing today."

"You're not still angry?" He leaned back in his chair and cocked his head to the side.

"Your intentions were good." I shrugged. *Play it cool*, I told myself. *Don't let him know what a big deal it is to let him hang out with my son.* "But next time call me."

His mouth twitched upward on one side. "So far, we've skipped that part and I've stuck to just barging into your home."

"This isn't my home." I fought my smile. "But you have been barging in here a lot."

"I'd like to barge in tomorrow if that's okay." He watched my face carefully.

"I think Marty would enjoy that." I kept my face neutral.

"And what about you, Meredith?" With a smooth movement he leaned forward and reached out to touch the back of my hand with his fingertips. "Would you mind if I came over tomorrow?"

My immediate response stuck in my throat, surprising me. I looked into his green eyes and swallowed. How did this man continually make me feel like I was sixteen again? I was used to being the one in charge—the person who made decisions about where a relationship went. Which was usually nowhere.

"I . . . I would like that." I tried to keep my tone nonchalant, but failed miserably. This wasn't a relationship. This was just a person helping another person. Right?

Something in his expression shifted and I realized that he had been tense, waiting for my response. Maybe I wasn't the only one feeling at the other's mercy.

"What time would be a good time to show up?" His fingers were still on my hand. My skin tingled under his touch.

"Why don't you come with your sister and sister-in-law?" I tried to keep my nerves to myself. So far my father hadn't come out of his room, but who knew what tomorrow would bring?

As if he was reading my mind, Max's eyes

darted to the stairs. "Maybe I could come a little earlier."

"We'll be fine," I said. We would. I'd dealt with this a hundred times before. *But not without my grandfather in the background,* my mind whispered.

"What have you decided about going back to England?" His eyes had taken on a serious cast and the light highlighted his sharp cheekbones.

"I have to wait until the will reading." I shrugged.

"Your grandfather left a will?" His eyes brightened.

I tried to keep the frustration out of my voice. "I found out this morning."

"How?" His fingers rubbed gently along my knuckles and I wondered if he was doing it on purpose.

"Rachel. The woman your mother sent to take care of the family." Gently, I extracted my hand from underneath his. It was hard to think when he touched me. "She said that he entrusted it to the queen."

He sat back in his chair and rubbed his chin. "That's not completely unusual."

"Even you didn't sound convinced when you said that." I shook my head. "I don't know what to expect." I shivered. What if Granddad did do

something crazy in his will? What if he left everything to my father, expecting him to do the right
thing? I would hope that he had left money for
Marty and me, because if he left it all to my father,
we'd be screwed. Thank God I had been squirrel-
ing away money and living well within our new
means.

"Who will be here when the will is read?" He
looked at me with serious eyes.

"I'm not sure. Who comes to the reading of a
will?" I snorted. "A lawyer? Rachel will be here.
Me and my father. I don't know who else."

"If he entrusted it to the queen, then she will
have a representative present." He narrowed his
eyes.

"Rachel will be there. She sent Rachel to repre-
sent her interest." I frowned.

"If she has taken the will in trust, either my
mother or one of our family must be present." He
leaned back in his chair, his eyes half lidded. "I'm
sure that my brother would be willing to step in."

"The last thing I want to do is have more of
your family involved in my drama." I clenched my
teeth. "Seriously. What is it with your family sticking their nose in my business? My granddad died.
Lots of people die. Every day. Why are you guys
not bothering them?"

"Because they aren't you." He lowered his voice. "My mother uprooted your family, changed your entire world, and feels responsible for you."

"Is it that or the fact that my father is a drunk? God help us if we do something embarrassing." I stood up. "I've been dodging his issues for years, cutting him out of my life, moving to a different country. The last thing I want is to have everyone standing around, staring at me with sad eyes. I just want to have a normal life. I *was* having a normal life. And then—then my granddad died. He died and he left us with a giant mess."

"Meredith." He said my name softly.

"No. Don't you dare look at me like that." I pointed my finger at him, ignoring the tears that were threatening to overflow. I was too tired, too sad, too broken. "This is like reliving my childhood all over. I'm covering for my father at a school dance or praying that he doesn't show up to a parent-teacher conference slurring. Only it's all there for the media to show the world. The embarrassing new royal family. And all because the one man that held us together died."

"Meredith." He stood up and walked slowly around the table. "This is why I'm here. Why mother sent Rachel. No one should have to deal with all of this on their own."

"Having all of you here makes it worse." I was shaking. Our calm, almost peaceful dinner was now a thing of the past. "Don't you get it?"

"You're embarrassed." He said the words quietly. "You don't need to be."

I snorted and wrapped my arms around myself. "My father tried to deck me in front of a prince. Of course I'm embarrassed."

His hands clenched at his sides and I wondered what was going through his mind as he stared at me.

"I need to go give Marty a bath. He's waiting on me." I took a deep breath. I couldn't afford to lose control right now. I couldn't afford to lose control at all.

"Let the nanny give him a bath."

"It's my job." I lifted my chin and stared at him. "It's not the nanny's job to be his mother."

"It's the nanny's job to help you when you need it." He moved closer to me. "When my mother reinstated your title, she wasn't just giving you your inheritance. She was bringing you into a world where much would be asked of you. For some, it might seem like winning the lottery, but the truth is that it isn't always easy to wear a royal title. That's why you have a cook, a butler, and a nanny. That's why I'm here to help during a difficult time."

I just looked up at him. I wasn't sure I knew how to let other people help me.

"Go take a hot shower." Gently he placed his hands on my shoulders and steered me toward the door. "Take a long hot shower and let other people help you for once."

I let him guide me through the hallway and to the stairs. "Are you going home now?"

The light in the foyer was dim and his face was cloaked in shadow as he looked down at me. "No."

"What will you do?" I shivered. I was more worn out than I had realized.

"Stay."

With that one word, relief crashed over me. How could this man, whom I barely knew, make me feel safe?

"Thank you." I stood on my tiptoes and kissed his cheek.

He turned just enough so that I could feel his breath on my own cheek. "Get some rest, Meredith."

"Yes, Your Highness." I trudged up the stairs with a backward glance over my shoulder. He was watching me, one hand on the stair rail, but my barb had made him smile just a little.

I stopped by Marty's room. He was sitting on his bed, playing his video game.

"Did you get your pajamas?"

"Yes, ma'am." He glanced over at me.

"I think Katie's going to come give you a bath. Is that okay?" I leaned against the door frame.

"Ah, I can bathe myself." He scrunched up his nose. "I don't want her to see my butt."

I laughed. "Okay. She can stay in the other room and just make sure you don't drown. How's that?"

"Works for me!" He turned back to the television.

I crossed the room and kissed the top of his head. "Good night, monster."

" 'Night, Mom."

It only took a moment to swing by Katie's room and ask her to handle Marty's bedtime routine. She was reading a book and folded the page to mark her spot. I couldn't detect any annoyance at being interrupted. Instead she seemed happy to help.

"Do you need help with anything else?"

"No, I'm going to call it a night." I tugged at my shirt.

"Yes, ma'am. I'll see to it that Marty gets to bed." Katie smiled.

"Thank you." When I got to my room, I closed the door and leaned against it. There was a prince somewhere in my house, doing God knows what. I let someone else handle my son's bedtime routine. And I was very close to falling apart.

I stripped as I walked to my bathroom and turned the water to scalding. Without thinking, I stepped in and let the water run over my body. It only took a few minutes before the tears started and mixed with the water running over my face.

There was a sense of relief, knowing that no one was waiting on me, there was nothing that I had to do right that moment, and I just let myself cry. I cried until the water turned cold and then cried some more.

By the time I dragged myself out of the bathroom, I could barely hold my eyes open. I wanted nothing more than to fall on my bed, but I wouldn't be able to sleep unless I checked on Marty one more time.

Grabbing one of the throw blankets from a chair, I wrapped it around my shoulders and tiptoed down the hallway. Holding my breath, I opened the door and hoped that it wouldn't creak. Sticking my head in, I listened to his steady breathing and sighed.

I could sleep now.

Back in my room, I crawled on top of the blankets and let myself fall into oblivion.

TEN

SOMETHING NUDGED MY foot and I jerked awake.

"Don't you have a castle of your own somewhere?" Meredith's father stared down at me.

"Yes, sir, I do." I sat up and chose to ignore his sarcasm.

"Then why are you sleeping on my sofa?" He sat down in the chair across from me.

"It was rather late last night for me to make the drive home." The butler had offered me a guest room, but I had declined. I didn't want Meredith to feel like I was trying to move in and take over. Though I had accepted a room for my bodyguard.

"And what? You just came for a visit?"

The last few times I had seen this man, his eyes had been blurry and his voice had been heavy. Right now, he was alert, if irritable.

"Yes, sir. Marty and I went fishing." I tugged

at the collar of my shirt. The couch hadn't exactly been the most comfortable place to sleep.

"Fishing." He grunted. "Boy would spend his life fishing if he could."

"He certainly seemed at home out there." I looked around on the floor for my shoes. I had kicked them off at some point during the night.

"Why are you really here?"

"What do you mean?" I tried to keep calm, but I wasn't known for being overly sociable. Especially in the morning.

"Did the queen send you to make sure we didn't do anything wrong?" He grunted. "Keep the dirty cousins from making a scene?"

"No, I'm here to help Meredith." I paused for a moment. "And you."

"Help us with what exactly?" He ran his hand along the arm of the chair he was sitting in.

"Helping with the ceremony, keeping Marty busy . . ." I was running out of polite explanations. I didn't care if the old man wanted to make an ass out of himself, but I did care about how it affected Meredith and Marty.

"That's it?" He drummed his fingers on the chair.

"I also agreed to be a pallbearer." I shrugged and ran a hand across the back of my neck. Having a conversation with the man who tried to hit Meredith was pushing my patience.

"Where's your bodyguard?" He leaned back in his chair.

"I don't require him all the time." I narrowed my eyes.

"Huh." He grunted again and his eyes flicked toward the liquor cabinet in the corner of the room.

"A little early to be hitting the drink, isn't it?" I didn't regret the words, which was probably a bad thing.

"Don't come in my home and judge me." He smacked his hand down on the chair arm. "What I do in my own home has nothing to do with you."

"It does when it endangers Meredith and Marty."

"They are only here for the funeral, then back to England they go." He scratched at the scruff on his chin. "Bet they're dying to get back."

"It might be easier on them if you cut back on your drinking while they are here." I sat up straighter and put my hands on my knees. "You could try actually spending time with them, instead of being passed out in your room."

"They can spend time with me anytime they want." His eyes darted back to the cabinet.

"Not if they're afraid you're going to hit them."
I ground my teeth together.

"I wouldn't have hurt Mere." He rolled his eyes, and it took all of my willpower to keep from leaping across the table between us.

"If I hadn't been there, you would have hurt her." There was no disguising the anger in my words.

"Ah. I see. You want to champion my daughter." The old man leaned forward, just begging to be punched. "Be her knight in shining armor and steal her away from this horrible life." His laugh made my muscles tense.

I didn't say anything. There was nothing to say. I did want to whisk Meredith and Marty away. Whisk them right back to their place in England, where they would be safe. He made it sound wrong, dirty somehow.

"Let me tell you something, boy. My daughter is using you. Trailing you along like she does all the men that come sniffing around her door. She'll use you, get what she wants, and never look back." His smug smile made the hair on my arms stand up. "I don't know what you have that she wants, but there's something. Fuck, you're a goddamn prince. She might want to be queen." His mirthless laugh filled the room. "Or she wants to use you to get attention for her singing career. I don't know. But I can tell you this; this family isn't anything but trailer trash. You can give us a title, lands, and money, but it doesn't change a thing. Deep down, we'll always be the poor neighbors."

I stood up and stared down at the miserable man across from me. "Meredith has more breeding, backbone, and strength than anyone I've ever met. You, on the other hand, are exactly what you say you are."

"High-and-mighty, aren't you?" Arthur stood up and walked to the liquor cabinet. "You'll see."

"Dad?" Meredith's sleepy voice came from the hallway.

"In here." Arthur turned around with a smug expression. "With your boy toy."

"Stop that." Meredith rounded the corner and pulled her robe tight. "Prince Maxwell is a friend."

"As you say." He motioned with his full tumbler.

"For the love of God, Dad. It's barely eight o'clock in the morning." Meredith put a hand on one hip. "We have company coming today."

"I didn't invite anyone." The old man shrugged and took a sip of his drink.

"The royal family is coming to pay their respects." Meredith glanced toward me and then back at her father.

"Looks like he's already done that." Her father raised an eyebrow. "Kicked him out to sleep on the couch when you were done with him?"

"Father." The warning in her tone was ignored.

"You could have at least let him have one of the guest rooms." He leered.

"I offered to stay and help this morning." I stood up straight and glared at Arthur. "Nothing inappropriate happened."

The old man grunted. "Play the game all you want."

"Can you manage to stay sober for a few hours?" Meredith's mouth turned down. "It's your job to host the visitors."

"And again I say, I didn't invite them."

"It's customary in Lilaria for people to stop by the deceased's home and offer their respects." I said the words as calmly as possible. "When a person of title passes away, the royal family always comes to pay their respects."

"Please." Meredith said the word quietly. "If we can just get through the next couple of days, everything will be fine."

"Leave me be, Meredith." Her father's eyes narrowed. "I have to bury my father tomorrow and if I need a little drink to get through it, so be it."

She froze in place, her eyes the only indication of her anger. "Do what you want, just be sober enough to help carry the casket in the morning."

"Who the hell decided to do the funeral in the morning?" He tipped his drink back. "Why wasn't I consulted?"

"You were passed out in your room. As the next of kin, I had to make the decisions alone." Meredith dropped her hands to her sides. "The royal advisor suggested holding the funeral early so that the township could have a day of mourning."

"Royal advisor." He chuckled. "The queen sent someone to take over, huh?"

"Her Majesty sent someone to help you during a difficult and confusing time." I said the words calmly, aware that the tension in the room had continued to mount despite the cool words.

"Well, where are they?" He looked around the room. "What are they doing to make sure everything goes smoothly?"

"She will be here this afternoon." Meredith's shoulders tensed. "Did you know that Granddad left a will?"

"What?" Arthur froze, his glass halfway to his mouth. "The old man made a will?"

"He entrusted it to the crown." Meredith's knuckles whitened from how hard she clenched her fists. "There will be a reading the day after the funeral."

"How did you know?" Arthur slammed his glass down on the table. Amber liquid splashed over the edge and ran down the leg.

"The assistant that the queen sent told me." She shook her head. "I didn't know anything about it."

"Everything passes to me." He said the words like there was no question. "I'm the Duke of Thysmer now."

"Then you should act like it." I raised an eyebrow. "Stop leaving your daughter to shoulder everything by herself."

"Max." Meredith widened her eyes.

"Get out of my house." Arthur raised his hand and pointed at me. "Get the hell out. And don't come back."

"The house isn't yours until the will is read." I kept my voice calm. "And don't think for one minute that the crown can't take away what has been given."

"The hell it isn't my home. I'm the duke."

"I'm more than happy to leave, but not while

you are drinking. It is my responsibility to make sure that your family and staff are safe from abuse."

"I don't plan on stopping any time soon. You may be a prince, but you don't dictate what I do to my liver." As if to demonstrate, he picked up his glass and downed the rest of the contents.

"Then I will dismiss your staff and find suitable arrangements for your daughter and grandson." I could feel Meredith's glare, but I didn't look her way. I never used my title, never forced anyone to do anything. I never expected anyone to treat me differently, but I'd be damned if I was going to let this man hurt anyone else.

"You can't dismiss my staff." He shook his head.

"Your father took an oath that gave me that power." I stepped forward. "It is my job to see to the safety of my citizens, and if that means taking measures to remove them from a duke's bad decisions, then that is what I will do."

"Then go. I don't need them." He laughed. "I can take care of myself just fine. Been doing it my whole life."

"Meredith, please go pack some things for you and Marty." I turned and looked at her. The anger in her eyes was intimidating, but she didn't say a word, just turned and stalked out of the room.

"I will be letting the queen know that I've dismissed your staff and take care of their pay while things are handled." I started to turn, but paused. "If you show up for the funeral inebriated, I will make sure that you regret it. That is an order from the crown."

I walked out of the room and was roughly yanked by small hands to a dark corner.

"What the hell are you doing?" Meredith hissed. "Having a pissing contest with my father! Why? What good is this going to accomplish?"

"I can't leave you here with him." Wasn't that obvious?

"The hell you can't. I thought you were going to help, not make things worse!"

Her words felt like a slap. "Of course I'm trying to help."

"Jesus. If the staff is gone, if I'm gone, then there will be no one here to make sure he doesn't do something terrible." She ran a hand through her hair.

"He is a danger to everyone around him." I fought my frustration. She was obviously panicking.

"Where the hell am I going to stay? A hotel? Don't you think that's going to make the town talk?"

"You can stay at D'Lynsal or the palace. There is plenty of space at both." I shrugged. "I have an apartment in town if you want to stay there."

"I can't just go stay at your place, Max. People will talk." Her cheeks were pale.

"Stay at D'Lynsal. It's only two hours from your township and we can say that it was an invitation from my sister. She won't mind. You can say that you and Marty needed some time away from Thysmer. People will assume that it's grief." I reached in my pocket and pulled out my phone. "I need to call them and tell them that we're coming there. Okay?"

"Damn it. Stop making decisions for me." She turned away from me and I could hear her mumbling under her breath. When she turned back around, she poked me in the chest. "Fine. We'll go to your family's home, but you better start asking me what the hell I want. No more making decisions willy-nilly. Got it?"

"I didn't make the decision 'willy-nilly.'" Her robe had come open and I couldn't help but notice the tops of her breasts exposed by the tiny tank top she was wearing. Damn it, now was not the time for that shit. "I meant every word I said in there."

A glass tumbler flew out of the door and exploded against the wall across from us. Meredith jumped and I reached out to steady her.

"I'm going to go get Marty." She looked up at me. "It's just going to get worse."

She turned to leave and I reached out to grab her hand. "Meredith."

"What?" Her eyes looked from me to the open doorway and back.

"I'm sorry." I really was doing what I thought best. "I really am trying to help."

"Later. We'll talk later." She pulled out of my grasp and took the stairs two at a time.

I turned my phone on and headed down the hall to where some of the staff were standing. Dodging the liquid and broken glass, I motioned for the staff to move back.

"I'm putting you on leave." I held up my hand to stop questions. "You will be paid by the crown while not working until things are cleared up. Someone will contact you when it's time to come back."

"Sir, I'd like to stay." The butler stepped forward.

"I think it best that you leave." I started to turn but he cleared his throat.

"I made a promise, sir."

"To who?"

"The late Duke of Thysmer." He stepped forward and lowered his voice. "He requested that I make sure his son didn't do anything to hurt himself."

"I see." I frowned. "It's your decision, but I urge the rest of you to take leave until notified."

"Yes, sir."

I started to turn but stopped. "What is your name?"

"Gerard, sir."

"Please keep me advised of the situation."

"Yes, sir." He bowed his head.

"And make sure that the rest of the staff leave."

Taking a deep breath, I walked through the kitchen to find my bodyguard, but he was already heading in my direction.

"Sir, I heard there was a problem?"

"We're leaving. Lady Meredith and Marty will be accompanying us. Would you please go upstairs and make sure that no one bothers them while they pack?"

"Yes, sir."

"Thank you." I glanced down at my phone. Deciding that it would be easier to call, I dialed Cathy's number and held the phone up to my ear.

"Hello?" I could hear the faint sound of the car in the background.

"Cathy, are you on your way to Thysmer?" I looked around the kitchen, while some of the staff put things away.

"Yeah. Where are you?" Her voice sounded amused.

"Thysmer." I lowered my voice. "Go back home. I'm bringing Meredith and Marty to D'Lynsal."

"What's wrong?" Her voice took on the cool and calm tone our mother used when she was being careful.

"I'll explain later." I could hear Sam asking questions in the background. "Please."

"Sure." I could hear her juggling the phone as she did something. "Should I get guest rooms ready?"

"Yes." I tapped my fingers on the counter. "And see if you can have some food made for them. They haven't eaten."

"Sure." I could practically hear her begging for an explanation.

"Thanks." I hung up the phone and tucked it back in my pocket.

"I put together some snacks. The little one wakes up starving." The cook held out a bag to me.

"Thank you."

"Thank you, sir." She bobbed her head and turned back to getting the kitchen cleaned.

The mess in the hallway had been cleaned up and the door shut. I climbed the stairs quickly and went straight to Marty's room. Charles was standing just outside the door, his arms crossed and his face neutral.

Marty was sitting on his bed with a backpack while his mother shoved clothes into a small suitcase shaped like a car.

"Can I help?" I stopped in the doorway.

"I think you've helped enough for today." Meredith looked up at me and blew some of the hair out of her face.

"Have you packed?" I looked around the room wondering what else the kid might need. "Did you get his toothbrush?"

"His toothbrush?" She looked at me like I was crazy. "No. I haven't gotten his toothbrush yet."

"I'll get it." I ducked into the boy's bathroom and found the toothbrush. I handed it to her and she tucked it into the front pocket before standing up.

"I'm going to change and pack." She ran her fingers through her hair. "Can you stay here with Marty?"

"Of course."

"I'll hurry." She took off down the hallway with quick steps, her hair floating behind her.

I met Charles's eyes and jerked my head in her direction. He nodded once before moving down the hall toward her door.

"Why are we leaving?" Marty looked at me with sleepy eyes.

"What did your mom say?" I cleared my throat.

"Just that we were going to go stay with you." He rubbed at one eye. "She looked mad."

"Yeah, she's a little angry with me." I sat down next to him.

"What'd you do?" He looked up at me with big eyes.

"That's a long story." I sighed.

"Do you have a pond at your house?"

"We have a lake." I smiled when he grinned.

"A big lake or a little lake?" He narrowed his eyes. "Are there fish?"

"It's pretty big and I hear the fishing is great." I bumped his arm with mine. "Maybe you'll have time to go down there."

"Awesome."

"Brought you some food for the ride." I handed him the bag of pastries.

"Thanks." He took the bag and smashed it into his backpack.

Neither of us said anything else, just sat there in a comfortable silence while we waited on his mother. When she finally showed back up, she'd changed into a pair of jeans, boots, and sweater. Her hair hung around her face and while she looked annoyed, she couldn't be any more beautiful.

"Ready?" I stood up and helped Marty off the bed.

"Yep!" He hitched his straps up higher on his shoulders.

I looked back over at Meredith and tried to not frown. Knowing she was angry with me was like a kick to the balls. But I wouldn't change my mind. I couldn't.

"As ready as I'm going to be." She turned and held out her hand. "C'mon, Marty."

I sighed as I followed them down the stairs. How the hell had I gotten involved in all of this? And why the hell couldn't I seem to leave it alone?

"If you leave with him, don't bother coming back!" her father hollered from the sitting room door. "I'm not going to take care of you if you go get yourself knocked up again. We don't need any more bastards running around."

Meredith tensed but tucked Marty's head against her side and kept walking. I, on the other hand, stopped dead in my tracks and looked at the man.

"Do not speak to them again." I said the words quietly.

"I'll say what I want to my daughter and her bastard—"

I moved without thinking, covering the distance between us in the space of a heartbeat.

"Max!" Meredith's worried voice snaked through my fury-riddled brain.

I stared at Arthur and took another step forward so that there was barely any space between our noses. The thick smell of alcohol on his breath made me wrinkle my nose.

"Please, Max." Meredith's small hand touched my shoulder.

"We will be back for the reading of the will." I didn't want him to think that he had banned Meredith from her home. You should always be able to go home.

Meredith grabbed my hand and tugged me backward. I let her lead me out of the house, her hand shaking in mine as we put distance between us and her father.

My SUV and Charles's car stood idling in the curved driveway. Marty was standing at the door where Meredith must have left him his little face covered in fear, and I felt like I had been kicked in the gut. Had I done that? Had I made him scared?

Meredith grabbed Marty's hand with her free one and let me lead them to my car. I watched as she buckled Marty into the backseat and pulled out a coloring book and crayons for him. I opened her door before going around to the other side to drive.

"All ready?" I looked in my rearview mirror at Marty. He nodded his head, and some of the fear had started to fade away. I looked over at Meredith and she jerked her head once.

As we drove to D'Lynsal no one talked. I tried the radio, but gave up and turned it off. Meredith stared out the window, much like she did the day I showed up to tell her about her grandfather. I didn't know what she was thinking. Would she stay at D'Lynsal? Or would she fight to go somewhere else?

She could go back to England. There was nothing saying that she had to be at her grandfather's funeral. Maybe I could find a way to make sure she got a scholarship. Something that would set her and Marty up if the will left her with nothing.

I pulled up to D'Lynsal and waited for the guard to open the gate. Landscapers worked around the front gardens, trimming and cutting. I pulled around to the back and parked next to Alex's car.

"I didn't know you lived in a castle." Marty stared at the stone walls of D'Lynsal.

I ruffled his hair and helped him put his backpack on. Meredith walked around to the back and opened the rear door. I hurried around to grab the bags so she wouldn't have to carry them.

"I can carry my bag." She shook her head.

"I know that." I offered her a small smile. "But I wanted to carry them anyway."

Cathy met us at the back door with a big smile. "Hi!"

My little sister stepped forward and hugged Meredith before looking at Marty. "How's my favorite dancer?"

Marty's cheeks turned pink and he giggled.

"Come in!" Cathy held the door open and I followed Meredith and Marty inside.

A butler took their bags from me. "I've readied rooms on the family wing, sir."

"Thank you, Lawrence."

"Should I take the young man's backpack?"

"I think he's fine."

I half listened as Cathy chatted with Meredith. She had pulled herself together and looked completely comfortable as she walked through the house. When we passed the suits of armor near a large picture window, Marty grabbed her hand excitedly.

"Look! Look! Real armor." He stopped in his tracks and looked up at the armor in awe.

"Those were used in a war a long time ago." I pointed out some of the dents and scratches that hadn't been buffed out.

"Whoa." He leaned forward. "Is there any blood?"

"Marty." Meredith laughed.

"There probably was some a long time ago, but not anymore." I winked at him.

"Max and Alex got in big trouble for trying to use the swords when we were little," Cathy whispered.

"Don't even think about it, buddy." Meredith poked Marty in the shoulder.

"That is so cool." Marty looked up at me. "What else is there?"

I laughed. "Well, there's the lake, the stables, the birds."

"Birds?" He grimaced. "Like parakeets?"

"Like the ones that would eat parakeets."

"Oh man." He whispered the words and I laughed.

"I figured you guys didn't have time to eat, so I had the cook make something for you." Cathy opened the door to the dining room. "We weren't sure what you liked, so we made a little bit of everything."

Samantha stood up from her seat at the table and smiled. "Hey guys!"

"Ah, no wonder you made so much food. The pregnant woman is eating with us." I pulled a chair out for Marty and then Meredith.

"Shut it, dork." Sam sat back down and mock-glared at me.

"I'm glad to see you too." I smiled at my sister-in-law. Some of the tension that had gripped me for days melted away. It was good to be home.

"Thank you for having us over on such short notice." Meredith unfolded her napkin and placed it in her lap. "I hope we're not causing any trouble."

"Not at all." Cathy sat down next to Sam. "We're glad you're here."

"Well, it's very kind of you."

I snorted and Meredith glared at me.

"What?" Sam looked between me and Meredith.

"I didn't really give them much choice." I shrugged. "It was either here or the palace."

"Didn't give her a choice?" Sam stared at us. "You kidnapped them?"

"I didn't kidnap them!" I sat up straight. "Let's talk about this later."

"Yes, let's." Meredith narrowed her eyes at me and I realized I was in trouble. The weird part was that I kind of enjoyed knowing she was going to let down her guard and rip into me.

ELEVEN

BREAKFAST. OR WOULD it be brunch? Brunch with the royal family. Not exactly what I had planned for the day.

I tried to focus on the conversation, but I kept going over what had happened with my father. I knew that he was going to be upset about the will, but I had underestimated his reaction. I had thought he would be more understanding this morning, having slept off the alcohol from the night before.

And then Max! Telling me that I had to leave, dismissing the staff. I'd never seen someone stand up to my father in that fashion, but it went exactly the way I would have expected. Horribly.

Then again, we were out of the house, and for once I didn't feel guilty about it.

"Do you have any Pop-Tarts?" Marty's voice pulled my attention back to the present.

"Marty," I admonished. "Look at all of this great

stuff that they have for us." I grabbed a bowl of fresh fruit and picked out some of his favorite pieces.

"Sorry, I just thought I'd ask." Marty looked down at the table.

"I like those!" Cathy smiled at my son and his cheeks turned pink. Lord help me, the boy was already noticing pretty girls.

"Would you like an apple turnover?" Samantha held out the tray. "I've been craving these for the last month."

"You'll like that." I picked one off of the tray and set it on his plate.

"Is Alex here?" Max asked. His deep voice made my heart speed up. Whether it was from anger or what, I wasn't sure.

The truth was that while I was angry with him, I was also a little grateful. He had taken me out of the house and away from my father's abuse. And while normally I would not have stayed, I felt trapped by Granddad's passing. It seemed like I had to stay to try and keep things from going haywire. And honestly, I hadn't been doing such a good job.

"He'll be back this afternoon," Sam replied. "He had a meeting today at the palace. Some of the ambassadors from the Future Bird Trust are in town."

"Fun." Max was busily filling his plate with food. "Better him than me."

"What is the Future Bird Trust?" Marty asked around a mouthful of food.

"We are a group that educates people about birds." Sam smiled at him. "We have classes that work with children. You should come out sometime. One of our centers isn't that far from here."

"Will I get to hold a bird?" Marty sat up in his seat.

"You might be able to work up to that." Sam leaned forward. "It takes a lot of training to learn how to hold a bird."

"Cool."

Brunch with the royal family was far more normal than I had thought it would be. They talked about work, about family, and teased one another. It wasn't long before I could feel myself relaxing for real, no longer playing a role.

"Are you going to sing tomorrow?" Cathy smiled at me. "I've heard that you have a beautiful voice."

"Yes, I'll be singing."

Max looked up at me sharply. "You're going to sing tomorrow?"

"Yes." I felt my eyebrows pull together. It would

be my final tribute to my granddad. Of course I was going to sing.

"It won't be too . . . difficult?"

"I'm a performer." I shrugged. "I can keep it together for one song."

His eyes took on a worried cast and I wasn't sure if I wanted to smile or smack him. Why did he seem to think I couldn't take care of myself?

"I'm sure it will be beautiful." Cathy reached out and touched my hand. "It's so hard to lose someone."

I nodded my head, not really trusting myself to speak. If there was one thing I knew about the royal family, it was that they knew about personal loss. When King Joseph died, it had been splashed across the headlines. I hadn't paid much attention because I'd been young and dealing with things that life had thrown my way.

"What do you have planned for today, Meredith?" Samantha asked.

"I'm not sure." I shot a look at Max. "I need to call and let Rachel know that I won't be at Thysmer."

"Do you have an assistant?" Cathy cocked her head to the side. "I'm sure they could take care of that for you."

"No, I don't have an assistant." I pulled my

phone from my pocket and quickly sent a text to Rachel. As savvy as she had seemed, I figured a text would work. "I really didn't need one in England."

"No bodyguards?" Sam raised an eyebrow. "No one following you around?"

"No." I frowned. "Is that weird?"

"It sounds amazing." Sam sighed. "Not that I would trade my Chadwick for anything."

"Chadwick?"

"My assistant." Sam shook her head. "No, he's more than that. He's my rock. He takes care of everything. I don't know how I would have adapted without him."

"We had someone that helped us when we first took over Thysmer, but Granddad didn't keep them around for long. He said it felt weird to have someone following him around when he just wanted to fish." I smiled, remembering how he would jump whenever Bernard would come up with a question.

"Do you handle your own events, then?" Sam frowned. "That's a lot of work, especially if you're in school."

"Actually, I haven't had any tasks given to me." I kept my face calm. Did that mean the queen hadn't trusted my family with anything important? Not that I could really blame her.

"I believe I overheard my mom telling some-one to leave you be while you were in school," Max spoke up. "They were looking for someone to partner with a food bank. Mom said that while you were in school, you weren't taking any as-signments."

"Oh." I frowned. I hadn't even realized that I was somehow dodging "royal work." Not that I was going to complain. The school and rehearsal schedule had been rigorous enough.

"Lucky." Cathy leaned back in her chair. "I only escape during the semester. I still get sent on errands during the summer."

"Well, I've been attending through the sum-mers." I was trying to finish as quickly as possible. I wasn't exactly looking for the typical university experience. No clubs or drunken binges. No dates or relationship drama. Just class and singing. And hanging out with my little man.

"I wish I could do that. I really don't have a choice." Cathy frowned. "Not that I don't love my work with the Liberty Anne Foundation. It's re-warding in a very different way."

"What do you do there?" I sat back in my chair and tapped Marty's hand when he started fidget-ing with the tablecloth.

"We raise money for the local schools' art

programs and we also work with children with disabilities." Her eyes turned thoughtful. "We've made some huge steps forward in the last couple of months."

"Hey, would you guys like to see where you will be staying?" Max stood up.

"Sure." I cocked my eyebrow at him. "Will there be shackles, Your Highness?"

"That can be arranged." His eyes took on a dark look and I found myself blushing. Talk about having your words turned around. I guess that's what I deserved for being snarky.

"Oh, I like her," Sam whispered loudly to Cathy as they exchanged a look.

"I don't think you're the only one." Cathy smirked at her brother, and I wondered if they had forgotten I was sitting there.

"What are shackles?" Marty asked.

Everyone at the table turned to look at him.

"Back in the old days, they were used to keep prisoners from escaping." Max kept his eyes glued to mine. "Nowadays they are mainly just for show."

"Like the suits of armor?" Marty hopped out of his seat.

"Just like that." Max smiled. "But if your mom would like I could look to see if we have any that are in good shape."

"Thanks, but that's not necessary." I stood up and set my napkin on the table.

"Thanks for the food." Marty smiled at Samantha and Cathy. Much to my surprise he folded himself in half to perform a little bow.

"You're very welcome, sir." Cathy bowed her head in return.

We left the dining room and walked through a large sitting room. For being such a big space, it had a homey feel that I appreciated.

"We put you guys in the family wing. I hope you don't mind." Max led us up a flight of stairs.

"Worried we might sneak away?" I raised an eyebrow and smiled.

"Everything wakes up Sam nowadays. She's like our alarm system." Max smiled back at me, but I could see something worried in his eyes. "I really hope you will stay at D'Lynsal."

I didn't say anything, just kept walking. I might joke about him having kidnapped us, but I knew that he had done what he thought best. It wasn't like he had forced us into the car with him. If I pushed to go somewhere else, he wouldn't stop me. And going back to Thysmer was completely out of the question at this point anyway.

"This is Marty's room." Max pushed open a door and Marty bounded through.

"Awesome." My son flew straight to the TV to check out the game consoles.

"No games until I see what they are." Just because we weren't at home didn't mean he was going to play a game not rated for him.

I looked around the room and nodded. It was similar to the one Marty had at Thysmer. A large bed, a desk and chair, a wardrobe. The only difference was that everything felt much newer than at Thysmer.

"This will work great." I smiled over at Max, hoping to show him that I really was okay with the accommodations.

"Good." He leaned against the door frame.

"Can I play, Mom?" Marty looked up at me with big eyes. "They have the new Turbo Man."

"Is that the space one?"

"Yes! You fly your ship around the galaxy and kill bad guys." He folded his hands together. "Please?"

"I guess so." I frowned. "But you need to play outside some too."

"I will! I brought my football." He shrugged out of his backpack and held it up.

"I bet Cathy would play with you if you asked." Max smiled. "She's a great player."

"Really? Maybe I should go ask her now." Marty looked excited. "Before she gets busy."

"You're going to give up on Turbo Man?" Shock widened my eyes.

"Well, I might as well play while it's nice outside." He shrugged, but there was red in his cheeks.

"She's probably still in the dining room. Do you remember how to get there?" Max pushed off from the wall while Marty wrestled his ball out of his bag.

"Yeah." He threw the mostly empty bag on the bed.

"Can I go, Mom?" He looked up at me with his big blue eyes and I frowned.

"I guess so." He tore off down the stairs and I stuck my head out of the room. "Come find me if she's busy."

"Yes, ma'am!"

I looked up at Max and shook my head. "He's been begging me for that game for weeks. I can't believe he gave it up to play football."

"Never underestimate the effect of a pretty girl on a guy." Max's eyes traveled over my face and landed on my mouth. "It's a powerful thing."

"But he's only six." I took a deep breath.

"I was five when I fell madly in love with the head housekeeper." Max smiled. "I followed her around folding towels."

"You did not." I laughed.

"I did." He reached out and touched the hair next to my face. "She was Irish. Red hair, blue eyes, and didn't let me get away with anything."

I didn't say anything, just watched as he examined my face.

"I guess I have a type that I prefer." His smile was slow and lazy.

"Well, good thing I'm not Irish." The words came out softly, as if I hadn't been able to find much force to say them with.

"Three out of four isn't bad." He chuckled and tugged on my hair. "C'mon. Let me show you your room."

"Okay." I swallowed and followed after him. My eyes dipped down to his rear and I couldn't help but appreciate the way his jeans cupped his nice ass.

"This one is yours." He opened the door and stood back so I could enter.

The room was huge, and that was saying a lot. Where Thysmer Manor had preserved the past, D'Lynsal was incredibly modern. The room was a soft gray color; the furniture was all white except for the large four-poster bed, which was ebony. Fresh flowers filled the room and I found myself wanting to climb into the soft-looking comforter. This was the room of a princess. Absolutely decadent.

"Wow." I whispered the word. My suitcase had been set on a small bench near a closet.

"You like it?" Max's deep voice was quiet.

"I do." I nodded my head. "Very much. You guys might have to kick me out."

"You're welcome as long as you like." He tucked his hands into his pockets and nodded his head toward my suitcase. "If there is anything you need steamed or pressed for tomorrow, just hang it on the door."

"Thank you." I had already picked out my outfit for the funeral, thank goodness, so it had been waiting on me when I was packing to leave.

"We wanted you to be comfortable." He frowned. "I wanted you to be comfortable."

"I appreciate what you've done, but I really wish you had gone about it in another way." I turned to look at him.

"If I had suggested you stay here before your father blew his top this morning, would you have come?" Max stood up straight. "Meredith, you're a strong person to have put up with all of that.

Stronger than I am. I couldn't leave you there while he drank himself into oblivion."

"Sometimes it's easier when he's completely wasted. He passes out somewhere and I have nothing to worry about." I sighed and sat down on the bed. "Really, I haven't lived with him in years. I came to Lilaria with Granddad. How could I not? It meant a better life for Marty. But I found a way to get us out of the house with my father as soon as I could. I was lucky enough to be accepted into the program in England. I left and only came back for short visits."

"And now you're just waiting on the will." Max took a deep breath. "I'm sorry I got involved, but when I saw him try to hit you that day . . ." He shook his head.

"It's not always that bad. I mean, it's not great, but usually he leaves me alone." I frowned. "Says I remind him of my mom too much."

"What happened to your mom?"

"She left. When I was little." I shrugged. "No clue where she is or why she left—though I can guess it was because of my father."

His jaw tensed and without him saying anything, I knew what he was thinking. That it was deplorable for a parent to leave a child in such a situation. I agreed with him, which was why I didn't mourn the loss.

"What about . . . what about Marty's father?" He looked down at the ground. "Do you share custody with him?"

"No." I guess we were going to air out all of my dirty secrets. "Jared disappeared as soon as I told him I was pregnant."

"You must have been young." He watched me with thoughtful eyes. "That would have been hard."

"I've done easier things."

"You're a really great mother." His eyes were sincere.

"Thanks." I smiled at him. "I try."

"It shows."

My heart felt a little lighter with that simple sentence. "I never wanted Marty to want for anything."

"It would seem like you've given him everything that he needs." He pulled out the chair from the desk and sat down. "He's a great kid."

"I think so." I smiled at him.

We sat there for a minute, just looking at each other, and I couldn't help but laugh. "Is that an artist thing?"

"What?" His eyebrows furrowed.

"Staring at people." I shook my head. "You were staring at me."

"Well, you're beautiful." He said the words as if it should be obvious.

I looked away from him and laughed.

"What?" He smiled.

"I'm not even wearing any makeup." I shook my head. "And yet you saying that made me feel more beautiful than I ever have."

His smile took on a hint of pride. "Do you remember dancing with me at Alex's wedding?"

"I do. You looked rather grumpy when you asked me to dance." It had been one of those pure moments of deliciousness. Something I thought I'd look back on with fondness. The night a prince flirted with me and asked me to dance. That wasn't something that most people could claim.

"Well, I hate being paraded around." He shrugged. "That many people get to me."

"Then why'd you ask me to dance?"

"You were gorgeous that night, but I like you like this just as much." His eyes watched me closely and I tried to hide my smile.

"Do they teach princes to say things like that when you're growing up? How to Melt a Woman's Heart 101?"

"Actually the class is called Panty-Dropping 101." He raised one eyebrow.

I looked down at my feet. "Nope. They're still in place. Maybe you need a refresher course."

"I'll have to get the ol' schoolbooks back out." His eyes twinkled.

We were flirting. I was in a room in his house, my son was playing outside with a princess, and we were flirting.

"You realize that my father kicked you out of his house earlier and now you're flirting with me." I shook my head. "I thought you didn't like drama."

"Well, I would have flirted with you there, but that option was taken away." He stood up and held his hand out to me. "C'mon."

"Where are we going?" I let him take my hand.

"I figured I'd give you the grand tour." His fingers twined with mine and my heart raced like a schoolgirl's. "Unless you have something else to do."

"No, I think my schedule has been cleared for today."

He walked me through the house, pointing out his family members' rooms. I tried hard to ignore the fact that his room was directly across from mine. I was the mother of a six-year-old boy. Why was I so nervous to let this man lead me around?

"This is my studio." He opened the door to a large room full of bright sunlight. "It used to be my mother's office, but she gave it to me. The lighting in here is perfect."

"Where does she work now?" I stepped into the room and took in the canvases leaning against the walls, the drop cloths that were speckled with paint, and the pictures that were tacked along the walls.

"In a room downstairs." He watched me as I walked around the space.

There were tons of half-finished projects around the room, sketches pinned to boards, and photographs taped to a desk. Finished pieces leaned against the wall as if they were trash or forgotten.

I knelt down and looked at a painting of a city scene. New buildings were interspersed with old buildings. Brick and metal caught with casual strokes. I could imagine the sounds that he would have heard while working on the piece. On the terrace of an apartment sat a grandmother with a small boy. The old and the new.

Standing up, I walked around the room, uncovering treasures that were half obscured with discarded projects or trash. He followed behind me as I walked through his sanctum and I wondered what he was thinking.

"You're messy." I glanced at him.

"Comes with the trade." He shrugged.

"I would figure your studio would be full of fur rugs and images of nudes."

"Well, you haven't seen my room yet."

"Ah, that's where you keep them." I cut my eyes at him, a little worried that he wasn't joking. "And is your bearskin rug in front of a fireplace?"

His eyes sparkled down at me. "I spilled chocolate milk on the fake bearskin rug when I was little."

"Naughty."

"You have no idea." He took a step closer to me and my back hit the wall.

"I have a pretty big imagination." I whispered the words, but my attention was focused on his mouth.

"We should test that out."

"Could be dangerous."

"I'm willing to take the risk." His reached up to touch my face with one hand, his other hand pressed against the wall next to my shoulder.

"Max." I wasn't sure why I said his name. Did I want him to stop? Was I begging for more? I wasn't sure.

"Tell me now if you don't want me to kiss you." His eyes met mine in all seriousness. His fingers caressed my jaw, sending shivers down my body. "Because it's all I can think of doing."

I licked my lips and watched as his pupils dilated. His breath fanned across my face and I reached up and placed a hand on his chest. His heart beat against my fingertips and I couldn't drag my eyes from his.

I shouldn't want him to kiss me. I shouldn't. I didn't kiss men. It was too real.

But I did want him to kiss me. I wanted so much more than just a kiss.

"Kiss me."

Something akin to victory lit his features, but he didn't rush for the prize. Instead he leaned forward and barely grazed my lips with his. I could feel his heart jackhammering under my touch, matching my own.

"Are you sure?"

"Kiss me, damn it." I fisted my hand in his shirt and tugged him toward me.

He wasted no time. His lips pressed against mine as he tilted my head up. There was nothing held back this time, nothing left to the imagination. He nipped my bottom lip between his teeth and I gasped in pleasure. He was in control of the kiss, his tongue soft but determined as it tangled with mine.

I ran my free hand through his hair, grabbing a handful so that he couldn't pull away until I was ready. His body pressed into mine so that I could feel every delicious muscle under his shirt, the strength in his thighs. His hands went to my waist, pushing my shirt up so that his fingers were touching my skin.

It was just as good as the first time he had kissed me. Maybe even better. I could become addicted to the way he felt pressed against me, the way he tasted.

When he broke the kiss, it was only to trail soft kisses down my neck. His breath rushed over my cleavage and I felt my nipples tighten in excitement just before his lips glided across my collarbone. Warm fingers inched upward under my shirt until they were tracing the wire of my bra. His mouth covered mine again and I let my hands explore his chest. Tracing the hard lines of his body all the way down to where his plaid shirt was tucked into his jeans.

I let my fingers run along the top of his belt, tracing the dips created by his muscles, and around to his back, where I tugged at his shirt. My fingers ran over his skin, delighting in the way he had increased our kiss, as if I had pushed him to the edge. His hand moved to cup my breast and

I moaned into his mouth. His traced my nipple through the thin material of my bra with his thumb and I arched against him.

"Meredith," he whispered against my ear. "You're killing me."

"I'm not done yet." Pulling his face back to mine I sucked his bottom lip into my mouth. If I was going to break my cardinal rule for men, then I was going to shatter it to pieces.

His free hand slid down to cup my ass, pressing his excitement against my side. With soft fingers he rolled my nipple before gently pinching it. My head fell back and I groaned. It felt good to be touched. It felt right to be touched by Max.

I slid my hands around to the front of his shirt, untucking it so I could touch more of him. He slid one leg between mine and I bucked against him. He groaned before pulling his mouth from mine. He trailed his teeth down my neck, making me shiver.

I should stop. Should tell him that I didn't sleep with people, hadn't slept with anyone since Marty's father, but I didn't. I couldn't. I needed what he was offering me. I needed Max. The man who created beautiful paintings. The man who had stood up to my father. The man who had whisked me and my son away to somewhere safe.

His hand left my breast, but only to lift me off the ground so that he was pressed between my legs. I ground against him and moaned into his ear while he kissed my neck.

"Damn it." He groaned. "Door. Gotta close the door."

He pulled me away from the wall and kicked the door shut before turning the lock with one hand. Pressing us back against the wall, he pulled my boots off and threw them to the side.

"What about Marty?" I lifted my eyes to his.

"He'll be fine. I promise." He set me down and ran a hand along my cheek. "I wouldn't leave him if he wasn't."

He kissed me again, this time tenderly as he worked my sweater up over my body. When he moved back to pull the sweater over my head, I started working on the buttons of his shirt, quickly making my way down before pushing the shirt off his shoulders. Reaching behind him, he grabbed the collar of his undershirt and pulled it over his head, discarding it with my sweater.

Looking up at him, I worked his belt loose and pulled it from the belt loops before dropping it on the ground. His chest was perfectly sculpted muscle, and my mouth begged to run over it. He brushed some of my hair out of my face before leaning down to kiss me. One of his hands fisted in my hair at the base of my neck while the other reached around to undo my bra.

He slid the straps off my shoulders and I stepped back just enough to let the flimsy material fall to the ground between us. His warm fingers undid the button to my jeans and traced along the top of my panties.

One of his hands grazed my breast and I closed my eyes in pleasure.

"You're beautiful," he whispered. "Perfect."

"You're not so bad yourself." I gasped as his fingers dipped into my panties, teasing me.

Pulling me away from the wall, he worked my jeans down and I kicked them to the side. I had a momentary bit of fear as I worried about whether or not I had shaved my legs, but it was forgotten when he stood back up and caught one of my breasts with his mouth. His tongue stroked my hardened nipple before raking it with his teeth.

His hand slid between my legs, teasing me, and I moaned loudly before biting my lip. It had been so long. So long since I'd been touched that way.

He lifted his head and pressed his mouth to mine, his tongue eagerly exploring. The sound of his zipper filled my ears and panic shot through me. Was I really going to do this? And then his hand was pulling my panties down and the cool air rushed across my bare skin. When his hardened shaft pressed against my skin, I sucked in a lungful of air.

Sensing my panic, his kiss slowed. "Are you okay?"

"Yes." I looked into his green eyes and took a deep breath.

"We can stop."

"I don't want to." I said the words quietly. There, my barriers were gone. The truth was out. "I want you."

"Thank God." He pressed his mouth back to mine before lifting me in his arms. He laid me down on a small sofa before covering my body with his. Hungrily I pulled at him, eager for the feel of his skin pressed against mine. I felt like he had lit me on fire and only his touch would put it out.

His mouth covered my breast while his hand slid between my legs. I bucked when he dipped one finger inside and then groaned when another joined the first.

His mouth captured my groan as I writhed beneath him. Reaching out, I stroked along his stomach until I could wrap my fingers around his manhood. He hissed in pleasure before shifting so that I could stroke him better. He mumbled things in Lilarian as we touched each other; half words and phrases while lost in pleasure.

When I was nearing my peak, he pulled his hand away and moved so that he was hovering between my legs.

"Not yet." He leaned down and tugged on my ear with his teeth. "I want to be inside you when you come."

He rubbed at my opening before slowly filling me. The light streaming into the room made his eyes shimmer with a symphony of colors. My own eyes started to drift shut, but he touched my cheek.

"Watch me, Meredith," he whispered in Lilarian. "I want to see your eyes when you finish."

When he began to move, it was slow and steady. Long, deep strokes, as he pulled out and then filled me again. And again. My body arched with him, meeting him thrust for thrust. With the hand that he wasn't using to brace himself, he cupped my breast, kneading it softly.

My eyes closed in pleasure and he gave a deep, masculine chuckle. "Not yet. I want to see you."

I opened my eyes, giving him what he asked. I'd give him anything he asked for at that moment.

He shifted and I groaned loudly. He found just the right spot and I could hold on no longer.

"Yes," I whispered as he picked up the pace. "Yes, please. Yes."

His eyes clouded and I could tell that he wasn't far from the end. Reaching around him, I grabbed his ass and urged him on. Faster. Harder.

I looked up into his eyes just as I fell over the edge. It was blinding; far more intense than I remembered it ever being before. Triumph filled his gaze as he stared down at me as he finished.

He pressed his face to the crook of my neck, breathing heavily, and murmured sweet nothings as he pressed his lips to my shoulder.

"Beautiful," he whispered. "Perfect."

I closed my eyes, enjoying the weight of his body pressing into me. Enjoying the sense of contentment we had created.

Enjoying Max.

I had warned him that this would be dangerous. And I'd been right.

I was losing my heart to this prince.

A prince who would hate everything about the career I was trying to build for myself.

TWELVE

Ｈｅｒ ａｒｍｓ ｗｅｒｅ still wrapped around me, one hand cupping my ass as we lay on the tiny sofa in my studio. Her breathing had slowed and I shifted so that I wasn't crushing her. Carefully, I rolled so that we were facing one another, her soft body tucked against mine.

I wasn't sure what to say. There were too many emotions rattling around in my head. But the dominant one was victory. Quickly followed by a sense of possessiveness that surprised me.

"I'd like to paint you like this." My eyes ran over her face, enjoying the way it was highlighted by the sun.

"Nude?" She laughed, and her perfect breasts moved against me.

"The look on your face right now." I touched her nose. "You look satisfied."

"Feeling proud of yourself, Your Highness?" She wrinkled her perfect nose and rolled her eyes.

"Absolutely." I grinned down at her.

"You're something else."

"So are you." I let my hand slide down her back and over the curve of her hip. She had such perfect lines.

"I bet you tell all the girls that." Her eyes looked down between us.

"No, I don't." It was truth. No one had compared to Meredith.

She hummed under her breath. "And is there anyone that I should worry about making jealous?"

Her guarded eyes looked up into mine and I let out a chuckle and then realized maybe I had something to worry about. Way to get the information backward, Max.

"No." I tilted her chin up. "Is there someone in your life?"

"There hasn't been anyone since Marty's father." She shrugged, but shock filled my body.

"No one?"

"No." She sat up and pulled away from me. "Did you believe my dad when he called me a whore?"

"Of course not." How could I explain that I was surprised no one else had taken the time to get close to her? "Thank you."

"For what?" She looked at me, surprised.

"For trusting me with something so important."

Something soft filled her eyes as she leaned down and pressed a gentle kiss to my mouth. "You're welcome."

"I suppose we need to get up and join the world?" My eyes ran over her body and back to her breasts. I really hadn't spent enough time playing with those.

"Stop staring at my chest." She laughed.

"I'm not sure I can help it." I moved so that I was a little closer to them. "They're begging for more attention."

"I don't hear anything." She pushed at my shoulder and started to stand up but I penned her with my arm.

"At least let me tell them good-bye before you leave." I captured one peak with my mouth and enjoyed her gasp of surprise.

Her skin was perfect. Soft and creamy, made for being kissed. Letting go of that peak I grabbed the other, flicking it with my tongue.

When she moaned gently, I pulled away.

"That was a hell of a way to say good-bye." Her voice was raspy.

"Imagine saying hello." I raised one eyebrow.

There were a lot of things I wanted to do to Meredith and we'd only touched the tip of the iceberg.

She smiled but didn't say anything. Instead, she stood up and looked around the studio. I tucked my arms under my head and watched as she walked around retrieving her clothing.

"Are you going to stay there all day?" She looked at me as she put her bra back on.

"I could." I stretched, enjoying the way her eyes ran over my body.

"Don't you have things to do?" She stepped into her jeans and zipped them back up.

"Didn't anyone tell you? I'm the slacker prince." I raised one eyebrow. "I lie about and paint things when I feel like it."

"Slacker." She snorted. "You organized an entire art event in England, came to my rescue, and then fought a dragon."

"My dragon-slaying skills were getting a little rusty." I sat up on one elbow. "I needed a refresher."

"I think you poked him with a stick." She shook her head and looked away from me. Her shoulders drooped a little and I tensed.

"I forgot my sword at home." I sat up and grabbed my pants from the floor. Things had been going so well. What had happened?

"I need to check on Marty." She bit her lip, but still didn't look up at me. "I shouldn't have left him alone like that."

"You didn't leave him alone." I pulled my shirt on and turned her to face me. "He's in the very capable hands of my sister and sister-in-law. I told you I wouldn't leave him if he wasn't safe."

As I looked at her face I watched as she pulled on a mask, changing into someone else. Before my eyes, she became aloof and distant, the opposite of the woman I had just been holding in my arms.

"Don't do that." I lifted her chin with my fingers. "You don't have to play a part with me."

Her eyes widened a bit, but she managed to keep her face intact. "What do you mean?"

"This." I narrowed my eyes. "Just a minute ago you were alive, open and real. Now you've shut it all down. Tighter than a prison cell."

"I don't know what you're talking about."

"Don't do this, Meredith." I sighed in frustration. "I don't know what's going on in your head, but you don't have to shut me out."

"It's for your own good." The words tumbled out of her mouth.

"What is?" I felt my eyebrows arch.

"We did something amazing together." She touched my chest. "But we can't do it again."

"What? Why?" That blew my plans out of the water. I'd planned on doing it a lot more.

"I have too much going on." She shrugged. "I can't handle the complications that come with any kind of relationship. And you don't want what comes along with me."

I stared at her, picking my words carefully. "It's too late for that."

"Complications?"

"A relationship." I let go of her chin. "There's something between us. Whatever you want to call it. Friendship, a relationship, attraction. It's there already." Shit, things had gotten out of hand fast. When was the last time I was in a relationship? I avoided them like the plague, but here I was arguing that we were in the middle of one.

"What about when I go home?" Her mask cracked and I could see the worry swirling beneath. "When I go back to singing and have to make public appearances? What then? That's not the life you want."

"Let's take it one day at a time, okay?" I took a deep breath. Again the thought of her leaving twisted my gut, but she was right. I hated being in the public eye. Hated the press that would go along with having a famous girlfriend. "No expectations."

Her face froze and I watched as she worked through something. "I'm everything you want to avoid, Max."

"Not everything." I shrugged. Oh shit. Was I changing my mind? No. Not about the press. That would never happen. But maybe . . . maybe it didn't matter if she was in the spotlight as long as I wasn't. "I don't know. All I know is that I want to spend time with you. And with Marty."

Her eyes closed for a minute. "Okay."

"Then let's go downstairs and see if we can teach Marty something about football." I sat down and pulled my shoes on.

She nodded her head, but didn't say anything. Whatever was bothering her was still there, nagging at her mind. Until she worked through it or decided to tell me what it was, there was nothing I could do.

Taking her hand in mine, I led her downstairs and through the back door. I wanted to touch her, needed to cement what had passed between us.

"You're cheating!" Marty yelled as Cathy picked up the ball and ran away from him with it.

Cathy laughed loudly as she ran back and forth, keeping the ball out of Marty's reach.

"Cheater!" Sam yelled from her shaded spot under a tree.

"I've got to!" Cathy yelled back. "The kid is good!"

"Should we go help Marty?" I squeezed Meredith's fingers gently.

"I think I'd be more of a hindrance than a help." She flashed a brief smile. "I'm terrible."

"It's all for fun." I pulled her toward the field. "Get some sunshine. It'll do you good."

"You're as persistent as Marty." She shook her head. "You're going to regret this."

"No I'm not." I laughed. "You're on Cathy's team."

She looked at me and started laughing. "That's cruel."

"She's making Marty chase her all over the place. This way it'll be fair."

"Fine." She pulled her hair back away from her face. "If I break a leg, it's on you."

"I can live with that." I ran ahead, catching Cathy from behind so that Marty could grab the ball.

"Penalty!" Cathy shouted.

"It's an all for all." Marty took the ball and started dribbling it toward the large tree.

Meredith chased after him, desperately trying to kick the ball away from him while the boy laughed loudly.

Letting Cathy go, I chased after Marty and Meredith. "Pass!"

Marty kicked me the ball and I dribbled it a ways while Cathy gained ground on me.

"I'm open!" Marty called, Meredith still doggedly pursuing him.

"Here." I kicked the ball to him and hollered in triumph when he scored a goal between two trees.

Samantha cheered from the sidelines, her hands in the air.

"Good job." Meredith held her hand out for a high-five.

"You too." Marty hopped up and smacked her hand.

We spent hours playing in the sun, chasing the ball back and forth. Meredith scored a goal, which was cause for celebration, even if it looked like it wasn't on purpose. I picked her up and she laughed as I spun her in a circle. Marty giggled at his mom as she tried to get me to put her down.

"It was an accident." She smacked at my shoulder.

"Don't admit it." I set her back down. "And that's a hell of an improvement."

"Gee, thanks." She playfully punched my shoulder. When she turned to go back toward the ball I smacked her ass.

"Fair's fair." I winked at her shocked expression.

By the time dinner rolled around I had almost forgotten how the day had started out. Meredith and Marty fit into my family's routine smoothly. In some ways it felt like they'd always been a part of it. In fact it was a little scary how easily they got along with my sister and sister-in-law.

"Alex should be home soon." Samantha was sitting on the floor, putting together a puzzle with Marty. We had all taken up spots around the room after eating. Cathy was working on her computer and I was idly sketching the room.

"He's coming back tonight?" It was a long drive to D'Lynsal from the palace.

"You know how he is." She shrugged, but I could see her smile. Alex barely let her out of his sight now that she was pregnant. For some reason that didn't seem as annoying to me today as it normally did.

"Are you coming tomorrow?"

"Of course. We all are." Sam shot me a pointed look before tilting her head in Marty's direction.

"Right." Clue understood. I wasn't to speak about the funeral in front of Marty. No reason to upset him.

Looking back at my sketch pad, I frowned. I

needed to pick out an appropriate suit before the morning. We'd have to leave early to make it back to the Thysmer township in time.

"All right, buddy. Time for a bath." Meredith came down the stairs, her hair still wet from her own shower.

"We're not done yet!" He looked up at her with worried eyes.

"It's a six-hundred piece puzzle. You're not going to be able to finish it tonight." She leveled a stare at him.

"Can we work on it tomorrow?" Marty looked at Sam with big eyes.

"We'll leave it here until we can, okay?"

"Okay." He hopped up and ran toward his mom.

She chased him up the stairs, telling him to not make a mess.

"Spill." Sam looked at me with serious eyes.

Cathy shut her computer and moved closer to me. I sighed and shut my sketchbook. There was no escaping this. They needed to know, especially with the funeral tomorrow.

"It was bad." I leveled my gaze on them.

"What happened?" Cathy shook her head at me. "You can't just say it was bad. What was bad?"

"Her father." I had to walk a careful line here.

I didn't want to tell them all of Meredith's dirty laundry. "He drinks."

"You mean he's an alcoholic." It wasn't a question.

"Yes." I frowned. "I'm guessing that Mother knew or had a heads-up, because she sent someone to help out."

"Sounds like something she would do." Cathy nodded her head. "But why did you bring them here today?"

"Turns out that the old man left a will. Meredith's father thought everything would just pass to him. Needless to say, he was not happy."

"How so?" Sam climbed up off the floor and sat down in a chair.

"He's an angry drunk." I leaned forward and put my elbows on my knees. "I couldn't leave them there."

"You think he would hurt them?" Cathy lowered her voice. "Was it that bad?"

I nodded my head.

"Surely he wouldn't hurt his daughter or grandson." Cathy shook her head. "What did he do? Yell at them?"

I debated before answering and decided that they deserved to know the truth. "The first day I went over there, Arthur tried to hit Meredith."

Cathy covered her mouth, but Sam sat up straighter.

"What did you do?"

"I pulled her out of his path and penned him until he calmed down." I shrugged. "I wanted them to leave that night, but she wasn't having any of it."

"She probably felt like she had to stay until after the funeral." Sam frowned. "God, that makes me so mad. I wish you had hit him."

"I came close today." I frowned. "He called Marty something and I was ready to beat his face in."

"But you didn't." Sam cocked her head to the side.

"Meredith asked me not to." I leaned back in my chair.

"You are in so much trouble." Sam laughed.

"What do you mean?" Why did everyone keep hinting that I was headed for trouble?

"You're in deep, boy." Sam looked over at Cathy with a smile. I hated that smile. It was the one they used to convey womanly thoughts. Silly things and ideas. Like they knew something I didn't know. Fuck, they knew something I didn't know.

"I'm just helping them until they can get back

to England." I glared at my sister-in-law. I think I even sounded like I meant what I had said.

"I don't think so." Cathy shook her head.

"She has a life back in England." Shit, did I sound dejected?

"Maybe." Sam shrugged. "Or she may have a life here. You won't know until after the reading of the will."

"It doesn't affect me."

"Blind. He's absolutely blind." Cathy grinned at me. "I like seeing you all discombobulated. It's fun."

"I'm not discombobulated. Jesus. Who says 'discombobulated'?" I ran a hand over my jaw. I need to shave before the morning. Christ, I had to carry a casket tomorrow.

"You look at her and that boy like they are yours." Sam's eyes softened.

"I do not." I remembered that strong sense of possessiveness I had felt while holding her in my arms. Did I really look at her differently? I'd been around her for only a few days. A few very emotionally charged days. "They aren't mine."

"Maybe they should be." Sam smiled.

"Stop that."

"Stop what?" Her smile turned mischievous.

"Stop trying to plant ideas in my head." Especially when there was already a seed there.

"You know, once upon a time, a very smart person told me that it's easier for people on the outside to see what's going on." She paused for a moment. "Especially when you're in love."

"That's stupid." I leveled my gaze at her.

"You have much to learn, grasshopper."

"Don't you have pregnant things to do? Like looking at baby clothes?" I rolled my eyes.

"I'm getting the dirt on your girlfriend." Sam shifted in her seat. "Duh."

"She's not my girlfriend." I leaned my head back and closed my eyes. It was like being back in grade school.

"Hm." Cathy tapped her mouth with her finger.

"Out with it." I cracked my eyes open.

"I think you'd be good together. She pulls you out of your shell and you give her something stable."

"I'm not stable. I'm an artist." Stable sounded boring. Sounded like a job.

"It doesn't matter what you do." Sam shrugged. "Alex is going to be king one day. Not exactly who I saw myself ending up with."

"You guys are killing me, you know that?" I closed my eyes again.

"Okay, back to the serious topic." Cathy darted her eyes up toward the staircase. "Is her father going to be at the funeral?"

"He better be." The words came out in a growl. "And he better be sober."

"What are you going to do if he isn't?" Sam asked.

"I don't know." I shrugged. "I ordered him to be sober. I guess I could have him thrown in jail."

"You can't throw him in jail for coming to his father's funeral." Sam laughed at me.

"Actually, if he gave him an order from the crown, he could," Cathy said quietly, and looked at me. "Did you?"

I didn't respond. When was the last time I had ever given an order from the crown? Oh yeah. Never. I didn't do things like that. Until today.

"Are you kidding me?" Sam looked between us and I shrugged. "You can't do that, Max. It would be a PR nightmare. Not to mention it would probably upset Meredith and Marty."

"What would be better? Letting him beat on his daughter in front of everyone? Or let him call Marty a bastard in the middle of the church?" I sat up and looked at them. "You tell me, because I don't know. I've tried to figure it out, but I just don't know. What would hurt them the most?"

Sam frowned and looked down at her hands. For the life of me I couldn't believe what I was seeing.

"Are you crying?" My eyes widened in horror. "Why are you crying?"

"I'm not. It's just such a terrible situation." She sniffled but didn't look up.

"Way to go, ass-face." Cathy got up and knelt next to Sam.

"I'm sorry." I didn't even know what I had done, but I was really sorry I had done it.

"It's just really sad." Sam rubbed at her eyes. "And I'm hormonal. And you're an ass-face."

"Please don't cry." I stood up and took a step toward her, then a step back. I wasn't sure if I'd make it worse by hugging her or not. "I shouldn't have said it that way."

"It's true though. There are no good solutions." She looked up at me. "What are you going to do?"

"I don't know." I shrugged. "I—that man makes me so angry I snap. I've come close to hitting him twice now and I'm not sure I could stop myself a third time."

"I didn't know it was so bad when I sent you to help." She looked up at me and my heart broke. Giant tears glistened on her cheek and I wanted to slam my head in a door. "It's my fault."

"Hey." Giving up, I crossed the room and sat on the arm of the chair and hugged her against my side. "It's not your fault. I'm glad you sent me. I shouldn't have told you."

"Damn straight." Cathy shot me an evil glare. "What were you thinking?"

"I don't know." I held my hands up in surrender. "I'm frustrated and just blurted it out."

"I'm okay." Sam shook her head. "I'm fine. Really. But we have to help them." Her eyes darted toward the stairs.

"I'm trying." I sighed. "But right now there is no clear path. They're stuck in limbo for the next couple of days."

"Hopefully things will be clarified after the reading of the will." Cathy looked over at me. "Do you think he left something for Marty and Meredith?"

"I don't know. She thinks very highly of him, but he also thought his son would turn around. I guess it could go either way."

"What if they're left with nothing but her father to depend on?" Cathy's brow furrowed. "Will she stay with him?"

"I don't think so." There was no way she would leave Marty in the same house with that man for an extended period of time. How they would fare on their own was another question. But I'd learned my lesson and wasn't about to say anything about that in front of Sam.

"She's a fighter." Sam took a deep breath. "I can't see her staying with her dad."

"You're right." I hugged her tightly. "I'm sorry I upset you."

"It's okay. We knew something big was bothering you, but I didn't expect that. And I'm overly sensitive right now." She balled up her fists and looked up at me. "I can't believe he called Marty a bastard. Was it where Marty could hear him? You know what, it doesn't matter. If you decide to punch him, give him one for me too."

"I'll be sure to remember that."

"Let me know if you need me to run interference for you," Cathy said. "I can try to keep her father distracted and away from them at the funeral."

"Absolutely not." I frowned. "I don't want him to turn on you."

"Please. He's not going to do anything to me. And I have bodyguards, anyway." Cathy shrugged. "It'll be simple."

"We spread out the family." Sam nodded her head. "You stay with Meredith and Marty while me, Cathy, and Alex manage Arthur."

"I don't know." I shook my head.

"Really. It'll be simple. The media will see it as though we're showing Arthur special support. I'm betting he will see it that way too." Sam nodded her head. "Alex will help. He's good at putting people at ease."

She was right about that. My big brother was excellent at making things appear easy and simple. I'd say I was envious of that trait, but I'm not. It would mean I'd have to take on more responsibility.

"We'll see." I stood up. "I'm going to check on Marty."

"And Meredith." Cathy grinned at me.

"Shut it, brat." I messed up her hair when I walked by her, content to see her annoyed expression.

"Jerk."

I took the stairs slowly. I didn't want anyone to think I was in a hurry. Was I in a hurry? Why was I even checking on them? They probably wanted to be left alone.

As I neared Marty's door I could hear the two talking softly. I hesitated, not wanting to intrude. Then something changed. Instead of talking, Meredith began singing softly. I leaned against the wall by his door and listened. It wasn't a lullaby, but a soothing, soft song. Her voice was effortless as she worked through the verses. Perfect without any accompaniment; it was like the song had been written just for her voice. It was a powerful thing, when someone could touch something inside you without even being in the same room.

Her voice quieted and I could hear her moving away from the bed and toward the door. I waited where I was, unashamed that I had listened to their song.

"Oh." She looked at me with big eyes when she stepped into the hallway. "I didn't realize anyone else was up here."

"I came to see how you two were doing." I placed my hands in my pockets.

"I was just tucking Marty in." She looked back toward his sleeping form and quietly pulled the door closed.

"What song were you singing?"

"Just something I heard growing up." She frowned. "He hasn't asked me to sing for him in a while."

"He's very proud of your voice."

"Is he?" She smiled.

"He was bragging on you." I chuckled softly. "With good reason."

"Thank you." She leaned against the wall and looked up at me.

I took a step closer to her. "Are you ready for tomorrow?"

"I think so." She took a deep breath and let it out. "I'm nervous."

"About what?" Honestly, I was nervous and I wasn't the one singing or burying their grandfather.

"About my father. I have no idea what to expect tomorrow." She smiled shyly. "And a little about singing."

"You? Nervous about singing? The same woman that tells me she lives for the spotlight?"

"It's different this time. It's not a show. It's . . . personal. Real. I can't become another character." She lifted one shoulder and let it fall. "I'm proud to sing for my grandfather, but that doesn't mean I'm not a little nervous."

"Well, how do you deal with the nerves?" I leaned against the wall with one shoulder.

"Distraction." She lowered her eyelashes. "Trying to not obsess over things."

"Hm." I looked at her, letting my eyes travel over her face. There were some things I'd like to do as distraction, but knew that now wasn't the time. "I have an idea."

"What?" She stood up a little straighter.

"Do you trust me?" I held my hand out to her.

She looked down at my hand, then back to my eyes. I waited while she fought through whatever was going on in her mind. My question hadn't been simple.

"Yes." She slid her hand into mine. "I do."

"Good." I lifted her hand to my mouth and pressed a kiss to her knuckles. "Come with me."

"What about Marty?" She looked back at his door.

"Cathy's room is right next to his." I pulled her away from the wall. "I'm sure she won't mind babysitting."

"Boy, you really have a habit of deciding things for everyone." A hint of amusement crept into her voice. "You're bossy."

"She's my little sister. I'm supposed to boss her around." I winked at her. "It was in the rule book I got when they brought her home from the hospital."

"Why don't we try asking her?"

"Oh, I was going to ask nicely and just expect her to agree." I led her toward the stairs. "I'm bossy, not stupid."

"That's up for debate."

"Hey, that hurts." I tugged on her hand a little.

"The truth often does." She looked at me with a grin.

Downstairs, Cathy was still working on her computer while Sam was snoring softly on the couch.

"Why didn't she go to bed?" I looked at my sister and nodded my head toward the pregnant woman.

"She's waiting on Alex." She looked up at me and noticed Meredith. "Hey. How are you?"

"Fine." Meredith smiled but her eyebrows pulled together.

"Good. That's good." Cathy pursed her lips and I wanted to mentally kick her. Way to be awkward, little sister. "Just checking, with the funeral and all tomorrow."

"Thanks, but we'll get through it." Meredith stood up a little straighter, but I was relieved to see that she didn't put up any front. "It's going to be tough."

"Actually, that's why I came down here." I cleared my throat. "Would you mind keeping an ear open for Marty? I thought I'd take Meredith out to the lake to take her mind off things."

"Sure." Cathy closed her computer and stood up. "I'll work in my room so I can hear him better."

"Thank you." Meredith smiled.

"Any time. I like him." Cathy rolled up her laptop cord.

"I think he likes you too." Meredith sighed.

"Meh, he just likes having his butt kicked at

football." Cathy headed for the stairs. "You guys have fun."

"Thanks," I said.

Just as she was turning, she winked at me. It took all of my inner strength to keep from rolling my eyes.

Turning from her, I let go of Meredith's hand and pulled a throw blanket off a chair. I settled it over Samantha's sleeping form before turning back to Meredith. It might be a while before Alex made it home.

"Ready?" I held my hand back out to the red-head next to me.

"I guess."

"You guess?" I raised one eyebrow.

"I'm going to stick with that answer." Her lips curved upward.

"Little dost thou know, disbeliever." I raised one eyebrow.

Pulling her with me, I headed out back. The moon was bright, the air was cool, and the stars were shining brightly. We didn't talk as we walked, which I appreciated. It wasn't that I didn't want to hear all about Meredith, but I wanted to let her relax and unwind.

"Do you have horses?" Meredith stopped near the stables.

"We have a few." I let my eyes run over her moonlit face. "Would you like to see them?"

"Do you mind?" She looked up at me with thoughtful eyes. "I've always liked horses."

"Of course." I led her to the doors and nodded at the man who normally tended the horses.

"They're beautiful, aren't they?" Her eyes locked on a light brown mare. "So sleek and powerful, but they can be nurturing and gentle."

"Hm." I agreed. Horseback riding was one of the few outdoor recreational activities I did on a regular basis. "That's Butterscotch."

"Perfect name." She walked over to the stall and held out her hand. "May I?"

I nodded my head in response.

"Hello, Butterscotch." I watched as she stroked the horse's head, humming to herself and whispering to the horse.

"Butterscotch is Cathy's horse." I walked over to a bag along the wall and fished out some carrots before holding them out to Meredith. "She's a sucker for these."

"Ah." Meredith took a carrot and offered it to Butterscotch. "Here, sweetheart."

Butterscotch wasted no time gobbling the carrot and then looking for more. I passed another carrot to Meredith and she offered it to the horse.

"All us girls have our weaknesses." Meredith chuckled.

"What's yours?" I reached out and scratched the horse behind her ear.

"Nuh-uh." Meredith grinned at me. "You have to figure it out for yourself."

"Chocolate?" I raised an eyebrow. I did have a sister, after all.

"That would be too easy."

"Flowers?" I shifted closer to her.

"I do love fresh flowers, but no." Her eyes sparkled at me.

"Tricky." I watched her as she continued to pet Butterscotch. "It's not jewelry."

"What makes you so sure?" She looked at me.

"You don't wear much. The little pearl ring on your finger is the only thing I've seen constantly on you." My eyes flicked to the simple ring on her middle finger.

"Observant." She looked down the length of the stables. "Do you have a horse?"

"I do." I walked a couple of stalls down to where Da Vinci was stabled. "This big guy is mine."

"Oh, he's gorgeous." Her eyes ran over his sleek black body. She looked at the plaque next to his stall. "Da Vinci, huh?"

"Well, I was pretty young when I got him." I

chuckled. "It was when I'd really just started to get into painting."

"It's a good name." She reached out and stroked between his eyes.

"Do you ride?"

"I haven't ridden a horse since I was little." Her eyes clouded. "It was a really good day."

"Tell me about it."

"Well, my father dried out for a while. Stopped drinking and acted like a real father. I don't know what triggered the change but I was more than happy when it happened." She shrugged. "For my birthday he took me to a camp where you could ride horses on trails. It was the most fun we'd ever had together. He even got me a present."

"Sounds like a good memory." I watched her face carefully. Her tone had taken on a fond quality.

"It is. I guess that's why I like horses so much." She shook her head. "I'm sure that's what a psychiatrist would say."

"Not a bad reason." I shrugged. "We all have fond memories that influence how we feel about things." And I was glad that Meredith did have some fond memories of her childhood. I was starting to wonder if she'd ever been happy.

"True." She smiled at me. "So, show me this lake."

I held my hand out to her, reveling in the way she immediately took it without thought.

I led her through the trees and to an outcropping of rocks that overlooked the water. I sat down and patted next to me. There was a light scuffle on the stone as she took a seat next to me. She tucked her legs against her chest and looked out over the water.

"This is a great spot." Her voice was soft.

"I come here to clear my mind."

"You mean the slacker prince worries about things?" She pushed me with an elbow.

"Occasionally." I tilted my head back and looked at the stars. "Sometimes I'll feel stuck on a painting. It's usually because I need to take a step back and let it simmer."

She hummed her understanding.

"I also come out here when I've been in the public too much." I looked over at her.

"You mean doing public events? Royal duties."

"Yeah. It's not the speaking so much as all that goes with it." I took a deep breath of crisp air. "It's what goes along with being in the spotlight. I feel like I have to be someone else. It's . . . draining."

"What about your art shows?" She cocked her head and looked over at me. "Do those make you uncomfortable?"

I thought about it for a minute. "No."

"Maybe it's because you're still being yourself." Her voice was thoughtful. "Being an artist is first and the prince second. You're doing something that completes you."

I let that roll around in my head. I'd never thought about the fact that doing art shows didn't bother me, but what she said made sense.

"Maybe."

"Maybe? I'm right and you know it." She grinned up at me.

"Cocky, aren't you?"

"Must be rubbing off from spending time with you."

"Now that definitely makes sense." I reached out with an arm and tugged her against my side.

"Thanks for bringing me out here."

She put her head on my shoulder and my heart did something funny. I looked up at the sky and wondered what I was doing. Meredith had been right. Being with her could be dangerous. Not because of her family or because of her love for the spotlight.

But because I was in serious danger of falling in love.

And that just didn't happen to me.

THIRTEEN

I LOOKED AT MY black dress and sighed. I looked nice. In fact, I looked great. Too bad my insides didn't match the outside.

The black dress fit perfectly. The sleeves fell to a comfortable but fashionable length, while the tiny belt I wore accented my waist. I hadn't brought many pairs of shoes with me, but I had thankfully grabbed a couple pairs of heels. I had debated over my shoes far longer than I should have. I'd brought black heels for the funeral, but after evaluation had decided to go with the pair that were such a dark red, they were almost black. It was just a tiny splash of color and it gave my confidence a boost.

I stepped away from the mirror and picked up my pearl ring from the nightstand. I slid it on my finger and felt my eyes grow teary. He was really gone. That man had been the only stable family I had growing up. He'd held a job, paid his bills, didn't have crazy rampages.

I wiped at my eyes and tried to pull myself together. I hadn't seen him since we'd arrived. It hadn't been required that we identify the body, and I waived the viewing. Granddad had always thought those were strange; staring at a dead body seemed odd to him. But right now, I wish I hadn't decided against it. I wish I had gotten to see him one more time. Just once more.

I closed my eyes and counted to ten. I needed to pull myself together before everything that was going to happen today. I'd been up for hours, getting messages from Rachel, my grandfather's friends, and even the press looking for a statement. It had already been a nightmare.

"Mom, I hate ties." Marty walked into my room and threw himself on my bed. "Do I have to wear one?"

"Sorry, babe, but today is a definite tie day." I walked over and held out my hand. "Here, I'll help you put it on."

"When can I take it off?" He stood up and lifted his chin so I could tie a proper knot.

"I'll let you know as soon as you can."

"Fine." He frowned. "Is this going to take a long time?"

"I'm not sure." I knelt down in front of him. "How are you holding up?"

"Okay." He shrugged. "I like being here, but

I'm still really sad about Great Granddad. And I miss my friends from school."

"Maybe we can call one tomorrow," I suggested.

"That would be cool." He looked at me with worried eyes. "Do you think I'm going to get in trouble for missing school?"

"Nah." I hugged him. "Things like this are excused."

"What about homework?"

"We'll talk to your teachers about that when we get back, okay?" I tweaked his nose before standing back up. "You ready to go downstairs?"

"Yeah." He sighed. "Might as well get it over with."

"Get breakfast over with?"

"Yeah. I miss my Pop-Tarts." He hung his head.

"I bet we can find some soon. Maybe we could ask someone to go to the store."

"Would they do that?" He looked up at me with bright eyes.

"They might if we ask nicely." I squeezed his hand. "Doesn't hurt to try."

Cathy was coming up the stairs and smiled at us. "Good morning."

"Good morning."

"Can I please have some Pop-Tarts?" My son smiled up at his friend.

"Marty, that is not what I meant."

Cathy laughed. "It so happens that I asked for the kitchen staff to pick some up yesterday. I wasn't sure what flavor you liked so we got a couple of boxes of each that the store had."

"Yes!" Marty made a little fist and pumped his arm.

"Thank you. That was very thoughtful of you." I smiled at her.

"It was no problem." She continued her climb up the stairs. "I'll see you guys in a little bit."

There were quite a few people downstairs in the large living space. Prince Alex was talking with a man who had bright red hair and was wearing a snazzy pink tie with his dark gray suit. And Samantha was on the phone, her face serious as she described something about talons. A couple of staff members were hanging about, doing different odds and ends.

But no Max.

I shouldn't be bothered by that fact. I should be putting as much space between the two of us as possible. And yet . . .

No, I couldn't deal with what happened between Max and me. Not today. There were only so many emotions a person could filter at any given moment and I felt like I was drowning. There was too much happening for me to be attached to a man who would probably prefer that I had never walked into his life. I needed to focus on getting through today and tomorrow before I even thought of anything else.

"Good morning." Alex bowed his head toward us and I dipped a slight curtsy. I was still getting used to the royal stuff. Was I supposed to do that right now, or should I be less formal now that I was staying at his house? Or more formal? Good grief, talk about overworrying things.

"Good morning." I offered the room a smile.

"Hello, I'm Chadwick." The man with the pink tie walked forward and held his hand out.

"It's nice to meet you." I shook his hand. "You're Samantha's assistant, right?"

"My reputation precedes me." He winked at me. "I'm not as terrible as everyone pretends."

"I've only heard good things." I chuckled.

"Good. That means you've been talking to the right people." He turned to Marty. "And good morning to you, sir."

"Hi." Marty leaned into my side.

"Are you ready for breakfast?" Chadwick motioned toward the hall that led to the dining room. "I believe it's all ready."

"Thank you." I looked around the room. "Will the others be joining us?"

"I'm coming!" Sam closed her phone and headed in my direction. Her black wraparound dress showed off her adorable pregnant belly. She was wearing flats instead of heels and a string of silvery pearls. "If I don't eat soon, I'll be sick."

The dining room had a huge spread of food, including Marty's Pop-Tarts. Maybe I was a bad mother for letting him eat them the last few days, but with everything else going on, I wasn't going to force him to eat sausage or eggs.

By the time we were ready to leave I had started to really worry that Max wasn't going to show up. What would I do if he wasn't there? I'd have to find someone else to help carry Granddad.

And even more importantly, why now? Why would Max flake out on me today of all days? I'd pushed and pushed to get him to leave me alone and he'd refused. Then the day I specifically asked for help he hadn't shown up. And no one was saying anything about it. I had slept with him yesterday—given him something important to me. And now? I didn't even know what to think.

"There are cars out front," Chadwick said. He handed Samantha a dark gray sweater to go over her dress.

Unable to stand it any longer, I looked over at Cathy. "Have you seen Max?"

"He's already gone." Cathy cocked her head to the side. "I thought he told you he was going early to make sure there were no problems."

"Oh." Relief flooded my body. He wasn't avoiding me. He was doing what he said he was going to do. Trying to help me. "No, he didn't mention it."

Or maybe he had? I'd almost fallen asleep last night while watching the water. I remembered him talking to me, but his deep voice had all but lulled me to sleep. I just remembered being content and relaxed before finally making our way back to the house. He had kissed my head before I went in my room and I had passed out easily on the giant bed. It had been the best sleep I'd had in years.

I let them lead us to one of the black limousines out front, not really paying attention to who all climbed into the car with me and Marty. Instead I took my phone out of my purse and looked up Max's number to send him a text message.

You didn't have to go without me.

I closed my phone and looked out the window. When my phone beeped I clicked on the message.

You didn't need to worry about everything.

I shook my head. What was it with him wanting to take care of everything for me? Pretty soon he was going to insist he wash my socks or help me bathe. That last thought brought heat to my cheeks. I'm not sure I'd mind letting him help me in the shower.

Thank you.

There, nice and simple. No talk of bathing each other. That was probably for the best. Probably.

Welcome.

Our ride to Thysmer was relatively quiet, except for Cathy and Marty. She had brought a handheld video game and currently was talking Marty through a level with tomato zombies. I was scared to even look at the game. The squishing sounds were bad enough.

The closer we came to the church, the more my nerves began to bubble and froth in my stomach.

I'd chosen a song to sing that I'd heard a while ago on the radio in England. The lyrics were beautiful and summed up the feelings of loss. It was something I'd fallen in love with the second I'd heard it. I knew the song by heart, so it wouldn't be something I'd be focused on getting right. I could just sing it and hopefully touch the people who had known my grandfather.

As we drove through Thysmer I noticed that flags had been lowered to half-staff. When the church came in to view it was surrounded by cars and people mingling outside. The media was a respectful distance away, which relieved me to no end. The last thing I wanted was to wade through people asking questions or wanting pictures. I wondered if that had been Max's doing.

As our limo pulled up, Max made his way out of the church, followed by Rachel, and headed straight for the car. He adjusted his suit jacket before opening the door. Cathy motioned for me and Marty to go out first.

Max held his hand out to help me, his fingers squeezing mine gently, before letting go to help Marty and his sister out of the car.

"My lady." Rachel bobbed a quick curtsy before moving to my side. Leaning close, she lowered her voice. "How are you?"

"We're fine." I nodded my head. "Is everything ready?"

"Yes, ma'am." She bobbed her head at someone she knew. "Everything is as you wished."

"Thank you. I should have come earlier to help."

"Not at all." She looked at me with wise eyes. "Your father is already here. He's been here for a while. Asked to see his father before the ceremony."

"Really?" I frowned. I hadn't thought he would care to see my granddad's body. I hadn't really thought he cared about any of it, to be truthful. "Has he said anything?"

"He's been quiet." She patted my arm. "I don't think you're going to have much to worry about today."

"Thank you." I couldn't explain how much I hoped she was right. "How'd my father get here? Did he drive?"

"Prince Maxwell has been a big help this morning." She offered me a smile. "He rode with a car to get your father. Said that he wanted to help escort the duke to the funeral."

"He did what?" I stopped and blinked at her. Marty grabbed my hand and waited with me. I could hear Cathy talking quietly with someone behind me. Surprise had me looking around the area for Max. He must've gotten up before dawn to manage everything. When my eyes landed on his, I felt my heart thump loudly in my chest. He was watching me with soft eyes as Cathy talked quietly.

"Prince Maxwell brought your father to the funeral. He felt it best that someone ride with him." She put her hand on my elbow and gently steered me toward the doors. I looked back to the church and took a deep breath.

My mind rushed through all of the scenarios that could have happened. Had he gone to make sure that my father came to the funeral? Honestly, I hadn't been sure he would attend.

"Mere!" An older man waved at me from near the door. "Marty!"

"Patrick!" I picked up my pace and walked toward my granddad's oldest friend. He was wearing a worn, dark suit and wire-rimmed glasses. As soon as I got to him, I wrapped my arms around him. "I'm so glad you were able to make it."

"Of course, love. I'm so sorry about your granddad." He squeezed me back before leaning down and hugging Marty. "He was a good man."

"Thank you." My eyes began to water and I wiped at my cheeks with my fingers. Seeing Patrick was like seeing my granddad's ghost. It cemented the awful truth of his death.

"Let me know if you need anything." He squeezed my shoulder. I looked into his eyes and realized that he was fighting back tears of his own.

"I really appreciate you coming out and helping today." I looked down at the ground. "It's not an easy thing to ask."

"I would have been offended if you hadn't asked me." He smiled at me. "It's my honor."

I leaned forward and kissed his cheek. "I've got to go inside."

"I'll be in there in a minute. Just need a little more fresh air." He took a deep breath.

"I understand." I hugged him again and picked up Marty's hand.

"Mom?" Marty's voice was quiet.

"Yes, baby?"

"I don't want to see Great Granddad." His chin trembled. I dropped to my knees, blocking the door for everyone else, and wrapped my arms around my son.

"That's okay." I squeezed him tightly.

"I just want to remember him fishing, you know? Fishing."

"I understand." I looked at him and wiped a tear from his cheek. "That's perfectly fine."

"Can I sit next to you?" Max knelt down next to us.

Marty looked from Max to me.

"We'd like that." I looked at Max. "It'll be nice for Marty to have someone to sit with while I sing."

Marty looked at Max and nodded his head.

"Okay, then." Max stood up and held his hand out to Marty.

Marty accepted it before turning and holding his other hand out to me. I took it and looked at Max. Did he realize that we looked like a family? A complete unit? Did he understand that Marty had opened himself up to him?

Marty and I were both so vulnerable and Max had stepped in and become our shield during the storm. It was frightening and amazing how quickly it had happened. How quickly he had become part of our lives.

Max nodded his head once and his bright green eyes locked on mine.

"Ready?"

"Ready," I whispered.

Together we walked through the church. It was full of people in black or gray. Some of the women wore hats, while others had chosen not to. They all had one thing in common, though. They turned to watch our little group make its way down the aisle.

Purposefully, I let my eyes sweep the room, never landing on the casket at the end of the walkway. I was scared to see if it had been left open or not. So I focused on other things.

I could see my father's head in the first pew, where the family would sit. His gray hair was neatly combed and he was wearing a suit. Our butler, Gerard, sat a few rows behind him.

When we neared the front row, my father looked over his shoulder and stood up. Despite his sour expression, I was relieved. His eyes were clear, which meant he was sober. Or at least at a level where he could function normally.

"Hello," I said. Marty's fingers tightened on mine.

"Hello." My father nodded his head at Max and then sat back down.

If he was anyone else's father, they might have been bothered by the distant greeting. For me, it was a small victory. He hadn't yelled at me, hadn't threatened me, hadn't caused a big scene. He had even spoken to me, when I had thought I'd be lucky to have him ignore us.

I took the seat next to my father, careful to keep a good distance between us. Marty sat next to me and Max sat on the other side of Marty. Samantha, Cathy, and Alex sat next to Max. Alex turned in his seat and greeted some of the people behind us. Shaking hands and being polite as people tried to get in a word with the heir to the throne.

When the minister stepped up to the podium, everyone began to quiet. I'd pushed to keep the ceremony simple. I didn't want to have people sitting there for hours, listening to endless droning on about my grandfather. Most of the people in this room had never met the man. And while I'm sure their intentions had been good in coming, it still felt invasive. I should have insisted that we keep the funeral small and personal, but Rachel had felt that it would send the wrong message to the town that had accepted us back. Understanding her point, I'd relinquished my stance and agreed to having a "proper" royal burial. Complete with flowers, music, and a real minister.

A Bible verse was read, which would have made Granddad cringe. And for some reason, that made me smile. Just imagining his reaction made me feel closer to him. I could practically hear him saying, "Oy vey" and rolling his eyes. My dad shifted in his seat and I dared to look at him. That's when I realized I hadn't imagined my grandfather saying his favorite phrase, it had been my father. With a look of amusement, he shot me a small smile, and I realized that in that moment we were thinking the same thing. Oddly enough, that made the whole situation feel a little lighter. This little connection with my father. I didn't forgive him for the way he'd been acting, the way he handled himself. But in a way, my grandfather linked us together.

A choir sang a hymn, the voices twining together through the rafters of the old church. Then the minister talked about Granddad, telling them about his life as a workingman, his love for his family and friends. He talked about how Granddad had fished with Marty, which made my son bury his face against my arm.

When it was almost time to sing, I took a deep breath and tried to gain my composure. It was like trying to grab silk line with oil-slathered hands. Feeling eyes on me, I looked to where Max was watching me. The light streaming through the stained-glass windows of the church splashed along his face, but it was his emerald gaze that held my attention.

I'm not sure what it was that passed between us, but it filled me with strength. If Max could come out and deal with the media, the spotlight, then I could get up and do what I did best.

"Lady Meredith is now going to sing a farewell to her beloved grandfather."

I kissed Marty's head and looked at Max. Without a word, he slid a casual arm around my son's shoulders.

As I stood up and walked toward the dais, I let go of my nerves and slid into the quiet zone I retreated to before a show. This was the place where I found my voice, where I found myself.

The minister stepped forward and shook my hand before leaning forward and kissing my cheek.

"I'm so sorry for your loss. I know that your grandfather loved you very much." He squeezed my hands.

"Thank you."

"The stage is yours, my lady. I've heard such wonderful things about your voice." He smiled. "I'm sure your grandfather will be listening."

"I hope so." Letting go of his hands, I stepped up to the podium and looked out at the audience.

The church was filled with people, but I didn't let that faze me. I'd sung for larger groups before. As the piano began to play, I closed my eyes and took a deep breath.

This was my farewell to a man who had taught me what family meant, to reach for my dreams, and never to take no for an answer.

This is for you, Granddad.

Opening my mouth, I let the words fall out. I reached deep and sang with my heart, the pain that I felt echoed by the melody of the song. I'd chosen a more contemporary song, something that had become popular on the indie music circuit. I'd fallen in love with the words. It spoke of carrying that person's love with you even if they were gone. Something about it touched my heart, and I wanted everyone in the room to feel it, too.

I didn't look at anyone in particular as I sang. Instead I imagined Granddad standing in the aisle. I knew his eyes would be full of tears, because he always cried when I sang. It had started when I was little and in school, and even the last time I had been practicing while I visited for a Christmas holiday.

As the song neared its pinnacle I let my eyes run over the front pews. The local government was well represented, as were the local businesses. But then my eyes found my father as he watched with a stone face. I'd never understood why he hated my singing. He treated it with disgust, and at best, he ignored it. Marty watched me with a small smile, his perfect little face warming my heart.

As my eyes met Max's, I almost stuttered. There was something in his expression that made me feel light. Pride and possession filled his face. I could practically feel his eyes like a gentle caress.

As the song drew to a close, I noticed that people were wiping at their cheeks and my pride swelled. Never had I sung better than I had for my grandfather. For the first time since finding out that Granddad had died, I felt as if I'd had my chance to say good-bye.

Stepping down from the podium, I went straight to Marty and hugged him, before taking my seat.

"You sounded great." Marty hugged me tightly.

"Thank you, baby." I kissed his head and looked up at Max.

When the choir began to sing, I looked back to the front and watched as the pallbearers took their spots around the coffin. Even my father strode up to the stage with steady steps. His face was a mask of confusion and pain. Seeing him struggle with reality without the aid of liquor was painful. It was obvious that he would rather be anywhere but here. And for a lot of reasons, I could agree with him.

Patrick looked pale, but determined. He stood just behind Max, whose face was composed into a vague sense of compassion. It was a practiced face, one that I'm sure he used for situations when he was uncomfortable, but needed to look the part. I felt bad that I had put him in that position, but I was even more grateful that he had agreed to do it. He had truly stepped up and helped my family.

He had helped me. Even when I begged him not to. Talk about being stubborn.

I watched as he walked with the others out of the church to the waiting cars outside. As a family, we were urged to stand and follow the casket. For the first time in my life I hated having everyone watch my every move. This was not the same as being on stage or performing. This was my real life—a painful moment in our family's history.

Marty held my hand and I was grateful to have my new friends following behind us. It took some of the attention away from Marty and me. I stopped in the foyer of the building, next to the guest log, so that I could thank the people who had attended. It was a blur of faces and hand-shakes, well wishes and condolences. I looked over my shoulder to see Max throw me a guilty look, but he didn't come to assist with the line. Instead I watched as he dipped into one of the cars. By the time it was over, I felt like I'd shaken every hand in Lilaria. And for some reason had a strong desire to wash my hands, or to dose them in hand sanitizer.

"My lady, your car is waiting." Rachel touched my shoulder. "Her Highness, Princess Cathy, is already in the car with your son. I put some snacks inside for Marty and you. I figured you might be hungry, thirsty at least, after that long reception line."

"Thank you, Rachel." I looked at the woman. "You've been a huge help."

Outside, the sky was at odds with the sorrow in my heart. Bright, puffy clouds floated in a clear blue sky, and I had to squint my eyes after being in the dark church for so long. Even from as far away as the photographers were, I could hear the whir and snaps of their cameras. Some of them called my name, but I kept my gaze down and continued on. Now was not the time for pictures or statements.

The driver opened the car door for me and I slid onto the back bench.

"Mom! Do you want some fizzy water?" Marty held up a green bottle of carbonated water.

"I think a regular water would be just fine." I looked around the interior of the limousine and my eyes fell on Max.

"I hope you don't mind if I ride with you." He cocked his head to the side. "Cathy, Alex, and Sam are riding with your father."

"No." I shook my head. "Not at all."

"I'm sorry I left you to deal with that line of people by yourself." He leaned back in his seat. "I figured Marty could use some company."

"And you hate lots of people staring at you." My mouth twisted into a small smile.

"And I hate having lots of people staring at me." He chuckled. "Makes me feel like a baboon at the zoo. People just looking at me because I have a title." He mimed having the chills. "Can't stand it."

"I think you've done more than enough for this family." I lowered my eyes and looked at my shoes. There was a small scuff on the left toe where a member of parliament had accidentally stepped on me.

"It's been my pleasure." His voice had lost its teasing quality and taken a turn for the serious. "And I'll be here to help as long as you need me."

What if that's forever? The question came unbidden to my mind. Silently I berated myself. I couldn't keep Max. I couldn't, even though I was really starting to want to. Not just because of the way he made me feel, but because of the way he looked at Marty. There was love in his gaze when he looked at my son, kindness and amusement.

Looking out the window, I tried to focus on the tasks at hand. Now wasn't the time to think about

Max. Was it? Maybe it was natural that my mind sought something happier to fixate on. Was that all this was with Max?

I surreptitiously glanced in his direction. Had I slept with him just because I had needed something good? As I watched him talk to Marty and open a package of crackers for him, I knew it had been more than that. Max had infiltrated our family bubble, our lives . . . my heart.

I never would have imagined that I would fall for a prince who hated the limelight. Hell, I'd given up on love all together. I hadn't been sure it actually existed. But here I was in the middle of it, completely confused by how I had gotten there.

And now I didn't know what to do.

In the limo on the way to entomb my grandfather in an old family plot, I'd realized that I had fallen in love with a man, completely my opposite, in only a matter of days.

So I did what any sane person would do in a situation like that. I laughed.

Loudly. Until I started snorting, which made me laugh even more.

"Does she do this often?" Max asked Marty.

"Sometimes," Marty replied. "She doesn't usually make that weird pig noise though."

I'd started to tear up I was laughing so hard. I

was in love. Love. Me. In love. Jesus, no wonder I hadn't kissed anyone in years. Apparently a good smack-a-roo was all it took to win my heart.

And I was in love with someone who would hate everything about the life I was trying to build. Living the life I wanted to live would be a type of torture for Max. I was in love. And I was completely stupid.

"Are you okay?" Max leaned forward and touched my knee.

"I—I am." I covered my mouth and tried to rein myself in. If anyone saw me right now they would think I was insane. Which is probably what Max was wondering right that minute.

"Do you need anything?" He looked at me with worried eyes, but didn't take his hand from my knee.

"I'm sorry. I'm fine. I just realized something." I wiped at my cheeks and tried to shrug it off. Could I make it work? Could we make it work? Would he even want to try?

"Must've been funny." He raised his eyebrows and grinned.

"Not really." I shook my head. There was nothing funny about being in love. The last time I'd fallen in love, I'd ended up with a baby and a broken heart.

The look on his face made me giggle again. I guess my brain just refused to handle any more stress or hurt. How could I convince him that we could make it work? I kept Marty out of the spotlight. Surely I could keep a boyfriend from being overwhelmed, right?

"Maybe you'll tell me someday." He reached out and tucked a strand of hair behind my ear.

"Maybe I will." That calmed my giggles. Would I, could I tell him that I was in love with him? Would that send him running for the hills? The thought almost made me feel nauseous. My eyes traveled over Max's face, taking in the darker eyebrows, bright green eyes, and strong jaw. He might be an artist, but he was a work of art himself. He shifted from the seat across from me so that he was sitting next to me.

He watched my face, trying to decipher what I was thinking. The thumb of the hand on my knee rubbed gently, causing goose bumps to erupt over my skin.

"Are you being mushy?" Marty's voice broke our staring contest.

"What?" My pulse quickened, and for a minute I felt like a girl caught by her parents.

"You look all gooey." He made a kissing face and I felt my eyes widen.

"Would that be okay?" Max asked.

My heart sped up and I started to speak but Marty beat me to it.

"I guess." He shrugged. "Can we still play video games?"

"You're not tired of losing to me?" Max laughed.

"I beat you twice last time!" Marty shook his head. "You need to practice."

"That's fine. I don't mind you beating me a bunch more." Max leaned back in the seat next to me and casually draped his arm along the seat. He looked at me with a calm expression and shrugged.

Could I really just leave it at that? Marty had never seen me with anyone before. When I'd dated people in the past, they'd had no contact with my son. Some of them hadn't even known I had a son. Which was exactly how I'd wanted it. They were never going to get that close to me anyway.

But Max. Max had come in to our lives from such a different direction. How could I have known we would be here today? I hadn't put up any walls or set any limits. Max had walked right into our lives and wouldn't leave when I tried to push him out. It was like he had found a hole and plugged it.

FOURTEEN

$\mathcal{M}$Y HEART COULDN'T beat any harder if I was running a decathlon. Asking Marty if he minded if I dated his mother—well, was mushy with his mother—had been scary. Not the jump-out-of-the-dark, haunted-house scary, but the real-life, this-shit-matters kind of scary.

Meredith hadn't responded and was still sitting rigidly next to me. When I'd asked Marty, I hadn't thought about how she might feel about the question. It burst out of my mouth without thought. I had wanted to know if it bothered him that I cared for his mother.

Care.

That's a word that covers all kinds of emotions. You care for your great-aunt Gertrude. You care about acquaintances. You care about your family and their well-being.

You also love your family.

"Have you beaten the Master Robot yet?" I cleared my throat and looked at Marty.

"Not yet, but I think I know how." Marty sat forward in his seat. "There's a hidden platform."

"How'd you find it?"

Meredith relaxed a little and leaned back in her seat. I left my arm where it was, not on her shoulders, but encasing the space around her. I was testing the waters without making a big splash. It was time to tread carefully.

"I was trying to reach the alien boomerang, but kept hitting something. I thought I wasn't doing it right, but then I realized there was something in my way." Marty waved his hands around in demonstration and I couldn't fight my smile. "How cool is that? When I grow up I want to make video games so people can find cool stuff."

"That would be an awesome job." I nodded my head.

"I thought you wanted to be a dolphin trainer," Meredith asked. Her voice was amused and she seemed to relax even more into my side.

"I can do both!" Marty held his hands up. "I could make a game with dolphins in it."

"Calm down, little man. You're rocking the car." Meredith laughed.

"But it would be so cool." Marty sat back in his seat and put his arms down.

"It takes a lot of math to make video games."

"Ew." Marty made a face and it was hard not to laugh.

"She's right," I told him. "I have a friend that does computer animation and he spends a lot of time working with numbers."

"Yuck."

"It's not that bad," I assured him.

"I hate numbers." He frowned.

I couldn't argue with him about that because I wasn't fond of math myself. "Cathy is pretty good at math. Maybe you could ask her to help."

"I don't know. I really don't like math. Maybe I'll just be a dolphin trainer."

"Pretty sure there's going to be math in anything you pick," Meredith warned.

"Well, that stinks."

Meredith shook her head, but didn't say anything. If I had to guess, I would say she was still trying to work things out in her head. Whether she was happy or not, I had no real clue. I'd gone and spoken without thinking again.

But I wasn't sure if I regretted that or not.

If I was going to pursue whatever it was that was between Meredith and me, then I needed to know that it would be okay with her son. I wouldn't want to make him upset. Well, it was one of the things I needed to know. I also needed to figure out how I would be able to handle her dreams of being in the spotlight. Just the thought of it made me cringe.

As the car pulled up to the Thysmer burial grounds, I climbed out and helped Meredith and then Marty. To my surprise, Marty held on to my hand, his little fingers gripping tightly.

"I have to go help carry the casket." I squeezed his hand.

"Will you come back and stand with me?"

"I'll come back and stand with you and your mom as soon as I can."

He nodded his head and let go of my hand. I looked at Meredith and stood there for a minute. Her face was full of emotions that seemed to swirl from one to the next.

"If that's okay with you," I prompted.

"We'd like that." Her words were quiet, thoughtful. Holding her hand out to Marty, she walked toward where my family stood.

Turning, I took my place by the hearse and prepared to carry the casket to the tomb. It was a somber task and not one I took lightly. People were gathered about, talking quietly and watching as we placed the casket on a marble table.

I moved through the crowd to take a place next to Marty. He reached up and wrapped his fingers around my own. I noticed a few people glancing in our direction but didn't pay them any attention. If they wanted to talk about me holding Marty's hand, then they could choke on their own tongues. I hated the back-talking, the gossiping, and the assumptions that came from being in the spotlight.

But nothing would get me to pry my fingers from that little boy's hand.

The minister took his time praying as we all stood shifting from foot to foot. All the bells and whistles had been pulled out for the duke's funeral.

By the time things were wrapping up, I was sweating in my suit. I wanted nothing more than to undo my damnable tie, throw my jacket away, and get the hell away from all of these people. Playing prince was one of the things I hated the most about my life.

As some of the people came forward to greet the grieving family, I fought my urge to fade away. Alex gave me the smallest nod to tell me to go, but I shook my head. Marty had a death grip on my fingers and there was no way I was going to leave him in this flood of people.

"I'm surprised to see you here." Lady Tabitha, one of my brother's exes, smiled at me. Her eyes flickered down to Marty. "I don't usually see you out and about."

"I came to help a friend." I offered her a small smile. I'd never cared for Tabitha. She was gorgeous, tall, thin, and blond, but her attitude had become crass over the years. And she was annoyingly involved in climbing social ladders.

"I see." She looked from Marty to Meredith. "I didn't realize that you were so close with the Thysmer family."

I didn't say anything. She was baiting me, trying to figure out if there was something going on between me and Meredith. And considering that I didn't know, I wasn't going to answer. Rather, I wasn't sure exactly what it was.

"The Thysmers are our neighbors. Arthur has come several times to visit with my father." She leaned close to me and lowered her voice. "He and Father drank most of our scotch in one sitting."

"I wouldn't think that a funeral is the place for gossip, Tabby." I narrowed my eyes. Tabitha loved to spread rumors. It was something she lived for; it fed attention in her direction.

"It's the perfect place." She reached out and straightened my tie. "It's been too long since I've seen you. Where have you been hiding?"

From the other side of Marty, I felt Meredith look in our direction and then quickly away.

"I've been putting together an art showing in London." I looked past Tabitha to the other people milling about. I was more than a little bored and edging into irritation.

"I heard about that. How long will it be going on? I'm going to London tomorrow. I'll stop by." She tossed her long hair over her shoulder and flashed a grin. "We could meet up and have dinner."

"It'll be running for a few more weeks." I shifted my feet and Marty pulled on my hand. "What do you need, buddy?"

"I'm hungry," Marty whispered loudly. I almost shouted in relief. Finally, a way to escape.

Besides, I was hungry too. Meredith was in conversation with the minister, but I saw her look down at Marty quickly and then at me. Did she need me here with her? Or would she be okay with me leaving to feed Marty?

My eyes ran over the line of people that were gathering to talk to her and my family and I made a decision. I just didn't have it in me to schmooze anyone else.

"Let's go see if we can find some snacks." I looked back at Tabitha. "It was nice to see you, but I must be going."

"Did his mother not bring something for the boy?" Tabitha shot a surreptitious glance in Meredith's direction. "And you? Playing babysitter? I thought you didn't like kids."

I took a step closer to Tabitha and lowered my voice. "I like that boy more than I like most people."

Turning to walk away, I caught a hint of a smile on Meredith's face.

"Come on, Marty, let's get out of here."

We headed to the limo, where Cathy was talking with Rachel.

"Got any snacks in your car?"

"I think we have some stuff." Cathy smiled at Marty. "Hungry? It's been a long day."

"Starving!"

"Climb in there and see what you can find." I opened the door and motioned for him to get in.

Marty threw himself headfirst into the car and slid across the leather bench.

"Watch the shoes," I said.

"I am!" He disappeared in the dark interior.

"How is Meredith?" Rachel asked.

I looked over to where Meredith was standing next to her father and grimaced. She was currently talking with Tabitha, and a pang of guilt slid through my body. I had taken the quickest way out of the receiving line that had formed.

"She'll be fine." Cathy read the guilt on my face. "She handles people as well as Alex."

I looked back toward where she was leaning forward and speaking quietly to an elderly woman. Her shoulders were loose and relaxed and she was smiling. If I wasn't looking for it, I would miss the way her body was angled away from her father's, the way she tucked her hair nervously behind her ear.

"It's not the people that I'm worried about." I glanced back at my sister.

"He is on good behavior right now," Rachel informed me. Apparently I wasn't the only one worried about Arthur. "I've kept a close watch on him today. Unless he's been sneaking stuff in the bathroom, he's sober."

I looked back over at Meredith and frowned. Samantha and Alex were right there with her and her father.

"The reading of the will is tomorrow?" I shot Rachel a glance.

She adjusted her glasses and frowned. "Yes. Tomorrow afternoon the attorney will be at Thysmer."

"Has my mother sent a representative?"

"I believe that she asked Alex to be present."
She looked at me over her glasses. "Unless you
want to be there."

"I'll do it. The old man already hates me
anyway." I shrugged before checking to make
sure Marty wasn't listening.

"You must have said something that made an
impact." Rachel looked back toward Arthur. "He
was sober when I arrived at Thysmer this morning and muttering about a prince."

"I gave him an order from the crown." I
frowned. It wasn't something that was done lightly.
In fact, I'd never used my title to force something
on someone. I was surprised that it didn't bother
me more.

"That explains it." Rachel sighed..

"Well, it worked." Cathy sighed. "I'm just glad
today has gone smoothly."

"Now we get through tomorrow." Rachel
nodded her head. "And things will sort themselves out."

"Do you have any idea what the old man left?"
I looked at the small woman.

"I wasn't privy to that information." She
frowned. "Though I'd be lying if I didn't say I was
concerned."

I let out a breath. If I was worried, I couldn't

imagine how Meredith felt. She truly felt a sense of responsibility to her township. Having her father take over as duke would leave them in a bad place. However, if her granddad did something drastic, it would change her course of life. It would be nearly impossible to be both the acting duchess and go to school full-time, much less having an active stage career.

Not to mention having a son.

"I found crackers and grapes!" Marty slid across the back bench of the car and held up his treasures. "Anyone want some?"

"I'm good." I ruffled his hair.

"Well, don't stuff yourself with fizzy water and crackers. I'm thinking we'll have a lot of food waiting on us when we get home."

"You mean Thysmer?" His face took on a worried cast.

"Um, no. I meant D'Lynsal." I looked over at Cathy quickly, but she shrugged her shoulders. How did the two royals with no kid experience end up with the munchkin? "Is that okay with you?"

"Yeah." He frowned and popped a grape into his mouth. "I like it there. Mom acts more like herself there."

"I'm glad to hear that."

"Is that because of the mushy stuff?" He cocked his head to the side and looked at me while he chewed.

"Um." I looked around at Cathy and Rachel. Cathy was smiling, but hiding it behind one hand, while Rachel looked distracted by her phone, obviously pretending that she hadn't heard what Marty had said.

"I'm just happy you both are comfortable there." My palms started to become sweaty and I wiped them on my pants.

"Yeah, we are." He popped another grape into his mouth. "My room is pretty awesome, but I miss my toys."

"I'm sorry about that." I frowned. "Is it anything in particular?"

"I dunno." He shrugged. "Just stuff."

"I've got some outdoor stuff you can play with," Cathy offered.

"And if you want, you could draw or paint. I've got some stuff you can use."

"That would be cool. Mom said you're a painter. Not like the ones that paint houses, but the ones that paint pictures of things. Mom likes a painter named Fan Golf."

"Van Gogh?" I chuckled.

"I guess. He painted lots of things about a missing ear." Marty took a sip of his water and made a face. "That stuff tickles my nose."

"There's probably some still water in there if you'd prefer."

"Nah. I like this." Marty took another swig. "Even if it tickles."

"You're kinda crazy." I chuckled. "A good crazy."

"Well, that's better than being a bad crazy." He took another swallow and made a face.

"Very true."

I looked back toward Meredith, and she had turned so that she was looking at where we were standing. I pointed at the open door of the car and she nodded her head in understanding. She had wanted to know where her son had gotten to.

There were a few more people left to speak to, but I could tell by her stance that she was tired. When the last person approached her, I watched as her father turned in her direction and began speaking. I started to go up the hill, but Alex beat me to it. Knowing my brother, he had left Samantha on the other side of Meredith on purpose when he went to talk to Arthur. Casually he placed a hand on the man's shoulder and joined in the conversation.

It was all friendly, but I also knew that it was

business. He was reminding the old man to stay on good behavior. It seemed to be working, because Arthur had taken to merely answering questions that were directed at him.

Once they were finished, they all started down the hill toward the cars together. Sam had looped her arm through Meredith's and was talking animatedly about something that had them both smiling. By the time they got to where I was standing I caught the tail end of the conversation.

"Tabitha could make the pope want to curse." Sam shook her head.

"I don't even know why she was here. Granddad thoroughly disliked her." Meredith shook her head, sending her red hair swirling around her shoulders. She brushed at the black dress she was wearing and looked back at Sam with a small smile. "Though it was fun to watch you put her in her place."

"It's a talent." Sam pretended to breathe on her fingernails before wiping them on her dress. "She's one annoying bitch with the memory of a goldfish."

Meredith laughed and her face lit up. Now that the funeral was over, I could appreciate how stunning she looked today.

Everything about her was understated elegance. She was the woman who walked down the street and caught everyone's eye. Though I had seen her dressed to kill at Sam and Alex's wedding, I was pretty sure I liked her naked best of all. My eyes ran over her body slowly, taking in every inch. Was it wrong that I wanted to whisk her away somewhere private? Probably, but I wasn't sure I cared. She needed to spend time with Marty; needed to relax and let some of her stress melt away. She needed more than what I could offer right now. I seemed to make her nervous when we were alone.

"So what do we do now?" Her eyes met mine. Her father was standing behind her, his hands stuffed in the pockets of his pants.

I kept my mouth shut. It was the only way I could make sure I didn't say what I was thinking out loud.

"If you have time, Arthur, I'd like to go back with you and set up a few things for tomorrow." Rachel looked at the man with a serious expression. "I'd be honored to help with some of the paperwork."

"All right," he grunted.

"Then we'll leave you now and get to business." Rachel bobbed her head at everyone.

"Thank you for coming." Arthur mumbled the

words, his face a frustrated mask as he nodded his head at Alex.

"It was my honor, sir." Alex reached out to shake his hand. With no way to escape without being rude, Arthur accepted his handshake before turning and swiftly heading toward the other limo.

I looked at Meredith as she watched her father walk away and I could see the worry etched in the planes of her face. There was also a good amount of guilt there that made me want to punch the old man again. She shouldn't feel guilty that he was going back to an empty house. He'd brought it on himself.

"Don't worry, dear, I'll take care of him." Rachel touched Meredith's arm and gave her a warm smile.

"Thank you."

"I think that after a day like today, we deserve to have fun and relax." Alex rubbed his hands together. "Marty, would you like to help me feed the birds today?"

"What do they eat?" Marty stuck his head out of the limo.

"Mice." Alex put his hand on the small of Sam's back.

"For real?" Marty's eyes got huge. "Can I, Mom?"

"Um, what will that involve?" Meredith looked at Alex with worried eyes.

"He'll wear a full glove and I'll be with him the whole time," Alex assured her.

"Okay," Meredith said. Her face still looked a little hesitant.

"I'll go with them," Sam said. "After I eat something."

"Food does sound like a good idea." Meredith rolled her head from side to side. "I didn't eat much this morning."

"Then let's head home." I opened the door for her and helped her climb in. It wasn't until I noticed Alex raise an eyebrow in my direction that I realized I had called D'Lynsal home. For all of us.

I helped Sam slide into her seat and looked up at Alex and Cathy. They were both smiling at me.

"What?"

"You're in trouble, brother." Alex smacked my shoulder before climbing into the car.

"You guys are really obnoxious, you know that?" I glared at my sister.

"Only because you know we're right." She laughed as she slid in the car.

Shaking my head, I climbed in after her and took the last seat available. The car ride was a jumble of talking, laughter, and good-natured ribbing. It was like we'd all decided to cut loose after a very intense morning.

Marty was draped over his seat so that his feet were in the air and his head hanging down by his mother's feet. He popped a grape in his mouth and Meredith rolled her eyes.

"Sit up before you choke."

"I was being a bat. Do you have any bats?" He looked at Alex.

"No bats." Alex laughed. "We have horses though."

"Oh cool!"

"When are you going to tell us if the baby is a boy or a girl?" Cathy was looking at Sam with an intense expression.

"What does it matter?" Alex asked. "You'll be an aunt either way."

"I want to know if I should buy pink stuff or blue stuff."

"Oh God. Do not swamp us with pink stuff. I hate pink." Sam shook her head.

Alex turned to look at her and smiled. "Purple wouldn't be so bad."

"Yes!" Cathy sat forward. "It is a girl! I knew it."

"I didn't say that." Sam frowned. "I just said I didn't want lots of pink stuff . . . if it is a girl."

"Come on." Cathy laughed. "It's a girl!"

Sam looked at Alex and he shrugged.

"Don't tell anyone else." Sam looked around the interior of the limo. "Yes, it's a girl."

"Ahh!" Cathy jumped across the cab and hugged Sam.

"Don't squish me!" Sam fended off my sister with a laugh.

"Names?" I leaned forward and looked at my brother.

"Not yet." He shook his head. "We're not going to decide for certain until we have the baby."

"I didn't pick Marty's name until after I had him," Meredith offered.

"Really?" Cathy asked. "I think I wouldn't be able to help myself from picking."

"I couldn't decide." Meredith shrugged. "Then when I saw him, the name Marty popped into my head and nothing else seemed to fit."

"Is it a family name?" I watched her face.

"No." She smiled. "I have no idea where it came from."

"It fits him." Alex nodded his head. "That's what we're hoping for."

"I would have thought you'd go with a family name." I looked at my brother. Knowing that Sam had lost her mother a few years before she lost her stepfather, I thought it would be a natural choice.

"We've talked about it, but we want it to be the baby's name. If it doesn't fit, then it doesn't fit." He shrugged.

"Cathy, I bet you twenty that they can't agree on a name in the first three days." I looked at my sister.

"Pfft. I'll see your twenty." Cathy narrowed her eyes and looked at Sam and then Alex. "I say five days."

"I want in." Meredith sat forward. "Two days tops. And I'll raise the bet to fifty."

"Accepted." I narrowed my eyes.

"You guys are going down." She lifted one eyebrow and smirked at me.

"Are you guys so sure that we're going to argue over our baby's name?" Alex looked around the car. "We have talked about it, you know."

"After I squeeze a watermelon out of my hooha, I have final say on the baby name." Samantha sat back in her seat. "His Royal Stubbornness can suck it if he doesn't like what I pick."

"That's not fair." Alex frowned and looked at his wife. "I helped make the baby too."

"You got the fun part." Sam huffed. "I get the final say."

"You two are so going to lose." Cathy cackled.

Meredith sat back in her seat and smiled. Either she had a great poker face—which I already suspected—or she knew something we didn't. Either way, I enjoyed watching her interact with my family.

By the time we'd gotten back to the house, Marty had fallen asleep on his mother's lap and Samantha was leaning against Alex. I waited outside of the car and when Meredith slid to the door I reached in and took Marty out of her arms, letting his head rest on my shoulder.

With my free hand I reached to Meredith to help her out of the car. Her face filled with an expression that I didn't completely understand. Her fingers wrapped around mine, and when she was standing next to me she stood on her tiptoes and kissed me softly.

The feel of her lips on mine sent a chorus of emotions rustling through my body. It wasn't excitement, but akin to satisfaction. She kept her fingers in mine as we walked back to the house while Marty snored softly on my shoulder. One of the butlers opened the door for us, and I walked straight to the room Marty was using.

Once I laid him on the bed, Meredith pulled his shoes off and tucked him under the blanket.

He had taken his jacket and tie off in the limo. She motioned for me to be quiet as we backed out of the room. With gentle hands she pulled his door shut and looked up at me.

"Thank you." She licked her lips. "I don't know how I'll repay you for all that you have done for my family."

Half a thought blossomed in my brain and I almost blurted out that she was family. She and Marty had inexplicably found a spot in what I considered mine. It was a tiny crowd, and the fact that they had slid into the select group so quickly was a bit scary.

"I was glad to do it." I tugged on a strand of hair that had slid out from behind her ear.

"It means a lot." She yawned and I chuckled.

"I think you need a nap too." I let go of her hair. "It's been a long morning."

"Even longer for you."

I shrugged. I hadn't wanted her to deal with a difficult father on the day she laid her grandfather to rest.

Reaching out, she grabbed my hand and tugged me toward her. I cupped her cheek and looked down into her bright eyes.

"Come with me." She chewed on her lip. "You're tired too. I can see it in your eyes."

She wasn't suggesting sex. She was asking for something just as personal; to sleep with me. I couldn't remember the last time I had slept with someone. Sex, I'd had plenty of sex. But I never stayed long afterward. And I certainly didn't have girls staying at my house. This was blowing my comfort zones out of the water. Then again, the entire week had pushed me past all of my set boundaries.

I studied her face and noted the nerves that made her eyebrows pull together, the way her teeth worked her bottom lip. This wasn't something that had been easy for her to suggest.

Taking her hand, I headed for my room.

I opened the door and let her walk in ahead of me. Her eyes traveled around before she walked to my desk and picked up the drawing on top. It was the one I'd done of her the morning after my nightmare.

I swallowed hard as her eyes traced the lines I'd drawn. For some reason it made me feel exposed. Could she see what I had felt while drawing her? After a minute she set the paper back down and walked toward the bed.

She stepped out of one shoe before using her toe to help pry the other off. Reaching up, she undid her earrings and put them on the bedside table. There was something in the little things she did that kept me spellbound. Such simple things like taking off her shoes shouldn't be exciting. But with her, everything was sexy. Even when she wasn't intending to be.

Clearing my throat, I slid my jacket off and hung it on the back of my desk chair. Kicking my shoes off, I undid the cuffs of my shirt before taking off my watch and setting it next to her earrings. I looked at the earrings for a minute, surprised by the amount of emotion that came from seeing her things sitting with mine.

Like that was the way it had always been.

"Could I borrow a shirt?" She looked at me from under heavy eyelashes.

I opened one of the drawers of my dresser and fished out a shirt. She undid the zipper of her dress before sliding it off and hanging it over my jacket. As she walked toward me in nothing but a bra, barely-there panties, and garter belt, I had to mentally remind myself that we were napping. Feebly I held out the shirt I had taken from my dresser.

With an amused smile, she took the shirt from me and slipped it over her head. Had my mouth been hanging open? Seeing her in *that* had been enough to make me forget my name.

She sat down on the bed and undid her stockings before rolling them down her legs. Turning around, she crawled across the bed toward the pillows, providing me with a great view of her perfect ass. She pulled the blanket out and lay down, tucking her hands under her cheek while looking at me.

I guess that meant it was my turn. Undoing the buttons of my shirt, I pulled it off and dropped it on the foot of the bed. I only hesitated for a moment before sliding my belt off and stepping out of my pants. I shifted so my body wouldn't give away my reaction to her climb over the bed. I slipped under the blanket and she immediately closed the distance between us.

Raising my arm, I let her tuck her lithe body close to mine and rest her head on my shoulder. Her delicate hand rested on my chest and I touched the tiny pearl ring on her middle finger.

"That's different."

"My granddad gave it to me when I had Marty." Sleep laced her voice. "He stayed at the hospital the entire time."

"He loved you two very much." I continued to trace the delicate ring.

"I miss him," she mumbled.

"That's natural." I turned my face so I could kiss her head. "It'll get better."

"Promise?" Her voice was so soft I almost didn't hear her.

"It takes time." I sighed. "But yes, I promise."

"Thank you."

"You don't have to thank me." I closed my eyes and listened to her breathing. As it slowed, I shifted on my pillow and threw my arm over my head. For a minute I wasn't sure if I would be able to sleep, but as I listened to her breathing, I found mine matching hers, and before I knew it I was asleep.

I must've been more tired than I'd realized because it wasn't until I tried to roll over that I remembered someone was in the bed with me. Meredith's leg was draped over mine; the T-shirt she had borrowed had ridden up to expose a delectable amount of flesh. My eyes scanned her face as her breath tickled my skin.

Her red hair was spread out around her head like a halo of fire. Her dark eyelashes rested against her cheeks. Delicate fingers twitched on my chest as she dreamed, and I wondered what she was seeing.

"You're doing it again." Her voice surprised me. I hadn't realized she'd woken up. Her eyes were still closed but her breathing had hitched.

"What?"

"Staring." She opened her eyes with a small smile.

"It's not my fault." I tilted her chin up so that I could see her eyes clearly. "You're worth staring at."

"Is that why you drew me?" She cocked an eyebrow.

"I had a nightmare." I watched her face, noting the way her eyes crinkled in the corners.

She scrunched up her nose. "That's not exactly a compliment."

"From the time my father died, I've had a recurring nightmare." I swallowed. "When it happens, the only thing that helps is drawing. For some reason the other morning when it happened, it was your face that made me feel better."

She reached up and traced my cheek with her fingers. Sitting up, she looked down at me for a minute before pulling my borrowed shirt up and over her head. The black of her bra and panties contrasted sharply with her fair skin. Shaking her hair out, she looked down at me, her eyes full of emotion.

My pulse sped up as she sat up on her knees and ran her hands down my chest before sliding them back up to my shoulders. Lowering her mouth, she brought her lips to mine in a butterfly-soft kiss. When her tongue traced my bottom lip, I had to grip the sheets to keep from trying to take control. There was something special about having her take the lead. Plus it was fucking sexy to know that she wanted me. I could get used to waking up this way.

She shifted so that she was straddling me and I let myself rest my hands on her waist. I needed to touch her, even though I sensed it was important that she was initiating this and that she was in control. Her kiss deepened, her tongue tangling with mine, and my brain fought to stay calm. Red hair curtained our faces as she kissed me senseless, narrowing my world until it was just the two of us.

My hands moved of their own accord, along her ribs, over her shoulders, until I traced the straps of her bra. With delicate fingers I slid the straps down her arms before running my hands up over her neck so I could cup her jaw. She sighed into my mouth, her fingers on my shoulders tightening.

Sitting up, she reached behind her, undoing the bra and exposing her pert breasts to my attention. Unable to resist the temptation, I sat up on one elbow and caught a pink peak with my mouth. She gasped and let her head fall back while she tangled her fingers in my hair. Her skin was creamy and smooth and I couldn't get enough of it. With my free hand I cupped her other breast, gently rolling the nipple between my fingers while I devoured the first tantalizing peak.

Her moan resonated through my body and I pushed up so that I was in a sitting position. I shifted her so that my shaft was pressed against her hot center, and gripped her ass with my hands. Yanking on my hair, she lifted my face so that she could kiss me. Her mouth was hungry and demanding, her soft lips firm as she took what she wanted.

When her hips shifted, rubbing against me, I groaned. I ran my hands over her lithe body, across the smooth skin of her back, and pulled at the clasp of her garter belt. As I fumbled with the hooks, she let go of my hair and reached around to help me undo the hooks. Grabbing her hands, I kept them pinned behind her back while I feasted on her flesh. I ran my lips over her neck and scraped my teeth along her collarbone, eliciting a shiver.

Her breathing increased, which made her chest rise and fall in front of my face. Unable to help myself, I caught one peak with my teeth, teasing it with my tongue while she wiggled on top of me. The feel of her hips pressing against mine drove me over the edge. I let go of her hands, which went straight back to my head, where they fisted tightly in my hair. Ripping her garter belt off, I threw it on the floor before rolling over so that she was on her back.

She looked up at me with hooded eyes before reaching for the band of my underwear. I sat up on my knees and helped her slide them off, closing my eyes when she wrapped her hand around me. She shifted so that she was on her knees, before leaning forward and pressing her lips to my head. Her warm, moist mouth slid over my dick in wet strokes, causing me to moan. Wanting to see her, I gathered her hair on the top of her head and out of the way. I watched as she sucked and licked me, her gorgeous eyes turned up at me.

When my hips began to move, I groaned. It was too good, too perfect. If I let her go on, I was going to lose it. When I tugged on her hair gently, she shifted back up so that I could capture her mouth with mine. Sliding my hands down over the curve of her back, I slid her panties down so that she could kick them off.

She pushed on my shoulders so that I was forced to sit down. With a determined look, she crawled onto my lap and grasped my shaft.

"I want you, Max." She positioned me at her opening before letting gravity do its job.

I groaned loudly; her slick excitement was almost too much to take. When she began to move, rocking against me, my head fell back and I groaned.

"Watch me, Max." Leaning forward, she caught my ear with her teeth. "I want you to see me."

"Fuck," I whispered in Lilarian. "You feel so good. So wet. For me."

"For you." She groaned, her hips picking up the pace. "Look at me. I want to see what I make you feel."

I opened my eyes and met her stare. She made me feel a lot of things. Could she see what she had done to me? She had changed my life in a matter of days. Would she be able to see that I had fallen in love with her?

The reality of that thought shot through my system like lightning. I loved this woman. Sometime when I wasn't paying attention, she had become mine. Did she know that? Would she object?

The tempo of her movements increased, her breasts rising and falling with each breath.

I fisted my hand in the hair at the base of her neck and pressed my forehead to hers.

"You're going to make me come, sweet Meredith." My Meredith. "You're too much, too fucking perfect."

She picked up her pace, her soft moans of pleasure rocking me closer to my edge.

"Max." She gasped my name as her eyes went wide. Her body jerked against mine as pleasure slammed into her, but not once did she close her eyes. Watching her topple over the peak of orgasm finished me. My body shook as an orgasm so intense I thought it would shatter me rocked through my body.

She watched me with heavily lidded eyes as I unraveled beneath her. I pressed my lips to her, kissing her softly, the tips of our tongues coming together in a gentle dance as we reveled in the pleasure our bodies had experienced.

Three simple words sat on the tip of my tongue when she pulled back to look at me. Her eyes were full of heat and pleasure. Instead, I wrapped an arm around her waist and buried my face in her chest. The need I felt to tell her—to try and keep her forever—scared me. She had busted all of my boundaries and walls without trying.

I had to figure out how I was going to keep her.

FIFTEEN

$\mathcal{I}$ WAS DONE FOR. The battle was over, if it had ever begun. I'd lost my heart to a prince. And I hadn't exactly been sitting around waiting for a prince to show up. I'd thought I didn't need anyone; I didn't need anyone. But I wanted him. All of him.

I wanted what I had seen in his eyes just a moment ago.

"Max . . ." I closed my mouth. Could I say it? The words that would leave me open for even more pain? How had I done this to myself again? And what was I going to do about it?

"You're gorgeous, Meredith." He lifted his head and looked into my eyes. "Every single inch of you is perfect. I could spend an eternity studying every nook and cranny."

"Well, I think you've gotten a good head start." I lifted myself off him and lay down on the bed. Feigning nonchalance, I stretched and watched as his eyes traveled over my body.

"So I have." He chuckled. Lying down on his side next to me, he trailed his fingers along my stomach and over the curve of my hip. "But there's a lot more I still want to do to you."

My heart sped up at that thought. "What do you have in mind?"

"I'd rather show you than tell you." His deep, masculine chuckle sent a wave of goose bumps over my body. "Hm. Looks like you approve of that idea."

"I'm not opposed—"

"Mom!" Marty's voice sounded from the hallway and I sat up straight, grabbing for the blankets.

Max hopped out of the bed and tossed me my dress. I pulled it on over my head and almost jumped out of my skin when I felt Max's fingers sliding the zipper up.

"Just a minute!" I called to stall Marty.

"Are you in Max's room?" Marty knocked on the door.

I glanced over my shoulder and shoved my hair out of my face. Max was pulling on his pants, his shirt already in place, and nodded at me.

"I'm here." I opened the door and looked down at my son.

"I couldn't find you." His eyes were accusing.

"I'm sorry." I looked back at Max. "I was talking with Max and we didn't want to wake you up."

I cringed. I never lied to Marty. Well, except about Santa Claus and the Tooth Fairy, but those didn't count. And technically there had been some talking. Some very . . . interesting talking.

"Oh." Marty's gaze shifted past me toward Max. "Were you sleeping?"

"Yes." Max nodded his head decisively. "We were sleeping."

"I thought you were talking." Marty narrowed his eyes.

"We fell asleep while talking," I rushed to clarify.

"Okay." He wasn't convinced. I didn't blame him. Max and I looked guiltier than a couple of kids found at make-out point.

"What did you need, sweetie?" Out of the corner of my eye I noticed my panties on the floor next to the desk and kicked them out of sight.

"I wanted to know if I could go feed the birds, but Alex said I had to let you know where I was first." He looked up at me with big eyes. "Can I go? I'll be fast so we won't be late for dinner. Please?"

I scanned the room, searching for a clock. It was late afternoon and almost time for dinner.

"Have you eaten anything?"

"I had some fruit." He smiled up at me.

"Grab your jacket. It's getting cold at night right now."

"Woo-hoo!" He tore out of the room.

"Your brother will take good care of him, right?" I looked back over at where Max was sitting on the bed. "He's not going to have his eyeballs pecked out or anything, right?"

Max chuckled and stood up. "Marty is in the safest of hands."

"Has he ever watched kids Marty's age?" I let my hands fall to my sides as he walked toward me.

"Alex is the favorite of all the cousins." He tilted my face up toward his. "We have a very large family. Lots of little ones running around all the time."

"Why aren't you the favorite?" He had such an affinity with Marty, I couldn't imagine him not getting along with all of his cousins.

He shrugged uncomfortably. "I suppose I never really tried."

"Were you scared of them?" I laughed, but his frown stopped me. "But you're so good with Marty."

"Alex has always wanted kids." His eyebrows drew together. "And they just gravitated to him."

"Huh." I studied his face. "So you don't want kids."

"No." He frowned. "I don't know. Maybe."

I cringed inwardly. He didn't want children? I was a single mother. Marty was my world. But he wasn't sure. Had something happened to change his mind? Had we changed his mind?

"Don't look at me like that." He reached out and tugged on my hair.

"What has you waffling?" I knew better than to put on an act. Somehow Max saw right through me. Instead I chewed on my lip.

He opened his mouth and then closed it. Mr. Confident looked nervous. "I don't know."

"Huh."

"Don't do that." He stroked my cheek.

"What?"

"'Huh' me." He shook his head. "It's what Cathy and Sam do when they think they know something I don't."

"Are they usually right?" I raised my eyebrow.

"That's not the point." He smiled. "The point is that I'm . . . I'm not sure what I want anymore."

"Not sure about anything?" The words fell from my mouth before I could rethink them.

"I'm sure that I want to do what we just did

again." He ran his thumb over my bottom lip. "I'm sure that I want to go fishing with Marty again. That I want to spend more time with both of you."

His eyes traced my face, looking for something.

"What do you want?" he asked.

You, my mind screamed. *I want you.* But my mouth wouldn't say the words. Instead I stood on my tiptoes and kissed him.

His arm slid around my waist, tucking me against his body. I leaned into his kiss, trying to convey what I hadn't been able to say aloud.

Someone cleared their throat and I broke our kiss, but Max kept me pinned to his side.

"Sorry to interrupt." Cathy was looking anywhere but at us.

"What do you want?" Max growled at his sister.

"Well, we just thought you might want to eat dinner, but if you're too busy, I'll just let the others know . . ."

"No, thank you. I'm starved." I lifted my hand to my mouth. Well, I guess the cat was out of the bag.

"Oh, thank God. I would hate to have interrupted and you weren't hungry." She motioned between us. "Because this could have been all awkward for no reason."

"Awkward is one word for it." Max narrowed his eyes. "Annoying is another."

"Well, that's one way of looking at it." She backed away from the door. "I'm going to go. And don't worry, I won't tell anyone what I saw. Not a soul. Except for Sam. Who will probably tell Alex. You know how they are. Yak, yak. No secrets."

"Get out of here." Max kicked the door shut, but we could still hear her laughing as she walked down the hall.

I turned to look at Max with wide eyes before busting out laughing. Max studied me with an amused expression. Running my hands through my hair, I took a deep breath.

"Are you upset?" His eyes watched me carefully.

"No." I shook my head. "You asked me what I wanted earlier."

"Yes." He touched my cheek and my eyes fluttered shut briefly.

"I want to keep spending time with you. I want you to go fishing with Marty. I want to frame that picture you drew of me so I can always remember that I was the one that soothed you when you were upset." I took a deep breath and opened my eyes. "And that's a problem. Because I want there to be something between us. But what I want in life doesn't add up for you. I want to sing on stage, on Broadway. I want to make people feel something, and that is the last thing you want."

Reaching down, he grabbed my hand and pulled it up to his lips. "That's not something you need to worry about right now."

My heart stuttered in my chest. I wanted that to be true. "Good, because I have a lot of other things to worry about."

"No you don't." He tugged me against his chest.

"Tomorrow is sort of scary." I looked up at him, and my voice cracked. "I don't know what to expect."

"Whatever comes, I'll be there with you." His green eyes stared down into mine. "You won't be alone."

It had been a long time since I'd been willing to depend on someone else, to count on anyone else. In the last few years I'd been the person Granddad had leaned on; I'd reminded him to take his medicine, made sure the staff was getting him to his appointments. All of that from London while being a single mom and going to school. Thank God I hadn't had to work a job too.

"Okay," I whispered.

"Then let's go eat."

He kept his fingers laced with mine as we walked through the house. Despite Cathy warning us to hurry up, we were the first people in the dining room. It was odd to sit at this huge, empty table full of food while everyone else finished what they were doing. It wasn't that the silence was uncomfortable, but I couldn't stop mulling over how things would end with Max. A mutual parting of ways? Slowly drifting apart? A fight? Would he wait until I was back to singing to decide it just didn't work?

"Wash your hands!" Samantha's voice carried down the hallway. It was followed by stampeding feet and the slam of a door.

I winced. "I hope he didn't break anything."

"This house has survived countless children. I'm sure it can handle Marty." Max chuckled, but his face took on a serious cast. "You look worried."

"Did you hear my child stampeding through your house? You should be worried." I tried to shrug it off. Hopefully Marty hadn't done much damage. I had enough to worry about.

"I told you not to worry about tomorrow." He rested his hand on top of mine.

"I'm trying." I smiled at him, a little relieved that he assumed it was about the will.

He kept his hand on mine, even as everyone

filled into the room talking animatedly. No one blinked an eye at us, not even Marty. He was too busy describing the birds he had seen.

"It was huge. Like half the size of me!" He held his hand up from the floor to demonstrate.

"They let you hold a bird that big?" I looked over his head at Alex.

"She's a sweetheart," Alex assured me. "Wouldn't hurt a fly."

"And I fed her a whole rat!" Marty tugged on my arm.

I leveled my gaze on the heir to the throne. "Not a fly, huh?"

"Rats are different." He cringed.

"He was actually really great with the birds." Sam reached out and touched my arm. "Very calm and patient."

"Thank you for letting him go with you."

"He livens the place up. You should bring him around more often." Sam threw me a sly smile. "We'd always be happy to babysit."

"Um, I'm not a baby." Marty pursed his lips.

"Excuse me, kid sit." Sam ruffled his hair.

"Actually, are you busy tomorrow?" Max asked as he pulled a seat out for me.

"I've got to go to Rousseau tomorrow. Did you need me to watch Marty?" She smiled at my son.

"I can call our nanny. Don't worry about it." I shook my head. "We've disrupted your schedules enough already."

"I wouldn't mind. He can keep me company while I take care of a few things." Sam smiled at me. "Really. It would be no trouble."

"Please, Mom?" Marty grabbed my arm.

Sending my rambunctious six-year-old with a busy, pregnant princess didn't seem like the best idea. I looked at Max and then back at Marty.

"She'll have Chadwick with her. It's not like she would be chasing him around." Max shrugged.

"We'll be fine. It'll be a good practice run for Chadwick." Sam laughed.

"Marty can be a handful." I frowned.

"I'm just going to sign some papers and then we can go fishing." Sam smirked. "Unlike some people, I actually know how to fish."

"Hey. I know how to fish." Max lifted his fork and pointed at her. "It's just been a while since I did it."

"Right." Sam shook her head. "The point is, you're busy tomorrow and I'm not."

"Are you sure?"

"Yeah! I miss being outside. I haven't been out for anything fun in a while." She dug into her food. "I'm getting antsy."

"That's true. She gets crabby when she's been stuck doing desk work for too long," Cathy added.

"If you're sure."

"Absolutely." She nodded her head. "Please let me take him with me? It'll be nice to have the company. Chadwick refuses to fish."

Cathy snorted. "He loves to fish. Just not with you."

"What?" Sam looked startled.

"He fishes when he goes on vacation. I've seen the pictures of him and Daniel." Cathy took a sip from her water glass. "Deep-sea fishing."

"You're kidding." Sam's eyebrows were creeping up toward her hairline. "He refuses to fish with me."

"That's because you are competitive." Alex walked into the room and kissed his wife on top of the head.

"So?" She scrunched up her nose.

"It's not relaxing to go fishing with you. It's a competition." Alex sat down in an empty chair.

"That'll be good for Marty." I bumped him with my elbow. "He's all about winning at things."

"It's on!" Sam winked at my son and he blushed.

If I'd been forced to guess what a dinner with

the royal family would be like, I would have thought it would be formal, punctuated with talk about politics and serious issues. I would have been very wrong. It was as if there was an unspoken rule to leave work at the door. The only time they talked about serious issues was if it involved something they were passionate about.

I didn't do a lot of talking. Partly because I was exhausted, but also because I was enthralled watching how this family worked. If I didn't know better, I would think they were a normal family getting together for a weekly dinner. Cathy asked about Max's art show in London, Max teased Alex about carrying a diaper bag, and Sam asked my opinion about the nursery.

"Did you co-sleep? I'm scared I'll squish her." Sam sighed. "Alex's family all co-slept when they were little. He thinks I'm silly."

"I didn't really have much choice." I shrugged. I'd been lucky to have a bed at all. My father had kicked me out as soon as he found out I was pregnant. I'd lived with my granddad until I could stand on my own two feet. "There are things you can buy to help with that. Little beds that go on your bed so you can't roll over and hurt him. Or bassinets that go right next to the bed."

"It must've been very difficult." Sam looked

at me with compassion-filled eyes. "But what an amazing job you've done."

"Thank you."

By the time dinner was finished, I could barely hold my eyes open. Marty was leaning against me, his little fingers wrapped around my arm as he fought to stay awake.

"Come on, big guy." Max stood up from his seat and swooped Marty into his arms. "I think it's time for bed."

"I just need 'nother nap," Marty mumbled into Max's shoulder.

"Sure." Max smiled at me over my son's shoulder. "You look tired too."

"Gee, that's what every woman wants to hear." I raised an eyebrow.

"Come on. I'll tuck you in." Max held a hand out to me with a mischievous smile.

"What did he say he was going to do to her?" Sam mock-whispered loudly.

"Tuck. He said he was going to tuck her in," Cathy answered in a stage whisper.

"Ah." Sam nodded her head. "I thought he said f—"

"Cut them some slack, ladies." Alex didn't bother to hide his smile.

"You guys are a riot." I shook my head. "Pay

back is a b— not good." I shot a look at Marty and changed my phrase.

"Ignore them." Max rolled his eyes. "Come on."

"Good night." I took Max's hand and let him pull me from the room.

He didn't say anything as he took us up the stairs and to Marty's room. He set Marty down on the edge of the bed and undid his shoes. My heart did something funny as I watched him. The tender way he pulled the shoes off and talked quietly to Marty made my mind spin. I swallowed hard and tried to keep my emotions in check. To keep myself from staring I went to the dresser and pulled out a pair of pajamas.

"Brush your teeth, buddy."

"But I'm so tired." Marty fell back on the bed and covered his face with his arm. "I don't wanna."

"Marty," I said his name in warning.

"Please? I can just brush them twice as much in the morning."

"You could be done if you'd stop arguing with me." I put my hands on my hips. "And change into your pajamas."

"Okay." Sighing, he slid off the bed like he was a puddle of goo and grabbed the checkered pants and T-shirt. "I'm going."

I raised an eyebrow.

"Ma'am. Yes, ma'am. I'm going now." Marty hurried to the bathroom and pulled the door shut.

"That's kind of hot." Max stood up and I could feel his eyes run over my body.

"What?" I wrinkled my nose.

"The whole 'mom' thing. It's sexy when you get all bossy." He walked toward me. "You tap your foot and put your hands on your hips. Very hot."

"You've lost your mind." I let go of my hips and shook my head.

"I think you're right." He narrowed his eyes. "But I'm okay with it."

"Are you sure?" I swallowed.

He put a hand on my waist and tilted my chin so that I was looking up at him.

"Yes." His eyes were serious as they studied my face. Leaning forward, his lips brushed mine in a gentle caress.

"Oh. Ew." Marty's voice cut through the room.

Max leaned back from me, his eyes twinkling in the low light.

"Teeth brushed?" I stepped away from Max and looked at my son. He was climbing into his bed.

"Yes, ma'am."

I walked over and kissed his head and tucked the blanket around his little form.

"Good night, little man."

" 'Night, Mom." He yawned. " 'Night, Max."

"Good night, buddy." Max lowered his voice and hit the light switch by the door. "Have fun tomorrow."

I made my way through the room carefully and out into the hallway where Max was waiting.

"Your turn." He nodded toward my door.

"You really don't have to tuck me in." I smiled at him. "I doubt I'll be able to fall asleep anyway."

"I could help with that too." His fingers wrapped around my wrist and tugged me after him.

Once inside my room, he turned me loose and closed the door. As he walked toward me, his eyes ran over my body, and my heart started to beat faster. He began to undo the buttons of his shirt as he walked toward me, and I didn't waste any time pulling my dress off. If I was only going to have Max for a little while, then I wasn't going to let any moment with him escape. His eyes stayed fixated on mine and he brushed my hair over my shoulders.

Tilting my head back, he kissed me. His lips were soft but hungry as he explored my mouth. His hands traced the lines of my body with just his fingertips. The feel of his hands on my skin elicited goose bumps, and I shivered. He chuckled, a deep masculine sound that sent my body into overdrive. When his lips left mine to trail down my neck I let my eyes close.

Pulling me closer, he swept me up into his arms and I squeaked in surprise.

"You're a tiny thing." He looked down into my eyes as he crossed the floor to the bed.

"Maybe you're just unnaturally large." I raised an eyebrow.

"Now, that's what every man wants to hear." His smile made me giggle.

He set me on the bed so that my legs were hanging over the edge. Kneeling in front of me, he slid my legs apart so that he could move close enough to kiss me. His hands grazed my breasts and moved down to grasp my hips, his thumbs tracing circles just inside my thighs.

Leaving my mouth, he trailed kisses over my body until his warm breath spread over my warm center. He looked up at me with a small smile before pressing his warm mouth to my skin. I sucked in a deep breath of air when his tongue darted out to trace along me. Long, slow strokes sent bursts of pleasure over my body.

Falling back on the bed, I closed my eyes and reached down to tangle my fingers in his hair. He shifted my legs so that they were thrown over his shoulders, giving him better access. My body bucked under his delicate attention, and his hands gripped my hips to keep me in place.

When the end came it hit me like lightning. I cried out before biting my lip as pleasure exploded over my body in wave after wave. Kissing my throbbing center delicately, he untangled himself from my legs and crawled onto the bed, pulling me up to the pillows.

I turned to him, ready to repay the favor, but he stopped me.

"Tonight was about you." He kissed my forehead. "Get some sleep."

He pulled the blanket out from underneath us, lay back and held his arm out to me.

I looked at him for a minute before doing as he suggested. His arm wrapped around my shoulders and he kissed my head. I'd never slept with a man before. Not even Marty's father. That had been all quick tumbles in a car or hasty, quiet meetings in dark places. I wasn't sure what had prompted me to ask him to take a nap with me earlier. My heart had been heavy and sore; I'd just wanted someone to hold me. No, not just someone. I'd wanted Max to hold me.

And now here we were again. Curled up

against each other as our breathing seemed to match. He reached out and ran his hand along my hip before pulling my leg up over his. His hand stayed on my knee while his thumb rubbed small circles against my skin.

I'm not sure when it happened, but I fell asleep. I had been prepared to spend the night stressing over what would happen at the reading of the will. Instead I spent the night in the arms of the man I loved. Too bad he didn't know it and I was too scared to tell him.

When I woke up, Max was snoring gently in my ear, and I didn't try to hide my satisfied smile. A girl could get used to waking up next to a man who looked like Max. I sat up on my elbow and looked around the room. The alarm clock blinking next to the bed said I didn't have long before I had to leave.

"Good morning." His voice rumbled beside me and I turned to look at him.

"Good morning." I leaned back so that I was propped up on one elbow.

"How'd you sleep?" He reached up and tucked some of my hair behind my ear.

"Good." Leaning down, I kissed him softly. "How about you?"

"Like a log." His eyes ran over the bits of me

that were exposed by the blanket. "I especially like waking up next to a gorgeous, naked redhead."

"Down, boy." I put my hand on his chest and lowered my eyelashes. "I've got to get ready."

"Go take a shower. I'll get Marty dressed." He looked up at me with warm eyes.

"Are you looking for brownie points?" I smiled at him. "Because you're definitely on the right road."

"Mission accomplished." He leaned up and kissed my nose before yanking the blanket away from me. "Now go get clean."

I shook my head and stood up, reveling in the way his eyes traveled over my body. As I turned to head for the bathroom, his warm hand smacked my ass, making me jump.

"What the hell was that for?" I shot him a glare and put my hands on my hips.

"Well, I didn't want you to start thinking I was too perfect." Lying back on the pillow, he tucked his hands under his head. "Plus you've got a really great ass."

I rolled my eyes at him but didn't say anything. I was scared if I opened my mouth I'd laugh. Instead I did as I was told and went to take a shower. I wasn't in there long. As a mother, you learn to be quick in the bathroom or you could walk out to find the house on fire. I was wrapped in my robe drying my hair when Marty walked into the bathroom. He was trying to stuff a jacket into his backpack.

"We're about to leave!"

"Already?" I set down the hair dryer and knelt down so I could hug him.

He rushed into my arms and squeezed me tightly. "Yeah, we're going to eat in the car."

"I want you to listen to Ms. Sam, okay? She's pregnant, so don't run her ragged." I looked him in the eyes. "If I find out you were bad I'm taking your game system"

"I'll be good." He almost rolled his eyes but caught himself. "I promise."

"Good." Pulling him forward, I gave him a big kiss and then pushed him toward the door. "I'll see you when I get back."

"Love you, Mom."

"Love you too."

Hearing someone shuffling in the hallway, I went to the door and stuck my head out.

"Sam?" I called.

"Hey." She turned around and gave me a small smile.

"Will you please let me know if he misbehaves? You can call me anytime and I'll find a way to come get him."

"Pfft." She rolled her eyes. "He's perfect. Don't worry."

"Thanks, but he has his moments." I shook my head. "No kid is perfect all the time."

"We'll be fine." She put a hand on her stomach and made a face. "This kid is going to play soccer. She's practicing with my bladder right now."

"Yikes." I winced in understanding.

"She'll move eventually." Sam shook her head. "It's nice to be able to say 'her' instead of 'it.'"

"With as much publicity as you two get, I don't blame you for wanting to keep something to yourselves for a while."

"It's part of the job." Her mouth turned down and something passed over her face. "Anyway, I hope today goes well. And don't worry about Marty. We're going to have fun. I'm looking forward to it."

"Thank you." I gripped the door handle. How had I gone from having no one to having so many people? "I owe you that spa day."

"I'm going to hold you to it." Sam smiled at me before walking away.

I closed my door and went about getting ready for the day. I only had what I'd stashed in my bag in my hasty retreat from Thysmer. Picking out dress pants, a blouse, and heels, I checked myself out in the mirror. My reflection looked tense and worried, but there wasn't anything I could do about that.

"Hungry?" Max knocked on my door before peeking inside.

"No." I shook my head. The thought of eating made my stomach flip and flop in a very uncomfortable way.

"Today is going to be okay." Max walked in. He was still tying his tie, but he cut a dashing figure in a suit.

"Yeah." I nodded out of habit. Today wasn't going to be okay. Out of all the outcomes I could come up with, there weren't any ones that left everyone happy.

"I'm serious." He put his hands on my shoulders. "No matter what happens, things will be okay. The queen can appoint a steward for the township if she needs to. Several of the older dukes have stewards that help in the running of day-to-day operations. Your father will not hurt your family or the township."

"What if . . ." I swallowed hard. "What if he doesn't leave it all to Dad? I've been thinking about it and I can't figure out why he would have sent a will to the queen if he was just going to pass the estate and title down to my father without any stipulations."

"Then we'll deal with it." He tipped my chin

upward so I was meeting his eyes. "You could have a steward while you finish school. There are always options. We just have to figure them all out."

"Why didn't he tell me though? I mean, why didn't he let us know he was making a will?" I shook my head. "It's so backward."

"I don't know." He pulled me against his chest. "My family has always lived by two mottos: Family first, and nothing is ever as good or as bad as you expect. So try not to stress yourself out before we even know what's going to happen."

I looked up in his eyes and was surprised by the honesty. He really felt that we were in this together.

"Okay. Then let's get going." I stepped out of his hands and grabbed my purse from the dresser near the door.

He motioned for me to walk in front of him and I took a deep breath. Alex was waiting outside by the car when we got there. He was wearing a suit and had his hands tucked into his pockets.

"Good morning." He smiled at me. I could see why Sam was so head over heels in love with the man. He was gorgeous and sweet. Not a normal combination.

"Good morning." I nodded my head at him.

"I thought I'd see if you two would like some company today. I'd be happy to lend my support."

"We've got it covered." Max smacked his brother's back. "Why don't you try taking a day off?"

"You're sure?" Alex frowned. "I know how much you hate the royal duties. I could play the bad cop. I don't get to do it that often. Sam is usually the bad cop."

"I've got this." Max looked at his brother, and something passed between them. Alex just nodded his head as if he understood something I hadn't heard.

"Okay then. I'll be here relaxing, if you need anything." Alex opened the car door for us.

Max held my hand to help me slide into the seat. It was one of those gentlemanly gestures that wasn't really necessary, but made a girl feel special. He didn't get in right away; instead Alex leaned forward and whispered to him quietly before slapping his back. Max nodded his head and then climbed into the car.

"Brotherly advice?" I raised an eyebrow.

"Just reminding me of something." He looked over at me with a small smile, but I could see the stress etched in the corners of his eyes.

"Hm." If he wasn't going to elaborate, I wasn't going to ask. After all, it really wasn't any of my business what passed between the brothers. Instead I straightened my pants and opened my purse to dig out my phone.

There were messages from my director at school, but I couldn't really answer them yet. I had no idea what was going to happen, not until this afternoon. Rachel had texted me to let me know that she and the lawyer were on the way to the estate. I did reply to her to let her know that we were on our way as well.

Talking was kept to a minimum, which I appreciated. It wasn't that I didn't enjoy small talk or a good conversation; I just didn't have the energy to focus on anything other than the reading of the will. It was like all of the worry and anxiety I'd been keeping bottled up had drained me dry.

Max reached out at one point and wrapped his fingers around mine, but didn't try to talk to me. Instead he played on his phone and let me stare out the window.

I tried to work out the appropriate response for how my father would react to different outcomes of the will. Would he lose his shit? Would he surprise me and stay calm? Would he gloat and kick me out of the house? Was I going to lose my cool?

Sighing, I leaned my head against the glass and closed my eyes. Max had been right. There was no point in worrying. What happened, happened, and it was out of my hands. The only person I could be responsible for today was myself.

I was sweating by the time we'd gotten through the gates and I was glad I'd decided to wear dark colors. We pulled up to the house, my heart beating as if I'd run a marathon. I felt like I was about to walk into a house of doom.

Max was out of his seat and opening my door before I realized the car had come to a complete stop. His cool fingers laced with mine as we walked up the steps, and I was grateful that he didn't say anything about my sweaty palms. The butler, Gerard, opened the doors for us as we reached the top, and motioned for us to come inside.

"Good morning, Lady Meredith, Prince Maxwell." He bowed his head.

"How is he?" I lowered my voice and took a step closer to Gerard.

"He is . . . better than usual, but not his best." Gerard frowned.

"Well, can't ask for much more than that. Where are they?" I straightened my shirt.

"The front parlor, ma'am."

"Thank you, Gerard." I looked back at Max. "Let's do this."

Stepping forward, I took a deep breath,

straightened my shoulders, and lifted my chin. If I was going into this blind, I was going to do it with confidence. Or at least a reasonable facsimile of confidence. I was an actress after all.

My father was sitting in a large wingback chair near the fireplace. The glass tumbler held loosely in his fingers was half empty. Rachel and an elderly man in an expensive suit stood up from their seat on the couch and bobbed a bow and curtsy.

"Your Highness, my lady, I am Daniel LeFave. I handle most of the legal matters for Her Majesty." The man held his hand out to shake. "I'm sorry for your loss. I know this has been a difficult time."

"Thank you." I shook his hand before taking one of the open seats across from the lawyer.

"Okay then. Since we're all here, let's get started." The old man clapped his hands together and smiled. "Prince Maxwell, I assume that you are here in an official position as your mother's witness?"

"Yes." He moved so that he was standing just behind my chair, and my father snorted.

"Isn't there supposed to be a witness? Someone who watched my old man lose his mind?" My father's voice was scratchy and annoyed.

"Yes, sir." Gerard closed the door and moved to the corner of the room. "I am present."

"The butler." My father chuckled darkly into his drink.

"Thank you, Gerard." I looked at the man who had done so much to take care of our family. He nodded his head before looking back at the lawyer.

"Okay, there is a lot of legal mumbo-jumbo, but if you'd like, I can cut straight to the meat of things." He opened his folder of papers and pulled out a piece of Thysmer letterhead. "The late Duke of Thysmer wrote this out himself, which I then translated for him into the proper legal form."

He passed me the paper, but before I could get a good look at it, my father was across the room and snatched it out of my hands.

"I'll take that." He set his empty tumbler on the table and scanned the paper quickly.

I watched as his face turned pale and then bloodred. My heart managed to lodge itself in my throat as I watched the veins in his neck strain against his skin. The paper shook in his hands as he looked up at me with furious eyes.

"As you can see, your father left very specific instructions." Mr. LeFave clasped his hands in his lap, his eyes trained on my father.

Max placed a hand on my shoulder and stepped around the chair as if he were going to shield me from my father's anger.

"The queen accepted his terms and has agreed to them," Rachel said quietly.

"How can he do this?" My father turned slowly to look at the woman on the couch. "He can't do this."

"What is he doing?" I licked my lips and scooted forward on the chair. "What are you talking about?"

"Basically, your grandfather has divided the title between the two of you, but with conditions." Mr. LeFave explained. "For your father to retain any of what has been left to him, he must successfully complete a course of addiction rehabilitation."

Every cell in my body froze. I wasn't even sure if I was breathing as I stared at the lawyer across from me. In one fell swoop, my grandfather had simultaneously validated my worry about my father and then turned around and ripped my dream out from under me. How could I be a performer and a duchess?

"She can't just take my title away because I don't go to rehab! That's ridiculous." Spittle flew from my father's mouth. "I don't need rehab. That's rubbish."

"We could schedule a consultation with a specialist. They could evaluate you and determine if you needed help or not." Rachel kept her voice cool and pleasant.

Everyone in the room was so calm. Very calm. Except for the vibrating exposed nerve that was my father.

"You expect me to trust a specialist you pick? This is some kind of ploy to take away what is rightfully mine." He turned his glare on me. "You're behind this, aren't you? You've been trying to push me out of the way for a long time."

"I've been covering for you for a long time." Something inside my chest snapped and my own rage boiled to the surface. I stood up and clenched my fists at my sides. "You see nothing but yourself, what's best for you! Granddad must have realized that you would hurt this town and our family. You think I want to stay here and babysit your drunk ass? Listen to you bitch and moan and abuse me or the staff? I haven't been trying to push you out; I've been trying to escape you."

My father stood there, fury running rampant across his face. The letter in his hand crinkled as his hands shook.

"We haven't gone over everything," Mr. LeFave offered. "The financial settlement is not based on your sobriety. Excepting the money from taxes that is used for the township, the family inheritance has been divided between Arthur, Meredith, and young Marty."

"I've still got my money?" Arthur turned and looked at the lawyer.

"Yes, sir. However, if you do not complete rehab or if you begin drinking again, you lose any rights to future moneys earned by your family. You will only receive a percentage of what is currently held in the family accounts." He flipped through papers in his folder and laid it on the table.

I glanced down briefly at the paper and then back at my father. I wasn't worried about how much money had been left to me. My largest concern at this moment was my father.

"What if she doesn't want to be Duchess of Thysmer?" My father's lip curled. "What if something happens to her? What then?"

The blood in my veins froze as I stared at the man in front of me. I'd always accepted that my father hated me. But did he hate me enough to try and kill me? For a title he seemed to loathe?

"Something happens to her?" Max's deep voice cut through the room. "What do you mean?"

"What are you worried about?" Dad sneered at Max.

"You wouldn't be the first person to try to gain a title by removing someone else from the picture."

"Grow up, boy. If I was going to kill my daughter I sure as hell wouldn't suggest it." My father shook his head and walked back over to the cabinet to replenish his scotch. "I told you she's using you. Now she has you all riled up because she's been shacked up with you for a few days."

"Do not speak about Meredith in such a disrespectful manner." The words snapped out of Max.

"Stop it." I growled the words at my father. "I am not using Max."

"Then why is he here following you around like a puppy?" He snorted. "That's what your mother did. Got me hooked with a few tumbles in the sheets. Then dumped you on me and ran off."

"Father," I hissed through gritted teeth. I wish I wasn't surprised that he was airing our dirty laundry.

"Embarrassed?" He laughed and swallowed what he had poured in one gulp. "You're just like your mother."

"Let's all take a seat," Rachel spoke up. "Wills are never a pleasant thing to deal with, and this one is a bit tougher than usual."

"I want you all out of my house." My father slammed his glass down on the table. "Now."

"Technically, the house belongs to both of you. Unless you refuse rehab. Then it goes directly to

Meredith and her son." The lawyer took on a stern tone. "I'm here by the crown's orders and will not leave until I have finished my job. Until you are sober and a functioning part of society, you will not be taking over any control of the current estate."

"Fine. I'll go." Standing up straighter, with only the slightest hint of a bobble, he straightened his jacket. "I'll go."

"We need to finish the will. There are things to discuss about personal artifacts, your father's dwelling in Germany, the family heirlooms." The lawyer stood up.

"I'm not entitled to any of it, remember? Unless I let you people make me into someone I'm not." My father glared at me. "Let the bitch have it. I know how to survive without a title. I won't live under the thumb of an idiotic queen and the mentally unstable ramblings of my old man."

I reached out and grabbed Max's arm when he took a step forward. His entire body was tense, even his jaw was clenched in anger.

"You would call your daughter a bitch and the queen—who granted your family lands back and bestowed God knows how much money on your family—an idiot." Max's arm shook under my touch. "You don't deserve any of it. Not the house, the title, or the money. But most of all, you don't deserve your daughter."

"Doesn't matter, does it?" My father sneered as he walked across the room. "It's all going to my little bitch."

I wasn't fast enough to stop him, even if I'd been strong enough. Every time my father had called me a bitch had been a stab in the gut, slowing my reflexes. Max was across the room in a heartbeat, grabbing my father's lapels with his fists and slamming him against the wall.

"Apologize," Max roared.

When my father started to laugh, Max pulled him away from the wall, only to slam him back against it.

"That is an order." He leaned close to my father and lowered his voice. "You will apologize to Meredith now."

My father stopped laughing and met my eyes over Max's shoulder. I put a hand to my mouth, my composure completely wrecked. Never had I been more mortified or hurt by the way my father behaved. And yet, on the other side of that coin was Max demanding I be treated with respect. It was like looking at the yin and yang of manhood. They were each other's opposites in every way.

No wonder I loved him so much. How could I

not? My prince that had charged in to save me and was now protecting my virtue.

"Let him go, Max." I cleared my throat. Stepping forward, I put a hand on his shoulder.

"He needs to apologize to you." His body could have been carved from stone.

"I don't need him to." I met my father's eyes. If anyone knew how to fight fire with fire, it was me. "He'd have to mean something to me for it to have hurt."

Something in my father's eyes shifted as if my words had hit him harder than I would have thought possible. Even when Max let go of him and he slid to the ground, his blurry eyes stayed focused on mine. If I hadn't known better I would have thought that I'd wounded him with my words.

Max took a step back and my father got up and adjusted his jacket before walking swiftly out of the room. Silence rang through the room until Max turned around and looked down into my eyes.

"God help me, Meredith. If he hurts you one more time I'm not accountable for my actions." He cupped my chin and tilted my face up toward his. "I can't stand seeing the pain in your eyes. It rips me to the bone."

My breath caught in my throat and I struggled to process what I saw in his eyes. His thumb moved over my cheek and wiped away a tear I hadn't realized I had shed. Was I crying because of my father? No.

I was crying because I loved this man—this prince who would go to war for me.

"Perhaps we should come back later." Rachel stood up and clasped her hands in front of her.

"No." Max kept his eyes trained on mine. "Meredith has been stuck in limbo for long enough. Let her know what has been laid on her shoulders."

"Very well." Rachel sat down next to the lawyer and motioned for him to continue.

"For the majority of the remaining things to be sorted out, they go to you. All of the family jewels are to stay with the estate, excepting pieces that may be handed down to family members that marry. Much of this stuff is the normal, mandated conditions of a duchy." His words began to blend together and I had to focus as he explained the details of the arrangement.

"For now, my lady, you are the acting head of the Thysmer family." Rachel took her glasses off and looked at me with compassion-filled eyes. "I realize that this is not necessarily the ideal situation, but until your father is sober and able to assist in the duties, it falls on your shoulders."

I took a deep breath and opened my mouth to speak, but couldn't find the right words. Max put a hand on my shoulder, offering his support. Rachel didn't say anything, just waited for me to absorb what had happened.

"I understand." Taking a deep breath, I closed my eyes and went to that quiet zone I used for performances. It was hard to reach today with so much swirling in my mind.

"She'll need help." Max's voice was quiet.

"I actually have a solution, if she's open to it." Rachel looked at me. "I'd like to offer my services as your assistant."

"My assistant?" My eyebrows furrowed together.

"Your grandfather refused one. As I understand it, they made him uncomfortable, but I could help you shoulder some of the responsibilities you're facing." She leaned forward and picked up a teacup. "I'm not sure that I would be able to cover for you being gone for whole semesters in England, but perhaps we can figure something else out."

"You would do that for me?"

"It would be my pleasure." Rachel nodded her head. "I've got a few good years left in me. And I'm quite fond of Thysmer . . . and you."

"I would be honored." I offered her a smile. "I think I'm going to need some help."

There was a sharp knock on the door frame.

"My lady." Gerard stepped into the room. He must have followed my father, but I hadn't noticed. Too wrapped up in Max's eyes. "I thought you should know that your father has left in the sedan."

"What?" I looked around the room, my eyes falling on the glass tumbler and empty container of scotch. "Where did he go?"

"Toward town, my lady."

"Oh God." Fear and panic slammed into my chest and I shot out of my seat. "He didn't have a driver?"

"No, ma'am. I tried to stop him, but he wasn't willing to listen to me."

I looked over at the butler and noticed the growing bruise under his left eye.

"Jesus, Gerard. I'm so sorry." I reached out and tilted his face. "Go put some ice on that."

"It can wait, ma'am." He stood up straight.

"I'm calling the authorities." Max pulled his phone out of his pocket. "He could hurt somebody."

Adrenaline pumped through my veins and I was moving before I realized. Grabbing the keys from a hook near the door, I ran out to the driveway.

"Meredith!" Max followed closely on my heels and grabbed my arm.

"I have to go after him." I looked at Max. "I'm not going to let him kill someone."

He looked at me, his phone still tucked to his ear.

"Fine, but I'm driving."

I handed him the key and jumped into the old work truck that was parked out front. Max said a few quick sentences as he climbed into the driver's seat before throwing the phone down on the bench between us.

His bodyguard ran up to the window as Max threw the truck in reverse.

Max stuck his head out of the open window and told him to follow us.

I sat back in the seat, gripping the door handle as Max sped down the driveway in pursuit of my father.

Silently I prayed that my father wouldn't hurt anyone.

SIXTEEN

THE ROADS WERE wet from an earlier shower and the old truck didn't have much get up and go, but I made the best of what I had.

Meredith sat next to me, her face a pale mask of nerves. Her knuckles gripping the door were white. She chewed on her bottom lip as she stared out at the road.

"Where would he go?" I asked as we rounded a bend on the curvy road.

"I'm not sure." Letting go of the door, she wiped her palms on her pants legs. "The local pub, maybe."

"Then we'll try there." We hit a pothole full of water and sent a wave of it crashing into the foliage along the road. "The police are looking for him."

"God, I hope he doesn't hurt anyone." She shook her head, and I didn't think she realized that she was rocking in her seat.

I didn't say anything. There was no way to make her feel better until we had the old man accounted for. At another curve in the road was what looked like fresh tire marks, suggesting that a car had slid, but no car was visible.

We were almost to town when the first of the wreckage caught my attention. There was glass strewn across the road and I slowed the truck and pulled over into the grass.

Just the rear end of the sedan was visible from where it was stuck among the trees. It must've rolled because it was upside down, the undercarriage exposed to the sky.

"Oh my God." Meredith threw herself against the old truck door, but it didn't open at first. She hit it with her hand several times before almost falling out onto the wet grass.

"Meredith!" I climbed out of my seat and ran after her. The last thing I wanted was for her to find her father dead.

"Dad!" She hollered as she slid down the slope and into weeds near the trees. "Daddy!"

"Meredith!" I slid down the knoll on my side, just barely catching her before she could get to the car. "Stop!"

"He's in there!" She fought against my arms.

"Let me go look." I turned her to face me. "Let

me look, Meredith. Go get my phone and call the police."

"Let me go!" She wiggled in my arms. "He might need us!"

I looked down into her eyes and let out a ragged breath before letting go. She turned and ran for the car, falling to her knees near the wreckage.

"Dad?"

I knelt down next to her and peered into the torn-up vehicle. He was hanging from his seat by his seat belt, but there was a large gash on his forehead.

"Daddy?" Meredith's voice sent chills over my body. There was so much pain in that one word that my heart almost broke in half.

"Let me look at him." I pushed her shoulder gently so that I could get a better look. He was breathing, but the cut on his head was bleeding profusely.

"Charles!" I hollered for my bodyguard.

"Here, sir." I could hear him sliding down the slope. "I've contacted the authorities."

"Come take a look." I wasn't sure if we should move him or not. On one hand he could have a broken neck or back, and on the other I wasn't sure that we should leave him hanging upside down.

Charles slid around to the other side of the car

and knelt down to peer through the broken windshield.

"We need to put a compress on his head," Charles's gruff voice instructed.

I pulled my jacket off and balled it up before placing it against Arthur's head.

"Should we move him?" I asked.

"No!" Meredith shook her head vehemently. "We don't know if anything is broken."

"She's right. I don't smell any gas or I'd say we need to pull him." Charles looked at me with serious eyes. "Has he said anything?"

"No." I grunted as I tried to slide into the car to apply better pressure.

Meredith scooted closer and reached out to touch her father. "Why did you do this?" Her voice was barely a whisper.

Her fingers touched his hair softly and I tilted so I could see her face. For a brief moment, I had a picture of the little girl that she had been. The fear etched on her face made her look younger. I swallowed against the lump in my throat.

I might loathe this man, but he was her father. No matter how horrible he had been, he would always be Meredith's parent.

"I hear sirens." Meredith sniffed and shifted on the ground.

"Careful, there's glass everywhere." I could

feel shards poking through the thin material of my dress shirt.

Arthur groaned and tried to move away from my hand, but I held him still.

"Don't move, Arthur. You've been in a car wreck." I tried to see if he had opened his eyes, but there was too much fabric in the way.

"Whaaa?" He shifted again.

"Stop moving, Dad." Meredith edged closer.

"Mere?" His voice took on a sad edge.

"I'm here," she whispered.

"Sorry." He let out a breath before coughing.

"Don't move. We don't know if anything is broken," I warned him.

"Hurt?"

"Yes, you're injured." I explained. "You have a nasty cut on your head.

"No." He groaned and coughed again. "Did . . . I . . . hurt . . ."

I realized what he was asking and closed my eyes. "No, you didn't hurt anyone but yourself."

And Meredith.

And I'd be damned if I'd ever see that much hurt in her eyes again.

The rain started again, running into my eyes and soaking my clothes. The cold water seemed to seep into my bones.

The sirens had reached us and I could hear

doors opening and slamming. Charles stood up and flagged them toward us.

"Down here. We have one injured." Charles's voice sounded like that of a drill sergeant.

The rescue crew pulled Meredith away from the car, and one of them slid in next to me to assess the situation.

"What's his name?" the man asked me.

"Arthur." I let him take charge of the wound care and backed up.

"Arthur, can you hear me?"

I sat up and tried to move out of the way but keep an ear open.

Looking around the ditch I was standing in, my eyes landed on Meredith. She was chewing on her bottom lip, a large smear of blood across her cheek and on her shirt. Moving quickly to her side, I checked her for cuts.

"Are you okay?" I asked.

"No." She shook her head and sniffed mightily.

"What's wrong?" I pulled the collar of her shirt to the side and looked along her neck. "Where are you hurt?"

"What?" She looked at me with blank eyes. Her red hair was plastered to her face; the thin material of her shirt was soaked through. She had never looked more fragile.

"You said you were hurt." I wrapped a hand around her neck and looked down in her eyes.

"No." She shook her head. "I said I wasn't okay."

I leaned down and pressed my forehead to hers and breathed a sigh of relief.

"I'm not. Not at all," she whispered. "How am I supposed to deal with all of this? I feel like I'm holding the world on my shoulders and doing a really bad job. I'm just so tired."

"You're not alone, Meredith." I opened my eyes and stared into hers. "You'll never be alone again."

Giant tears spilled from her lovely eyes and traced dirty tracks along her cheeks. Leaning forward, she pressed her face to my shirt and cried. I wrapped my arms around her, my heart aching with each hiccup and sob that escaped her. She fisted her hands in the wet material of my shirt and held on as if I was the only thing keeping her alive.

I watched as the crew worked to remove Arthur from the car, fitting him with a neck brace and loading him onto a stretcher.

The first of the journalists arrived as they were loading him into the ambulance. Leaning down, I swooped Meredith into my arms and headed for Charles's car. He opened the back door for me and I slid in carefully.

"I need to go to the hospital." Her voice sounded so tiny and broken. She had cried so hard and for so long, I was surprised she could talk at all.

"Let's get you changed first." I set her on the seat next to me and reached around to buckle her in. "You're drenched to the bone, and the paramedics said that your father was stable."

"Hospital." Her chin jutted forward and I sighed.

"Very well." Charles met my eyes in the rearview mirror and I nodded my head.

Picking up my phone, I called the Thysmer house and asked for Rachel.

"You found him?" Her motherly voice rang with worry.

"We're on our way to the hospital. Could you get some dry clothes together for Meredith? She's soaked to the bone."

"Yes. Do you need anything else?"

"No, thank you." I hung up and immediately called Alex.

"How'd it go?" My brother answered the phone with no greeting.

"Not so well." I lowered my voice. "We're on our way to the hospital."

"What happened?" His tone shifted. "Is Meredith hurt?"

"No. Arthur had a car accident." I frowned. I wasn't going to elaborate with Meredith sitting next to me. "He's stable, but I'm not sure when we'll get home."

"Don't worry about Marty. Samantha and he have been having a blast. He'll be safe here with us." Alex's crisp words flowed through the phone. "Family comes first."

He had said those very words to me before I'd gotten in the car this morning. I closed my eyes. He'd understood that Meredith and Marty were mine, even before I had. And in turn, Alex and the others had accepted Meredith and Marty as their family. "Thank you." I said the words quietly. "Don't tell Marty. Let Meredith handle that, okay?"

"Of course." Alex paused and I could practically hear his brain working. "Let me know if you need anything else. I can send someone to Thysmer if I need to."

"Rachel is there. I believe the place is in good hands for now." I looked over at Meredith. "I'll be in touch soon."

"Okay."

I hung up the phone and wrapped my arm around Meredith.

"I've been such a burden to your family." She

turned and looked at me. "Do they mind watching Marty a little longer?"

"Alex said that Samantha is having a blast." I looked down into her eyes and tried to figure out how to explain how my family saw them. "You are not a burden. My family . . . my family loves you. You'll be lucky if they ever let you leave."

"Maybe I don't want to leave." A small smile tugged at the corner of her mouth.

Picking up her cold hand, I brought it to my lips. "Good."

We were silent the rest of the ride to the hospital. Charles dropped us off at the emergency entrance and we were escorted back to the triage area where they were working on Arthur.

She never let go of my hand. Her fingers squeezed mine as she watched them pull glass out of wounds and go over X-rays. We were huddled in a tiny corner, out of the way as the staff worked. One of the nurses took note of our wet clothes and took pity on us. She disappeared and came back with two thin blankets. I wrapped them both around Meredith's shivering shoulders.

By the time Rachel arrived with clothes, they had taken Arthur back for surgery. One of his lungs had been punctured, but the surgeon seemed very confident that he would be able to repair the damage. Rachel handed me a bag of men's clothes before she ushered Meredith off to the bathroom to change.

I shrugged out of my ruined clothes in the men's room and tossed them in the trash. The clothes Rachel had brought were a little big, but that was better than being too small. Unfortunately I was stuck with my wet dress shoes. Going to the mirror, I looked at my reflection and frowned. I hadn't realized how much blood I'd gotten on my face and in my hair.

Turning the water on, I stuck my head under the flow and used the hand soap to scrub my hair. It wasn't exactly ideal, but it was better than having matted blood stuck on my head.

By the time I got out, the press had been alerted to our presence. Thankfully, one of the doctors offered us his office to wait in.

It was the longest four hours of my life. Meredith refused to eat the entire time, her face pale and her hands clenched together. The only time she moved from her seat was to talk to Marty on the phone. She paced back and forth in the tiny office while she cheerily talked to her son about the fish he had caught. When she was done, she collapsed in the chair next to me, and I pulled her into my lap.

"It's going to be okay," I murmured against her head.

"How can you know?" she whispered.

"I just do." God, please let him be all right. Meredith had dealt with enough.

"The last thing I said to him was that he didn't matter." She sucked in one of those horrible body-shaking breaths.

"He knows better." But maybe he had needed to hear that.

"He's an awful man, but I love him. God, why do I love him?" Tears gathered in her eyes.

"He's your father." I kissed her head. "And you had some good times."

"Yeah." She shook her head. "Maybe this will be his bottom."

"What do you mean?"

"Alcoholics have to hit bottom before they are ready to make a change. It's different for each person, but maybe this was his." She gave a wet chuckle. "I had a counselor explain that to me in school."

"I hope you're right."

"Thank you." She sat up in my arms and turned to face me.

"For what?" I cocked my head to the side.

"For being here. For treating me like family."

She closed her eyes. "For being so good to Marty. For showing me that it was okay to let some people in."

"Don't you get it, yet?" I brushed the hair out of her face.

"What?" She opened her eyes.

"Meredith, you are my family." I cupped her chin so that she couldn't look away. "I don't know when exactly it happened. Maybe it was when you yelled at me, or poked me in the chest. Maybe it was when I watched you stand up to your father, or how you take care of Marty. But sometime this week, I fell in love with you. You and Marty. You are my family."

Tears spilled down her face and I had a moment of panic. Should I have not told her? Should I have waited? I looked around the tiny office and frowned. I guess I could have tried to find a more romantic place. Or maybe she didn't love me and was now worried she was going to hurt my feelings.

"Meredith?" I brushed tears away from her cheek. "Say something. Anything. Even if it's that you hate me. But please don't cry."

"I—I—I have been trying—to." She hiccupped.

"I didn't mean to upset you." My heart sank in my chest.

"Would . . . you . . . shut up?" She wiped at her nose.

"Okay." I held up my hands in surrender.

"I've been trying to figure out how I was going to convince you that you love me, because I love you so much, so much, and I couldn't stand the thought of walking away from you." Her words fell out of her mouth like a flood. "I love you. I love the way you draw when you're upset. I love that you say things without thinking. I love—love the way you treat Marty. I love how loyal you are and how you love your family. I just . . . I love you."

She shook her head and started laughing.

"Is it funny?" I brushed the hair away from her face and kissed her nose. "Loving me is funny?"

"At the funeral, in the limo—I was laughing because that's when I realized I loved you. That you had swooped in and stolen my heart in a matter of days." She shook her head. "It's just . . . funny. I was lost the first time you kissed me and all I could think was that it was a good thing I had a strict no-kissing motto. Because apparently you could steal my heart with just one good smack-a-roo."

"Well, it was a really good kiss." I smiled.

"Yes, it was." She traced my jaw with her fingers. "And I want you to keep doing it for a long, long time."

"I think that can be arranged." In fact, I was already forming a plan. Leaning forward, I kissed her softly.

When I pulled back, she snuggled against my chest and promptly fell asleep. I shook my head when she started snoring and shifted her to a more comfortable position.

When the surgeon came to see us, I shook her gently to wake her up. She moved to the seat next to me and listened as he explained the surgery and told her that everything was going to be okay.

"His recovery won't be swift, but I've seen worse."

"He has a problem with alcohol." Meredith sat up. "Is there a way to make sure his medicine is regulated?"

"Absolutely." The surgeon nodded his head. "Detoxing and withdrawal will make his recovery more difficult, but still manageable. I'll let the appropriate staff know. We can also have him set up to enter rehab when he's ready."

"Thank you." She nodded her head. "When will he wake up?"

"Not for a while. You should go get some rest. One of the nurses will call you when he's up."

She chewed on her lip, and I knew she was trying to decide if she wanted to leave or not.

"I'm happy to stay," Rachel said from the doorway. "I brought my knitting supplies with me and will be just fine."

"I hate to ask you to do that." Meredith frowned.

"You didn't. I offered." Rachel made a shooing gesture at us. "Go tuck your boy in. I'll call you when something changes."

I put my arm around Meredith's shoulders and steered her out the door. "You need some real sleep."

"You're such a charmer, you know that?" She rolled her eyes. "Always telling me how tired I look."

"Baby, you're covered in blood but you're still the most beautiful woman here."

She laughed. "You need to get that panty-dropping book back out and study some more."

"Nah. You like my awkwardness. You already told me. You can't take it back now." I pulled her closer against my side. Pride filled my chest as we walked to the car. Mine. She was mine. How the hell had I managed to get so lucky?

By the time we made it to D'Lynsal, Marty was already asleep. Sam was snoring on the couch, her head on Alex's lap while he read through paperwork.

"How is he?" Alex whispered.

"He's going to be okay." Meredith yawned. "Thank you for watching Marty."

"It was our pleasure." Alex smiled.

"Okay, cut the nicey-nice stuff. I'm too tired for it. How'd he really do?" She put a hand on her hip and Alex's smile grew. The men in our family had a thing for feisty women, it would seem.

I snorted and set her purse on the table before kicking off my wet shoes.

"He does not like broccoli, lost a fishing rod in the lake, and accidentally squirted ketchup on Sam's dress." Alex chuckled softly. "But Samantha absolutely loved every minute of it. She took pictures of the fish they caught. He has them in his room."

"Now that I believe." Meredith smiled and dropped her hand from her hip. "I'm going to take a shower."

"I'll join you," I said.

Her eyes grew to the size of saucers and Alex chuckled quietly. When he started to hum softly, her face turned red.

"Are you humming 'Tubthumping'?" She looked incredulously at my brother.

"Oh good, I got the melody right."

I flung one of my wet socks at his head and smiled when it made contact. "Score!"

"Shh." He threw the nasty sock off to the side and motioned to his sleeping wife.

"Right, then." Meredith shook her head. "Good night."

I followed her up the stairs and into her room. Despite the way I loved her gorgeous body, I wasn't really looking for sex. I just wanted to be near her, to hold her.

In the shower I made her turn around so that I could work the shampoo through the knots in her hair. She took her time washing my body, scrubbing every part except my feet. She threw me the sponge to do those myself.

"I'm going to have to call my school tomorrow. I guess I can withdraw from classes." She frowned as she towel dried her hair.

"You could hire a steward."

"That just doesn't sit right with me. They welcomed us back, and look at all the drama we've caused. Dad's probably going to have charges brought against him for driving under the influence. Granddad just died . . . I can't leave them now." She shook her head. "Maybe I'll get a business degree locally."

"That would be a waste." I pulled up my pajama pants and looked at her reflection in the mirror. "Can you not go to England during the week and come back on the weekends?"

"Not if I'm in a show. It's constant practices, and showtimes are usually on the weekends." She looked down at the counter. "Being a singing duchess just isn't going to work. Really, I should have known better. At some point the title was going to fall to me. I guess I'd just hoped that I'd have a little longer first."

I didn't have an easy solution for that. Instead I threw the pillows off the bed and pulled back the covers while she got dressed. She crawled in and lay on her side looking at me.

"Are you not going to stay?" She frowned.

"I was waiting for you to ask."

"That didn't stop you with my shower." She gave me a sleepy smile. "Come on."

I slid under the blanket and pulled her against me. Tracing her arm with my fingertips, I thought about what she had said. She had to give up her dream to accept her family responsibility. Something she had been doing her whole life.

"You could always have family help you run Thysmer." I said the words quietly.

"Dad's got a lot of recovery to go through and there's no telling if he'll stay sober." She sighed.

I took a deep breath. "What about me?"

"I can't ask you to do that." She sat up and looked at me. "Thysmer isn't your responsibility."

"I told you that you were my family." I shifted so I was sitting and looked at her. "I want to make that official." A wave of possessiveness swept through my body. Mine. I wanted everyone to know that she and Marty were mine.

"What?" Her eyes widened.

"Marry me, Meredith." I didn't realize I was holding my breath. I hadn't thought those words would ever leave my mouth.

"Is this one of those times where you blurt out something and then realize you didn't mean it?" She gripped the blanket with white knuckles. "Is it?"

"Well, I blurted it out." I smiled sheepishly. "But I really mean it. I was going to ask you later, somewhere romantic, but I blurted it out."

"But . . . but . . . you can't . . . we've only had a week!" She looked at me like I'd grown a second head, and I was starting to think that maybe I was crazy. "You're only doing this because you feel sorry for me."

"What?" I frowned.

"You feel bad for me." Her eyes wouldn't meet mine.

I pulled her to me so that our foreheads were touching. "I want to marry you, Meredith Thysmer. I want Marty to teach me how to fish. I want to watch him grow up. And I want to sit in the wings, out of the spotlight, while you sing. You, me, and Marty. It's that simple. I don't feel sorry for you. How can you feel sorry for the strongest person you know? I just want to be part of your life every day. The good and the bad. Forever."

She looked into my eyes, and tears lined her eyelashes.

"I wasn't trying to make you cry."

"Yes," she whispered.

"Yes I was trying to make you cry?"

"Yes, I'll marry you, you idiot." She gave me a watery chuckle. "Yes. Yes. Yes."

"I love you." I leaned forward and kissed her. She fell back on the bed, pulling me with her.

"I love you too."

EPILOGUE

"*I* HATE HIM," SAM declared loudly.

"No you don't," I said.

"I do. I hate him." She glared over her shoulder at Alex. "And his stupid penis."

"It's going to be worth it." I pushed her IV as she walked around the large birthing suite.

"I want to put his penis in clamps." She grunted and bent over a bit. Alex was on his feet in a heartbeat but I waved him away.

"Breathe, Sam."

"I'm . . . breathing." She stood up once the contraction passed. "What was I saying? Clamps. Industrial clamps. That'll almost make it even."

I winced at the thought and had to consciously force myself to not fondle my goods. Looking toward the door, I wished that Meredith or Cathy were here to deal with this, but both had been hours away when Sam went into labor.

So, here I was, with my very pregnant, very

angry sister-in-law. Anytime Alex took a step in her direction she would growl. And honestly, seeing how much pain she was in, I didn't blame her.

"Have you picked a name yet?" I asked as we started walking again.

"Ha. I'm not telling you. You just want to win that stupid bet." She glanced at me.

"Nah. I'm just trying to distract you." I kept pace with her slow waddle. It was like walking with a giant penguin. A giant, pissed-off penguin.

"Where are Cathy and Meredith? You look too much like Alex."

"They're on their way." *Please, God, let them get here soon.*

"I brought a birthing ball!" Chadwick walked into the room with a giant rubber ball. It looked like something from a yoga studio.

"What?" Sam turned to look at her assistant.

"You sit on it and bounce. It's supposed to help." He put the ball down next to the bed.

"I'll try anything." Sam waddled over to the ball. I grabbed one arm while Chadwick grabbed the other. "I feel like I'm going to fall over."

"The instructions said to lean forward a little."

"Don't let me fall," Sam told us.

"Yes, ma'am," I said.

"Don't patronize me."

"Sorry."

"Now, just bounce gently. It's supposed to help get the baby in position and lessen some of the pain," Chadwick told her.

"Okay." Sam closed her eyes as another contraction hit her.

"We're here!" Cathy announced as she, David, and Meredith walked through the door.

Sam tried to stand up, and that was the moment her water broke. It dribbled down her legs onto the ball, the floor, and my shoes. It took some doing, but I was able to keep my face blank.

"Are you okay?" Alex was by my side before I could comprehend what had happened.

"Whoa." Cathy' s voice sounded small.

"Oh no." Sam's eyes filled with tears. "I'm so sorry, Max, Chadwick."

"It's okay." I leaned forward and kissed her head before letting Alex take my spot.

"Hey, that's exactly what you wanted to happen." Meredith took Chadwick's place. "This is good, it means the labor will go faster."

"I know, but it got all over them!" Sam's bottom lip trembled.

"They don't care," Meredith assured her. "Do you?"

"Nope," I agreed.

"Not at all. I even wore shoes that could get dirty just in case." Chadwick lifted his foot.

"Should we get the nurse?" Alex asked.

"Yes."

"On it!" Cathy hollered as she ran out of the room. David rocked back and forth on his feet, looking incredibly uncomfortable.

"Let's get you back in the bed. They're going to need to check you." Meredith steered Sam toward the hospital bed but glanced in my direction. "Would you go out with Marty? He's in the waiting room with Charles."

"I'll join you," David announced. "I think I'm just in the way here."

"Of course." I went to the bed and kissed Sam's head. "Don't kill anyone while I'm gone, okay?"

"Okay." She smiled at me briefly. "Thanks for letting me take it out on you."

"I'll find a way to pay you back." I winked at her as I left the room and made my way down the hall. The waiting room was full of other families waiting on their newest addition. Some of them watched me as I walked out, but for the most part they were more interested in what was happening with their own loved ones.

"We're over here." Marty waved at me. He was sitting with Charles next to a vending machine.

"What are you playing?" I looked down at his handheld game.

"Day of Doom Two."

"I thought your mom said you couldn't have that one." I frowned.

"Charles got it for me." The boy shrugged, never taking his eyes from the zombies he was killing.

I looked at my bodyguard and raised an eyebrow.

"I didn't know." His mouth twitched to one side in a half smile.

"Right." I looked for Marty's bag. "What else did you bring with you?"

"Racing games, a couple of space games. I grabbed whatever was on my dresser."

"Switch it out." I picked up the bag from the floor.

"Ah, man."

"Come on. I'm so not taking a beating for letting you play that." I narrowed my gaze at him. "You know better than to break your mom's rules."

"Are you going to tell?" He looked up at me with puppy dog eyes.

David snorted from where he was sitting, but managed to not laugh out loud.

"You better believe it."

"Are you going to take my system?" He held up his handheld device.

"I'm not that cruel. You can play while we're at the hospital, but then it's gone for a week." I leaned back in my chair. Being the bad cop did not come easily to me. Even with a few months of practice. But I was getting better at it.

The waiting room cleared of families as the hours passed. Marty was tucked against my side, his head rolling forward. Charles got up to stretch, walking around the open space and reading the plaques on the wall. David was dozing off, his arms crossed over his chest.

I'd had no idea it took so long to have a baby. Poor Sam.

"Are you and Mom going to have babies?" Marty's tiny voice made me jump.

"I thought you were asleep." I looked down at him.

"I'm not." He yawned. "Are you and Mom going to have babies? Zach, at school, said his mom and new dad are having a baby."

"That might be something you need to talk to your mom about." I shifted in my chair. There was not enough caffeine in the world to help me with this conversation.

"Don't you like babies?" He sat back and pulled his feet up into his seat.

"Erm." I looked around the room as if there was an easy answer waiting for me to find. "Sure, babies are great. But they are a lot of work. It's a big commitment."

"I think it would be cool." He moved my arm so it was draped over his shoulders again. "When you and Mom get married, you should have lots of babies."

I swallowed against my suddenly dry throat. "Maybe not lots."

"One would be fine." He said it as if he was giving me permission.

I'd always said I'd never have children. That it would be unfair to bring them into our lifestyle.

But now as I sat here with Marty under my arm, his soft snore reaching my ears, I wasn't so sure. Having one more might not be so bad. A little brother for Marty.

What if it was a girl? A sister for Marty.

Whoa. What the hell was I thinking about? I didn't even know if Meredith wanted more kids. We hadn't talked about it.

Cathy stuck her head out of the swinging doors and motioned for us to come in. Picking up Marty, I followed her to Sam's room.

Everyone was gathered around the bed, so I sat Marty down on the large chair and joined them.

"Do you want to hold your niece?" Sam smiled at me.

There was a tiny little blanket-wrapped bundle on her chest, with a tuft of dark brown hair on its head.

"Will it hurt her?" I frowned.

"No." Sam laughed. Her face was tired, but she radiated happiness.

"Okay."

Alex lifted the bundle off Sam and placed her in my arms. I shifted on my feet, and tried to get my arms just right. A tiny little hand reached out of the blanket and waved as if looking for something. Ever so carefully, I shifted her to one arm and let her grab my finger.

As I looked down at her tiny hand, button nose, and chubby cheeks, I was a goner. She was this perfect combination of Sam and Alex.

Eventually I had to let someone else have a turn, but it was hard to let go. My fingers itched and I wished I had thought to bring my sketchbook with me, but with Sam hollering and Alex freaking out, I was lucky I'd remembered to wear pants.

Meredith came to me and wrapped her arms around my waist.

"You look rather sexy holding a baby." She smiled up at me.

I grunted and watched as Cathy sat down next to Marty to show him his new cousin.

"What's wrong?" She tilted her head to the side.

"Marty asked me if we were going to have babies." I raised an eyebrow.

"Oh." Her eyes widened.

"Actually he said lots of babies."

"Lots?" She shook her head and looked over at her son.

"Yes, he gave his blessing. Apparently Zach has a new sibling on the way." I ran my hands over her back.

"Ah." She laughed. "I don't know about lots of babies."

"One might be nice," I said. "One day."

"I thought you didn't want kids." She cocked her head to the side, but her smile grew.

"Maybe I'm changing my mind." I shrugged.

"You've been doing that a lot lately." She reached down and pinched my butt.

"Hey." I mock-glared at her. "Stop that. I said someday. Not today. You'll get me all excited."

"So you'd really consider having a baby?" The tenderness in her expression almost killed me.

"If you want to be technical about it, you'd be the one having the baby. I'd just be the punching bag in the delivery room." Why did I blurt out idiotic things when I was nervous?

"I think that, one day, it would be nice to have another baby." She smiled shyly.

Leaning down, I kissed her softly. "Me too."

Life had changed. My plans for the future had shifted.

I was marrying a woman who had been contacted by several theater companies to perform for them. I was going to be the father to a six-year-old boy I loved more than drawing, painting, or breathing. I was helping run a duchy. Me, the royal who hated everything about being a royal. I still had my art. That would always be with me. And I'd keep making and creating things because I couldn't stop. It was part of who I am. But so were Meredith and Marty.

I wasn't where I thought I would be and I was incredibly grateful for that. I wouldn't trade my life for anything.

ACKNOWLEDGMENTS

SOMETIMES IT'S HARD to say good-bye. For me, the Royal series has been one of the most enjoyable, difficult, but rewarding series I've ever written. I'm going to miss these characters like crazy. They took on a life of their own and I loved watching their stories unfold.

This series wouldn't have been possible without a lot of help from my family and friends. It goes without saying that my daughter and husband have borne the brunt of the craziness that comes with writing a book. Without their patience and love, I wouldn't be able to write.

Thank you to my sister, who always talks me down when I panic about a book. Not only does she provide me with great scientific facts for books, but she's probably going to start charging me a fee for our therapy sessions.

Thank you to Nicole Mincey and Kate Savage for their medical knowledge. You guys really helped me out during a pinch! Thank you to Courtney Schriner for listening to me ramble about my books and for always being willing to read what I write. Thank you to Heather, my bestie, for not giving up on me when I disappear for months in a book.

For my friends in the FP, you know that you guys are my rock. A group of women that are always there for each other in some way; I'm incredibly lucky to be a part of it.

A huge thank-you to my agent, Rebecca Friedman, who has held my hand for almost a year now. She gets me, people. She really gets me.

KP Simmon, thank you for all of your hard work. I'm pretty sure that you're part robot or Super Woman. I have no idea how you do all that you do!

To the team at Avon, I owe you a huge debt of gratitude. Tessa Woodward is a saint. A very patient saint. Jessie Edwards has been a fantastic publicist. And she loves Doctor Who. It doesn't get much better than that, people.

Thank you to the readers who picked up *Suddenly Royal* and made my dreams come true. Without you, I wouldn't be here.